REAL LOVE

"Don't say anything you don't mean, Cordell. Please don't make a fool of me. My heart couldn't take it."

"I would never hurt you. I can't hurt what I love so much." He cupped her face in his hands and kissed her hard and long. "Lena, you are so beautiful. Believe me. I mean what I say."

Lena took a deep breath, attempting to quell the excitement building in the base of her stomach, the excitement bellowing through her blood. Rapture was shaking her whole body. "I'm in love with you, Cordell. I know it's soon. I know it almost seems unreal and unbelievable. But it's there, and nothing and no one in this world can make it ever go away."

Love had been a preciousness Lena assumed she knew, but it wasn't until Cordell entered her heart that she finally knew love.

NIGHTFALL

Louré Bussey

Pinnacle Books
Kensington Publishing Corp.
http://www.pinnaclebooks.com

PINNACLE BOOKS are published by

Kensington Publishing Corp.
850 Third Avenue
New York, NY 10022

Pinnacle, the P logo, and Arabesque are Reg. U.S. Pat. & TM Off.

First Printing: December, 1996

Printed in the United States of America
10 9 8 7 6 5 4 3 2 1

One

There is a place you reach by the way of pain. You can arrive there from the helplessness of losing a child or the astonishment of a friend betraying you, and even through your lover, slicing and slicing into your heart, until all it can do is break apart.

Lena Durant knew of the latter. Because she did, there were nervous flutterings in her stomach when she approached her apartment, then fumbled through her purse for a heart linked to a key. All day at work she dreaded returning home, but at the same time wondered what waited after she entered the door. The possibility drew beads of water across her forehead, but didn't sway her in finding that heart. Purchased from a street fair, it was supposedly more than a charm linking a key. According to the merchant who sold it, if your eyes sparkled when you looked at the golden veneer, one day they would sparkle before the man of your dreams while you were in his arms. Lena preferred being amused by the old romantic, rather than cry about how her love life really turned out.

The drift into memories stopped the instant Lena reached the key. Inching one hand toward the lock, she took a deep breath and challenged her lingering hesitation to enter. If only so much wasn't dependent upon today's outcome. If only Robert hadn't allowed it to be that way. She knew today's answers would mean everything.

The silence on the other side of 9C was unnatural. As Lena headed to the dining room, it enveloped her and somehow warned her about the man who perched at the table. He wore shorts and a T-shirt that bared his bronzed body, despite the blast of the air-conditioning in the dining room. The chill, in fact, matched his stare when Lena entered the room.

Sitting in a chair across from him, she asked, "Did you pass?"

"Pass?" He looked at Lena wryly, then slid a paper in front of her face. "There's a pass for you. There is your latest, greatest attorney for the state of New York."

Mink brown eyes pored over the results carefully. Afterward Lena stared up at him, while pushing her fiancé's misery aside. "I'm sorry, Robert. I know how much you wanted to ace the bar this time."

He chuckled dryly. "Yeah, well . . ."

"But, honey, you know you can take it again. Just try to meditate and focus next time. Just give it your all. You can do it. You have everything it takes inside you to do it. I know you do."

Lena didn't think she was sounding preachy, or weird, as Robert often claimed she was. Actually she was careful not to sound either way. His past eruptions made her cautious. Yet when she saw Robert's arms folding, his nostrils flaring, and his shoulders rearing back, Lena was aware she had pressed the wrong button again.

"I'm so sick of you jabbering that to me!" he blasted.

"But I hate to see you fail all the time."

"Fail?" His voice strangled on the word.

She winced at her phrasing. "I didn't mean it the way it might have sounded. I know you think I'm referring to those career choices, which didn't work out for you. But what I meant is that I hate to see you wanting something so bad and never getting it. Robert, all I want is for you to finally do whatever it is you want to do and be happy. Practice law or whatever it is."

There was tenderness in her tone. And in reaching her hand across to him, she was trying to show that her emotion wasn't solely compassion, but love. Except Robert's hands remained gripped on his arms. More disturbing, his glare was as icy as those other nights when his despair divided them.

"You know something," he told her, "maybe you should stop worrying about me so much. You need to look at your own situation and fix it before you can work on mine."

"Let's not get into that again, Robert. I was hoping all day that if you didn't pass, you wouldn't take out your frustrations on me."

"I'm not taking anything out on you!" He unfolded his burly arms and leaned forward. Burning his eyes into hers, he was adamant. "You think you're so together? What about you, Lena? When are you going to stop listening to some stuffy old man like you're a little child? When are you going to start living the life you want? Wh—"

"I'm fine! Being an actuary at a top insurance company is a pretty nice way to earn a living to most people."

"But not to you. You got into it just because it sounded good to your old man. Hell, if you can tell me what to do, what about yourself? You! When are you going to start that singing career? When exactly are you going to burst on the music scene as the latest, greatest singing sensation?" He sighed. "Oh, I can tell you when—when your gums are the only thing showing when you smile—that's when!"

"Stop it!" Her lithe form pounced from the table, her pumps clattering briskly toward the living room for escape. "I don't have to listen to this."

Robert was on her trail. "What's wrong? Can give criticism, but can't take it?"

"Why do you always do this to me?" She plopped down on the sofa, then glared up at him standing above her. "I try to support you and you turn on me. It's uncalled for!" She shook her head. "All I want is to help you! Help—that's all!"

"Help?" Crookedly he grinned. "Pretty lady, you better help yourself. For years you've been going to a job you hate, when you know that all you've ever wanted to do was use that voice God gave you. But no—just because you want to please your holier-than-thou father, you've missed out on so much! I bet you can't even sing like *that* anymore. And it would serve you right after turning down that record contract the way you did. They were offering you an opportunity that could have eventually made you rich, a star! You must have been out of your mind!"

"Just leave me alone! Go away somewhere!"

"What's the matter? Hearing how dumb you were hurts?"

"That is enough!" She hopped up from the sofa, her finger pointing at him, her rage breathing in his face. "I'm so tired of hearing you call me that! For months you've been saying that, disrespecting me like I'm your worst enemy, and I'm tired of it! Enough already!"

"But you did do something dumb. And when you do something dumb, it makes you look dumb. And all those crazy things you say sometimes about sending out positive vibrations in the universe, or that visualizing nonsense, it just proves what's in, or should I say, what's not, in your head—some common sense."

"I'm learning to be a spirit-connected person, and you should do the same. It will help you—and believe me, you need help."

"Sounds like just plain flakiness to me. Sometimes I think when God makes a woman as beautiful as you are, he says I can't give her everything, so he leaves out her brain."

Her gut twisted. "And sometimes the devil makes a man so weak, he hates when a woman succeeds at something she doesn't really want, when he can't even—" Lena stopped herself. His negativity had crept on her, and she was repulsed by the way it felt.

The statement predictably had called forth more of Robert's contention. Like in months past, he ranted on, attacking her unfulfilled dream, her father, her maturity, and her intelligence. It was as if all his life's mistreatments had been inhaled, and now the summed reaction was the indignation he exhaled at her. Whenever life indicated to Robert that he was falling behind, he let loose his tirade. Sometimes every day; sometimes every few days.

Lena could barely remember the affection that bewitched them in days gone by. Sweet nothings he had uttered so passionately during their times together were nowadays replaced with spears that raged from his lips straight to her heart. To her it still seemed unreal, and truly like a nightmare, that one's beloved could change so much. It all couldn't be real. Once upon a time, she believed the preciousness of their combined souls was not merely potent, and impassioned, but could surmount any obstacle.

Fairy tales aside, it was reality that made Lena's wide eyes then fill with water. Effortlessly they cascaded from her eyes, with Lena not even aware of them flowing until regret reflected vividly on Robert's face. His forehead was tensing.

"I'm sorry, baby. Like you said, it was frustration talking." He rubbed the back of his neck. "Because you know I love you. From the moment I saw you, I ached for you. Never had seen a woman that took my breath away, and when I came to know you, there was no way I could let you out of my life. And now we've shared so much. I was the one who pushed you toward your dream. I knew you could do it even if you didn't. And I was there whenever you were sick, nursing you back to health. And I was there to take you in my arms at night and enrapture you, love you senseless until you were tearfully blissful. I miss that. Hell, I miss just being close. I love you, and I just want to feel you in my arms again."

He dared to embrace her. Thus, unlike occasions before, when after hearing this Lena was weakened into letting him hug her, this time his arms remained untouched.

Moments later, Lena's Maxima was swiftly passing the bright lights of lofty buildings, and the roars of car engines racing by, and the lankily posed cables, all which enlivened the Brooklyn Bridge. Normally she would have relished towering above the water, feeling the wind on her face and seeing the remnants of a vanquishing sun illuminating the sky so picturesque it appeared like a portrait. Today, however, it was sweltering enough to raise your windows and put on the air-conditioning full blast.

Three years ago, Lena wouldn't have dreamed she could feel the anguish now besieging her. It was then she met Robert at the Bay Hill Towers, her previous co-op. As soon as she moved in, her bright-eyed downstairs neighbor was always flirting, joking with her and trying to get a date. Lena gently and humorously rejected Robert for two reasons. One was she had a boyfriend. The other was his unstableness. Whenever their paths crossed, Robert was always gushing about his latest career choice. Changing vocations was a constant with him. It seemed that he was forever dissatisfied, eternally on the move, sailing wherever the wind blew him, all for the search of something he never found. Lena couldn't understand it.

A year later she was single, and Robert was secure in one profession. At that time, he was teaching political science and appeared truly content to do it forever. So Robert started to appeal to her. Physically she had never missed his beauty. As well, there were his other alluring qualities. They were drawn together. Seasons passed with Robert making her laugh, think, feel beautiful and protected. She made Robert just as euphoric. And when Robert heard Lena sing, he was so astonished by such phenomenal talent, he confirmed what her soul already knew, what every dawn greeted her with, and what every night whispered: she was born to sing . . .

A right turn into a darkened street, brightened only by a neon sign, interrupted Lena's thoughts. She pulled her car aside. "Centerfields" was the happening place, according to the people at her job, for having an equal array of superstar and gong-show talent. She didn't intend to come here, but parked, locked up her car, and walked to the club's entrance.

As soon as she entered, Lena felt comforted by plushness. Soft, baby girl pink walls, the palest gray carpeting that crushed, and ice-cream-white tables made the atmosphere sophisticated and easy to feel relaxed in. There were also vibrant rose-colored vases with lofty, satin flowers, and mini-candles adorning each table, their brilliance granting everyone's skin a flawless tanned glow.

Many eyes shot up over at Lena, especially men's, as the ambience lured her farther inside. Others were content to simply look pleasantly at the stage as they patiently listened. A singer was trying his best. Veins were bursting from his stretched neck.

"If I could ma-yake you loooovvvvve me," he crooned.

"Not singing like that," a guy shouted. "I refuse to love you singing like that."

Lost in feeling, the entertainer didn't hear. Striving to maintain a straight face, Lena gave the performer her full attention. By now his gray eyes were exploding from his head, too. On his tiptoes, he was even yodeling, "But I wanna wanna love you. I wanna love you. I wanna wanna love youhoooooooooooo."

He looked like he was having an excruciating headache and couldn't breathe, and then there were the clumsy contortions he was doing with his back. It was an attempt to simulate a seductive, slow dance with an absent partner. *Chiropractor here he comes,* Lena predicted for this poor soul.

"I wanna wanna love youhooooooo."

That last wretched sound reached up in the back of

Lena's neck, shaking her head. No doubt this was the amateur night. She had heard about it from her co-workers. She was grateful to finally applaud.

A vacant table was available near the far right of the room. Promptly a slim, slick-haired waiter came over after Lena seated herself there. Looking young enough to be a freshman in college, he was wearing an oddly amused expression. Lena wondered what was so funny, but it didn't stop her from relaxing her posture, loosening her collar, and shaking away that lock of hair, which habitually dangled by her left eye.

"What are you drinking?" the waiter asked, his head wavering between her eyes and lips. His voice was deeper than expected.

"A strawberry daiquiri, please. No alcohol."

"Anything else?"

"Just the daiquiri. Thank you."

He sped away. Lena's thoughts drifted back to the concerns that gripped her in the car. Robert was on her mind. She, Robert, and the past.

Sooner than anyone predicted, Robert and Lena had gotten engaged. Since they were so committed to each other, it was the most natural step. However, something began to creep between them that eventually nagged Lena about her decision. Robert was showing signs of that instability again. The bouncing around from one vocation to the other began. Not knowing his purpose in life somehow took over their lives. To Lena it was a quiet madness, slowly growing, sweeping her farther within. It prompted the decision that they needed more time to get their lives together before making that ultimate commitment. She explained they had to love and know themselves fully before they pledged their lives together before God. For this reason, Lena talked Robert into a long engagement.

The union was opposed by her father, the Honorable Judge Angus Durant. Throughout his life, the judge had striven for the best for his only child, controlling her life with the meticulousness likened to his courtroom. Undoubtedly he knew she was smart and a rare jewel. At the same time, he was not blind to the sharks in the world mindlessly swimming, grabbing, taking, attacking because they didn't know who they were, but did know they had to survive. With all that he had, Angus had to protect Lena from them.

The judge longed for the best for his daughter, a man who knew his place in the world, not one who bounced around from being a teacher to a journalist to a talent manager and then to a student again. He wanted a solid rock that would stand side by side the flower he had nourished day after day, year after year—the flower who overnight had transformed into a bouquet so exquisite in every sense, that to Angus, no other garden could ever grow its kind.

After all, Angus and Lena had been everything for each other. Lena's mother and her older brother, Jared, were killed in a car accident when Lena was three. Thereafter father and daughter were the keepers of each other's souls. And it was purely because it put her father at peace that Lena forsook her dream, even if she couldn't relinquish the man she loved.

Angus opposed Lena wanting to be a singer. Not that he didn't think she was talented. On the contrary, that was clear to him each time her silky voice rolled through the air and reached in his soul, taking a part of it with him. Nevertheless, her gift also reminded him of something painful. His only sister, Lettie, was just as vocally gifted. In his youth, Angus loved Lettie to no end and encouraged her desire to be a famous R&B singer. Everyone thought Lettie had made it, too. She landed a contract with a major record company and created breathlessly beautiful love ballads. Unfortunately fame and fortune eluded her. Even with outrageous talent, the powers that make stars were not in Lettie's favor. She wound up terribly depressed, an alcoholic, and eventually committed suicide.

There were so many others that Angus knew about. There were so many who realized they were not going to be that one in a million. Therefore they didn't want to be at all. Over and over that was the song Angus sang to Lena. Despite it, working each day in her nine-to-five, the longing didn't die. So she attempted to assuage it with wedding performances for friends, solos in a church choir, or an occasional a cappella at a family gathering. It could be a hobby, she thought. That was safe. Hobbies wouldn't break your heart. Wanting and reaching for something with all your soul and never touching it would.

Still the passion burned. It burned when Lena heard a haunting ballad and closed her eyes and lost herself so that all she heard was herself and felt the fierce beating of her heart, because she was then truly alive and realizing emotions could make you high or help you accept that painful experiences are merely lessons you had to learn, to grow. The passion burned to share this from the oiliness of her throat, where she could feel magic escape and see it all around when it affected others.

So when Robert felt unsatisfied with his career choices and was constantly ricocheting from one vocation to the next, it was easy to rub his anxiousness on Lena. He persuaded her to record a demo tape. Wherefore, after work for three weeks, she opened her heart in a studio, performing songs composed by a professional song-writer/pianist Robert had hired. The result was an astounding work of ballads. Within only three days of Robert shopping it around, a recording contract was offered. Lena was thrilled. However, when she shared the news with Angus, his reaction was predictable. He would remind her of Lettie and so many others. He would convince her that where she was, was where she was meant to be. Why give up a good life to chase something that would never be? Lena couldn't bear breaking his heart.

But what about hers?

Lena asked herself this as the waiter returned with her drink. He set the cocktail on the table, handed her a fresh napkin, and surprised her by winking before he strolled off. As the frosty beverage rolled down her throat, she was flattered, particularly so since her twenty-nine years were probably a good ten over his. In spite of her troubles, Lena had to chuckle.

The next amateur hit the stage. She was big and beautiful, chocolate-hued black woman who had a powerful contralto voice. As she gripped the microphone and strode charismatically across the stage, Lena could feel the richness in her sound and emotions shivering all over and through her. Yet when the ballad reached the saxophone solo and the voice was no longer there to sustain her, Lena was transported back to her worries.

Yes, Robert was right in pointing out that she wanted to sing instead of be an actuary. But why taunt her about the unfairness time and time again? Why not simply encourage her lovingly like he used to? Indeed she was well aware that as decent as her position was, it didn't stop the restlessness that stalked her—especially in her office at work, when she was alone and hearing the murmurings of uneasiness churning within. It made her gaze out the window and wonder what might have been and what could be, and how long this unfulfillment could last within her, like an incurable sickness, before she exploded with the stark fear of looking out that window every day—of never seeing the vivacity in eyes like when people heard her sing—so she then had to gallop to it, to the passion, which she ached to do or otherwise go insane. But by then, by the time she understood that in this life you must not follow your mother's heart or your father's heart, but your own, would it be too late?

Both answers increased Lena's adrenaline as the owner of the club came to the podium and declared the winner of the amateur night show. The victor was the black woman. Lena studied her, her smile as high-charged as the spirit that suddenly infused Lena. Lena jumped up to the club's owner and surprised herself by announcing, "I'm a singer, and I want to sign up for next week's amateur night."

"You do?" Paper-white, short teeth lit up a pudgy face. A cigar balanced between two chunky fingers. The smell reached up into her memories, bringing to mind an adored uncle who smoked cigars, too. It didn't even bother Lena when his attention paused mischievously over her body until her gaze met his blue eyes again. "You're a model or something?" he inquired.

"No, but if that's a compliment, it's a very nice one."

He smiled and nodded. "You're gorgeous, darling. I'm Patty. I'm the owner of this place, and by now you realize I'm a connoisseur of beauty." He extended a chubby hand.

Unable to contain a huge grin, Lena reached to shake,

but her knuckles were abruptly brushed with a kiss. When Patty returned her hand, Lena's smile was bigger. "You sure are a shy one," she chimed with soft laughter. She liked him.

"So they tell me. But tell me something, can you really sing? I mean really sing like Nellie?"

She was puzzled. "Nellie?"

"You know, the lady who won."

"Oh. I don't know if I'm good as she is, but I've been offered a recording contract on the basis of a demo."

"No kidding. Who offered? I know a couple of A&R people. Some come in here checking out the new talent regularly. Two acts were signed up that way."

"Really?" Lena tried to keep the excitement out of her voice. Perhaps the Man upstairs would give her another chance. No way she would decline a contract this time. If she didn't accept it now, then when? She would show Robert something. And her father as well. "I know Shell Taylor and Michael Grierson," she revealed. "They tried to sign me."

"No kidding? I know them, too. They come in here regularly."

She blinked. "They do?"

"No joke. But why didn't you sign?"

"It's too complicated."

"So tell me one day."

"One day?" *Did this mean he wanted her to return?*

"And if you're good enough for them, you're good enough for me. Besides, no audition is required with us. We let the audience tell you if you're good or not. Just be here Wednesday morning around nine. Wednesday is our rehearsal day for the amateur show, and morning is the only time we do any kind of rehearsals since we open at noon and close so late."

"That's fine with me." She didn't mind missing a morning of work.

"Then Thursday night is the competition."

"I'm excited already."

The drive home contrasted with the ride into the city. Smiles replaced frowns. Glistening eyes displaced teared ones. Even when Lena opened the apartment door, a new scent greeted her: soyed lamb chops, onion rice, creamed carrots. They were her favorites. Robert was cooking.

Wearing his beige silk pajama bottoms and a well-oiled chest, he emerged from the kitchen. Coming to her, intensity was vibrant in his eyes. "I'm so sorry. I didn't mean any of that craziness I said to you earlier. You're the best woman I know. And I still believe in you. I'm always with you, by your side. Don't ever forget that. I'm just upset because . . . because I seem to always be on a fast road to nowhere. I'm so tired of living this way. Why can't things change for me?"

Lena gave him a probing look. She tracked a tear rolling down his narrow cheek onto his squared jaw. God help him, Robert was the only man she had ever seen weep and look like a warrior doing so. Oddly enough, this particular evening the tears made him look more gorgeous than ever. What's more, he had done something kind and thoughtful in preparing the food. He seemed pitiful and vulnerable, too. Lena knew he hoped some of these traits would finally reel her into his arms, where there would be incredible lovemaking with him. She hadn't let him touch her in nearly three months.

Except Robert wasn't guessing her thinking correctly tonight. Not only could Lena not imagine being intimate with him, but she had come to a great realization: she could no more marry this man than she could throw herself in front of a speeding train. All she ever wanted was a man to love her the way she loved him. She wanted him to be the one she had dreamed about all her life. He would fill her with a feeling she couldn't get enough of and couldn't live without. It had been a long time coming to see it, but Robert wasn't that man.

Two

At first, the sight of her beguilingly sashaying across the stage was jolting to the copious audience. From the same perspective, anyone could see that amid the spotlight highlighted against the purple drapes was exactly where the young woman belonged. On Lena's cue to the musicians, the ballad commenced smoothly, the haunting introduction building with instrumentation, poising every back upright and riveting each eye directly ahead.

Swaying subtly and sensuously to the intoxicating rhythm, Lena wore a buttercream silk dress. Sleeveless, a mini, with a sweetheart neckline, it snuggled a slender figure while emphasizing the pleasing curves around her bust and hips. Taupe sling-back pumps and nude stockings dramatized firm thighs meeting rounded calves. The outfit was enhanced with loose, shoulder-skimming curls. They framed an oval face with eyes so exotic, they alone classified their owner as beautiful.

When finally the voice began its initial caress into Anita Baker's "Sweet Love," with merely those faint intonations, its rumble was as arresting as its possessor's attractiveness. Staggering to Lena, her expression wasn't weak and trembling like her stage fright had predicted. Singing in a club was a major leap from entertaining family and friends. Painfully Lena's nerves affirmed that as she prepared to appear on the stage. That was why with every fiber of her being, with all of her effort, with all that she had to give, Lena concentrated on each utterance and was quickly relieved at how the notes rang so perfectly—her unique alto soprano masterfully and stunningly exercising her numerous octaves, granting the instruments accompanying her the full use of their ranges.

Within this moment, when no one seemed to breathe, there was louder, prettier, and stronger vocalizing as the mood progressed. Compelling Lena to close her eyes, the ballad absorbed her in its passion, draining out each ounce of emotion that she was further capable to give. The lyrics, the melody, and every component of the music sustained her, then exalted to that pinnacle where her spirit soared free. There, in that paradisal space, it was Lena and that faceless, consummate phantom she was singing to. At least if only for a duration of a song, she was loved passionately and unconditionally, and would be cherished forever by him, regardless of any unwelcome surprises their days together did bring.

Lena opened her eyes to a boisterous standing ovation. There were screams, more thundering claps, whistles, and such an uproar the most egocentric person's confidence would have been elevated. Patty hugged her. The slick-haired waiter, Manuel, hugged her. Plus there were the multitudes who attempted to meet Centerfields' newest amateur night superstar. They crowded around Lena, and one gentleman in particular was extremely impressed. Alone at his table, picking up a cocktail, he was captivated.

In his unyielding line of vision, confusion and exhilaration abounded where she was. Sipping his drink and

still whirling from her performance, he wasn't expecting
her to notice him over their considerable distance, but
she did. Among the myriad of enthusiasts circling her,
and those simply packing the room, their eyes met and
lingered. And although her fascination was erratic because of all the fan distractions, Cordell Richardson was
still picturing her dreamy image long after she had gone.
During her rendition of "Sweet Love," the boy within
fantasized that she was blowing those velvety pipes
solely to him, but it was the man who reminded him of
responsibility, and with that he decided it was time to go
home.

The house was so quiet and peaceful when Lena entered it, she suspected that Robert was asleep. Taking off
her shoes, then carrying them down the lengthy hall leading to their bedroom, Lena speculated about his reaction
to her singing debut had he been in the audience. For
fear of flopping and having him torment her about it
afterward, Lena was secretive. He was so negative lately,
he wouldn't have wished her the best. That's why Robert
had no inkling of her intentions when she left so casually
for work that morning, with a tote presumably packed
with a hearty lunch, when inside was actually a fitted
party dress.

Fortunately everything worked out better than she
dreamed. The racing energy was seizing her, apprising
Lena that tonight in some way she had climbed a mountain. Bizarre as it was, the elation was such that even
then she couldn't truly perceive herself in her home,
sauntering toward her room. On the contrary, it was as
if she were suspended in some mysterious but fantastical

haze, which made everything seem not quite real, or not really what it was. With it, she felt freed, fulfilled, purposeful, and perpetually on the brink of exploding with laughter. Even when she reached the bedroom and saw Robert not slumbering but engrossed in, of all things, an orthodontic textbook, nothing could diminish the high.

"Where were you?" he asked, his eyes instantly appraising her elaborate look. "And why are you dressed like that? No way you were working overtime looking like that." Frowning he put the book aside. "And what's the smile for? I want to be in on it, too."

"You won't believe it," she said, laughter unsettling her voice. Softly she sat on the bed, her eyes glittering, her skin basking in a glow that drew him nearer. "You just won't believe it."

"Believe what!" he shouted testily but promptly mellowed his tone. "Woman, you better tell me where you were and stop playing games." Playfulness tried to animate his words, but Lena knew cheer was the last thing in his heart. "Come on now," he urged. "Don't keep me in suspense."

Lena rested her shoes on the floor before assenting with a docile breath, "All right, I was singing."

"Singing!" boomed out of his bug-eyed shock.

She nodded, watching Robert's astoundment lurch his head forward. "Not at a studio, either," she enthused. "At a club."

"A club? *You were singing at a club tonight?"*

"Ever heard of Centerfields?"

"Of course," he answered, looking more bewildered. "It's that spot your co-workers talk about all the time. You said you wanted to check it out one night."

"That's the place."

Robert began rubbing the back of his neck and didn't stop until he flung himself out of bed and paced a few steps. "You mean to tell me you sang there and didn't tell me? You didn't even invite your fiancé?"

Lena bristled. *He wasn't her fiancé anymore, at least not in her heart.* With each day they shared, she realized this more and more. Lately the realization lasted long after his tirades, often bringing her close to the point of telling him the engagement was off and they were over. Luckily for Robert, though, she always stopped herself. Either Robert would say or do something so sweet and wonderful, guilt would make her postpone the dreaded moment. Other times Robert was in such a state about his problems—or just in such a hysterical state, period— that Lena was certain something awful would happen to him if she left.

"You could have screwed up everything!" jarred her from her musings.

Amazement twisted her face. "Because you weren't there? Because you weren't in the audience, I could have messed up?"

"No, because you're acting dumb. Stupid is more like. Getting mad at me, then running out, trying to make something alive that was dead. But what you're really trying to do is make me look bad. Trying to prove you can do everything, and I can do nothing! That's it, isn't it!"

The frustration coming at her reached into her soul, raking out the questions he couldn't deal with if she voiced them aloud. Was it her fault that he bungled the bar exam and so many other endeavors and was at a loss as to his bearing? God knows she had rendered everything in her power to support him, Lena thought to herself—to be there for him, to lift him up in every possible way. So why did she suffer and be his mouth's punching bag? She didn't. Refusing to let him destroy her gladness, she preferred to indulge in something that granted equilibrium to the highs and lows of this night. And that, she easily mused, was a strawberry-scented bubble bath. Hopefully, after it she could disclose her biggest news.

However, as Lena made a start toward the bathroom, "No, no, you don't!" swung her around and stopped her. "Don't walk away from me. Not yet."

"Why not?" she questioned irritably. "I just want to soak and revel in tonight. After I come out, we can get comfortable and talk about this more."

"I want to talk about it now." He ambled in front of her.

Smoothly Lena maneuvered away. "No, Robert, you want to do what you do best lately: argue. Argue over anything and everything. Why can't you just be happy? Happy that I made a step toward my dream? Don't you always tell me how I'm wasting my life at the insurance company? Well, I made an important step tonight in the direction I want to go in."

"But why couldn't I be a part of it?"

"Because!" she voiced sharply, then looked somewhere only her mind could see. "I didn't need you there to say anything negative! I had a point to prove to myself that I can make it in music regardless of what my father thinks my chances are, and regardless of what you said about it being all over for me. I had to find out if I could really be successful at it. I also felt ready." She peered back at him earnestly. "The right energy was around me that made me feel that way."

"Oh, brother, there's that crazy stuff again."

"Call it whatever you want! But something was telling me to do it! It started when I went there last week, after you made me so mad. I saw the amateur show and that's when I felt it. . . ." She paused, her eyes misting in a place only she could see.

"It?"

"It was a force or a surging, just something pulling me up out of my seat. At the same time, I could feel it coming from somewhere down deep inside me from a place so desperate. It was like I would suffocate if I didn't get up there and take this chance. Not taking it would mean dying while living. Not taking it would mean I never tried to know what it would feel like to be truly alive, doing what God intended me to do." She gazed back at him intently. "If that ever happens to you, Robert, you'll know you just have to do it. You won't have a choice. Something inside you won't let you have a choice. You just have to go where the spirit moves you."

"So the spirit moved you?" There was a hint of sarcasm.

"Yes. And it was the best thing I ever did."

"So you're telling me this wasn't to get back at me?"

"No, this was to come back to me, to what I love."

He plainly stared.

"I did very well, too. Standing ovation, lots and lots of applause, but most of all I won."

"Very good."

She couldn't tell whether he meant that.

"Not only that," she continued, "but the owner, Patty, invited me back for a three-week engagement." *There, her announcement was out.*

"A three-week engagement?" He pursed his lips approvingly.

"That's right. It pays well, too."

He nodded. "Great . . . really . . ."

"It sure is. I feel so good I could scream. But you know what the best part is?"

"What's that?"

"Shell Taylor and Michael Grierson come in there sometimes scouting for talent."

Sourly his lips downturned. "But you had your chance with them. You blew it."

She loathed the way he always spouted that, but was dogged not to let him destroy her spirit. "I honestly don't think my chance is blown. Maybe they'll give me another one."

"I doubt it. And even if they did, you wouldn't take it. You listen to your old man too much. Here you are a grown woman, and he has to okay every step you make."

"That's not fair, Robert."

"But it's true! He made you blow the opportunity of a lifetime. You were so dumb—"

"Stop—I don't want to hear it! Please don't insult me again!" Her eyes were suddenly so forlorn they beckoned a hush between them.

Within the soundlessness, Robert studied her, then gazed down ruefully. "I'm sorry," he apologized. Looking up, he made further amends: "Really I am. And speaking of your father . . . well, he called."

"He did? When?"

"This afternoon. Before he left."

"Left?"

"He went on a trip."

She was stunned. "My father went on a trip? Why didn't you tell me when I first came in?"

"I forgot . . . I guess . . ."

She eyed him warily. No love was lost between the two men. "Well, what did he say? How— Why did this come about so suddenly?"

"He said to tell you his chiropractor urged him to take an immediate medical leave of absence."

"Oh, yes, he has that back problem. He really shouldn't be sitting as long as he does during the day."

"Anyway, he claims that he'll be gone for a while. Said he was going with a—a Grace."

"That's Mrs. Atwater, his neighbor. My, my, Daddy." An impish grin crept onto Lena's face. "She lives down the block from him. She's a widow, too. Nice lady. She'll be good for Daddy."

"Whatever. He's going to be traveling to all these different countries. Said he'd write since calling is difficult and costly in foreign places, but if you need him contact Blue Sky Tours. Here, he left the number."

As Robert searched for the notepad, Lena was entranced with this news. Certainly she missed her father already. On the other hand, he wouldn't be around to thwart her dreams this time. But somehow, Lena sensed that even if he were nearby, there was a fire thriving in her that allowed no turning back. Moreover, as the spiritual awareness books she was reading lately indicated, one could feel when something out of the ordinary was about to happen, whether good or bad. Lena was starting to feel it then: something wonderful was coming.

Radio City Music Hall stood conspicuously, enchanting Lena like a moon in midnight's sky as she stepped toward it along Sixth Avenue. Imagining herself one day gracing its stage, she was scarcely alert to nearing the corner. Once there, dreaminess lingered while waiting to cross at the red light, until spotting a familiar face jarred her back into reality. Over six feet and suavely dressed in a navy blue suit, the guy from the club couldn't be missed among the horde of New Yorkers crossing the adjoining street. Virtually every night during her three-week engagement, he was seated at a lone table at Centerfields.

Try as she might not to notice him in the audience, Lena could never help herself. The lure was more than his handsomeness, that confidence and the sexiness about him, too. Undefinable, it was. What's more, she didn't feel guilty about admiring a man while still officially engaged. Like any normal woman who had a lover, Lena occasionally viewed other men as attractive. Nonetheless, that didn't mean she was attracted to them and therefore desired them lustfully. Always she was faithful, in mind and body, even lately when she didn't feel loved.

Out in the daylight, the mystery man's attractiveness was amplified. Coincidentally his skin's hue was identical to that lush, deep, Indian-brown that depicted Robert's complexion, but where Robert's striking eyes grabbed you, all of this man's calmly masculine features mingled together as easily as the blends of a sunset, each characteristic no more disarming than the last, it all fascinating in an undivided portrait of splendor.

The sunset was a few feet away sooner than Lena expected. The beauty was so awesome it made her uncomfortable. Childishly she whirled toward Radio City, feigning interest in the upcoming events on the billboards. No sooner than she took a breath, though, she sensed an overpowering presence behind her.

"Excuse me," sent a shiver down the small of her back, and for a split second froze her limbs. Finally turning around slowly, Lena encountered eyes that outshone the vibrant July sun.

"How you doing?" she said automatically, like they had spoken before.

"Hello. I'm Cordell Richardson." A large hand reached into hers, shaking it firmly. "Maybe you remember me from the club?"

"Yes, of course." She sounded more composed than she felt. She could still feel his hand on hers, even when it wasn't there any longer. "You always have that little table in the far left corner."

He smiled broadly, granting his serene features an excitement that intrigued her. "Well, I saw you standing here. And I just couldn't pass the opportunity to tell the incredible Lena Durant how much I've enjoyed her performances these past weeks. Your voice is unbelievable. You blew me away. I guess you can tell that by how much you've seen me at the club." He laughed gently, and its resound contradicted his appearance. From an upper thirties, sophisticated-looking gent, she didn't anticipate the deep controlled rumble of an old man. However, that was precisely what Lena heard. It brought to mind someone who had lived a long time and delighted in the stories of the naive, but was never patronizing. It was an infectious chuckle, and Lena liked its sound so much she joined him.

"Oh, I don't mind at all," she said sobering some. "I'm glad you've enjoyed the shows. As a matter of fact, I was heading to the club right now. This is the only day my boss gives out those golden pieces of paper called paychecks, and while I'm there I'm also going to sign a contract for another month at Centerfields."

"Another month? Can I reserve a permanent seat?"

"I guess this means I have my first groupie."

"That you do."

They both laughed lightly. It was gaiety where lips smiled but eyes didn't. Lena's were too busy noticing that he was even better looking up close. What she couldn't determine however, was his impression of her, and what specifically was he thinking at that instant. For he was looking at her in a way that made her very, very warm. And when unexpectedly Cordell's hand brushed aside that lock of hair that invariably fell by Lena's eye, she was even warmer. After he did it, there was a silence, stillness, and Cordell saw her uneasiness and knew he overstepped his bounds. It made him regret his natural instinct to make people he liked comfortable.

Heart pounding, Lena was caught off guard by the simple motion, and it took a moment to gather her wits and find her way out of a sudden secluded world, which she felt herself being drawn to with this stranger. Hundreds, possibly thousands, of people were around, but oddly enough she was beginning to feel as if there were solely two.

"My hair always falls in my eye," she said casually, pretending she was unaffected by his tender gesture.

"Beautiful hair." He smiled, examining it, then shifting to her face. "Very beautiful."

There was that stare again, the one that made her speculate what he was seeing and thinking. As much as Lena didn't want to, and as wrong as she knew it was, she could have easily lost herself within such a trancing gaze, whether she discerned its meaning or not. Stopping her was the reminder of the traffic lights. They had changed several times while they talked. If Lena didn't hurry up, she would arrive late at Centerfields, and in turn return tardily to the insurance company.

"I better get going." She spoke abruptly. "My regular job is an actuary at an insurance company, and I have to be back there by noon."

"An actuary and a singer. Now there's an odd combination."

"I know," Lena murmured sadly. Although hearing herself, she was exuberant when she asked, "What about you?"

"I'm an attorney at Rayborn, Richardson, and Brown. It's in the area. I'm on morning break now."

"An attorney." She nodded approvingly. "I'm impressed."

"I love it, too. Lately I've even taken on some new areas of law, which should spice things up more. But enough about me. Can I walk you to the club?"

"Walk . . . me?" Lena stammered, surprised by the offer. "I don't want to inconvenience you. I'm sure they need you back at the firm."

"Who cares about those guys?" he teased. "Especially when I'm in the company of the next R&B superstar of the world."

"I wish."

"You don't have to," he voiced with a sudden pensiveness. "It will happen, I'm sure. I can feel it. So with that, I guess I'll catch you at the club." Then befell a pause and with it, there was that look again. Roaming lowly behind it came, "Friday night?"

"Friday night it is."

Entering the club, Lena saw Patty setting up napkins and other adornments on the tables. When he caught sight of her, he ambled over with a huge grin. "Ready for a month more?"

"Ready as ever. Sometimes I have to pinch myself. I'm really singing in this beautiful club. And people actually pay money to hear me. A man even came up to me in the street today," she said, envisioning Cordell Richardson, unable to forget him. "He said he's coming to hear me again."

"You should be famous," Patty asserted, his joviality replaced with a seriousness. "Any woman as gorgeous and talented as you should be looked at and listened to by millions. You make people feel good. You're going to make it, Lena. You mark my words. And you know how much I believe that? You know what I did for you?"

"What did you do, Patty?"

"This is only because I love you, you know?"

"I know." She had to smile.

"Because this thing that I did for you is going to take from me. From my pocket."

"It is?"

"You bet."

He lit a cigar, then sat at the table in front of them. With the scent wafting about, he patted the spot in front of the available chair. "Sit, let me tell you."

Lena did as asked. Patty poised the cigar between his fingers, then, "I called Shell and Michael."

"You did?" Lena gasped excitedly.

"Yes, I did. They were out of town these last months. On the West Coast, I had heard. So when someone told me they were back in the city, I called them. I told them about you. They said they were trying to sign you before, some time ago, and nothing came of it." He took a drag of the cigar.

Lena looked worried. "I hope they aren't too upset about that?"

"Hey," he said, exhaling coils of smoke, "these guys are too busy to be upset that long. They just think about acquiring superior talent, producing a superior product, and making superior money. So they told me they might come this weekend to check you out. If you're still cooking, they implied they might give you another shot."

Lena jumped up and let out a scream.

Patty started laughing. "Sit down. Darling, you're crazy."

"About you." She scurried around the table and planted a smooch on his fleshy cheek. "Oh, Patty, I had a feeling about you the first time we met."

"Only weeks ago, too."

She collected herself, reclaiming her seat, her eyes growing misty. "Seems like longer."

"That it does." Sentimentality flushed his face, but he regained composure with a clearing of his throat. "But anyway, so you see why I say I'll lose money? I could sign you here for as long as I want and make a fortune. You could come out pretty good, too. But I know what you have, and you know what you have, and I wouldn't feel right if you didn't use it to its highest potential. I mean so everyone will know what you have. You see what I mean?"

"You're the best, Patty."

"I know."

Then something in the back of her mind pushed forward. Patty had thrown Robert out of Centerfields on the first night of her three-week engagement. Prior to the patrons' arrival, he was backstage loudly bickering with Lena, incensed about an outfit he thought too re-

vealing for her to wear onstage. As they escorted him
out, he went so far as to kick over a cart stacked with
glasses and dishes, breaking every one of them, and
shouting that he wouldn't reimburse a dime. From that
night forward, the shows had taken place without him in
the audience.

"What about Robert?" she thought aloud.

"What about him?" he mouthed blankly.

"Can he come back in the club?"

Patty looked bothered. He began scratching the top of
his head where hair used to be. "Look out for yourself,
Lena."

"But Patty, he won't be argumentative again. And I
told you, you can deduct the broken plates and glasses
from my pay."

He shook his head, gawking at her. "Why are you
looking out for that guy? Those things he said to you
were abominable."

Lena looked off recalling the ruthless words, then gazed
at Patty again. "Though it's no excuse for how he talks to
me, he's had it rough lately. So many disappointments in
his life have made him frustrated and bitter."

Patty took another puff of the cigar, then steadied it
in his grip. All the while he was still shaking his head.

"What?" Lena asked.

"What does he do? And what's been so rough for
him?"

"Well, a . . . he used to teach, and he did some other
things, and just recently he was in law school, but he—"

"Law school? I'd never know from the way he acted.
He made it that far in education, to law school?"

Barely, thought Lena. Yet she couldn't possibly tell
anyone how Robert almost ruined his prospect of being

a lawyer by scattering his concentration with everything conceivable, rather than focusing on his dreams and studying for exams.

"What's he doing now?" Patty queried. "What's the man's true calling? What does he want to do with his life? By now he should know. Hell, he has to be about thirty something or around there. What is he doing?"

"He just failed the bar, but he's planning to take it again."

"That so. But what is he doing now?"

Driving me nuts, Lena answered in her head, and soon couldn't hide the upset. Not knowing what to say, she peered down.

Staring at her, Patty frowned. "I see you don't want to talk about this, so enough of it already. Let me go get your pay and the new contract."

Why? Why am I still with him? Why can't I just tell him it's over? Alone that night, Lena lounged in bed for hours confronting the unavoidable.

Was it that she still cared about Robert so profoundly and was praying for the reappearance of his former self? Was it that she couldn't resist his sweet talk and actions after he verbally tormented her? Did they always interfere with her good sense? Was it that she empathized with him, and it ripped her heart to desert him at his lowest—the one who once loved her enough to ask for her hand in marriage? Could he fall completely apart if she left and there was nothing positive in his life? Or was it nigh impossible to relinquish the fairy-tale image of she and Robert having the ideal life, and marriage, all of which she embraced so dearly in her heart? Unequivocally it was a combination of all that made her hold onto something no longer magical, no longer even bearable.

Nestled underneath silken lavender sheets, facing a painting of a waterfall, Lena was relieved that Robert was visiting his parents. Before leaving, he heightened their woes, forbidding her to perform on Friday if he wasn't permitted inside. Furthermore, he contended that Centerfields was wasting time and stole too much of hers from him. He needed and loved her, he insisted, whereas her talents at the club were unproductive.

Well, he had a bombshell waiting when he entered the door, Lena contemplated, satisfaction granting her face a glow. Patty had made her day, informing her about the scouts coming to check her out. Not only Patty, though, but someone else transformed an ordinary day into one very special.

Lena lazily turned to her right side, where the terrace faced her. A striking view of the Brooklyn Bridge and the luminous buildings of various sizes, which were cast against it, was resplendent and brought with it a lightness of heart that streamed to her thoughts, suddenly softening her outlook of things, according a new mood. Therewith, instead of bemoaning Robert, she was recreating compliments, easy laughter, and covert stares. They were all compliments of a stranger she crossed paths with on a New York street. What did a man like Cordell Richardson do on a night like tonight? That was the mystery Lena pondered over and over as her mind sailed off to sleep.

Three

Friday night arrived with anxiousness, lending more inspiration for Lena's rendition of Whitney Houston's classic "I'll Always Love You." Her favorite song, its sound reverberated throughout a room so mobbed with music lovers that many who populated the nightspot had to stand. Word of mouth had made them rush to see Centerfields' new star. On top of that, all of the major papers had reviewed her performances, guaranteeing even the severest music critics that Ms. Durant's talent was unforgettable.

Manipulating every note for all its worth, presumably immersed in the drama of emotional intensity, Lena searched the audience. By the fifth number, appearances lied. No one knew the discouragement about the record executives' absence from the audience. Neither would they have guessed about the heartfelt wish for her one parent to behold her on that stage and hear the applause that capped the moment, which was soon enriched with adoration expressed with roses on the dressing room vanity, along with gifts and jumbo hugs.

Nevertheless, with these dashed hopes there was something else that added to the melancholy after showtime that night. Cordell Richardson wasn't among the fans like he assured Lena he would be. Considering that he was practically a stranger, and she knew hardly anything about the man, his nonattendance shouldn't have bothered Lena. Except it did.

That all being as it may, by other standards it was classified a fabulous night. Her vocalizing was electrifying. Never had she been more confident and in command of her abilities. Never had Lena felt more appreciated and basked in that sensation when Patty and she were the remaining occupants in the club.

Sliding onto the bar stool next to her boss, she watched him tallying the night's receipts. "Good night, wasn't it?"

Patty grinned, his cigar clenched between his front teeth. "Better than good. The money rolled in by the truckload. Boy, I'm going to miss you, darling."

Somewhat shocked, she reared back. "Miss me?"

"Yes. My waiter, Manuel," he mouthed with a chuckle, "he's really going to miss you, too. He has a big crush on you, you know?"

Dryly Lena smiled. "But who said I was going anywhere? There were no scouts here tonight."

Patty counted the last bills and piled them neatly in a steel repository with the capacity of a twelve-inch television. Locking it, he remarked, "The weekend is young. Believe me, before it goes you'll have what you've dreamed of, Lena. Mark my words."

"I hope so." She looked down.

"Now why are you blue?" Patty's voice raised her head. "Is it just because the A&R guys didn't come, or is there something else?"

Lena half smiled. "Don't pay me any mind, Patty. I'm just weird, that's all."

The somberness persevered on Saturday when neither the executives nor her new friend inhabited the audience.

As a result, Lena struggled to bury the dejection and get whatever joy, but also wisdom, out of this unforgettable season of her life. On Sunday she endeavored to do the same. Lena signaled to Patty, who was spouting corny jokes onstage. With that cue, she was prepared to treasure her gift, the moment, and mellifluously enlighten her audience about the bittersweetness of love. What Lena had no knowledge of then was how exquisite she had to come across this particular evening. Acutely she became aware, though, when Shell Taylor and Michael Grierson were spotted at a remote alcove table. Both gentlemen tipped their drinks toward her as she stepped in front of the microphone. The lights lowered dimmer than usual. The music commenced, charming Lena with its smoothness to close her eyes.

Darkly suited, with a self-assured stride, Cordell's noticeable presence emerged at the entrance of Centerfields, just as she reached the second verse of the slow, torrid strain. Stimulated and enthralled by the vision at center stage, he stopped and started several times while the waitress escorted him to a table. Once seated, his sight aimed straight ahead, and budging was impossible even if the world was ending that second. Amid thunderous clapping and shouting, Lena opened her eyes, seeing a blur of bodies overshadowed by the larger than life panorama of Shell and Michael motioning for her to join them. Nervousness trembled through her as she headed for their table, praying their hearts were in the same place as hers.

"The best drink in the house for this talented lady," Michael Grierson ordered with Manuel. "And two more beers for us."

Lena situated herself in a seat between the two men.

Manuel shot her a knowing glance. Afterward he hurried off.

"How are you two?" Lena asked. "I'm glad you caught the show."

"We're glad you didn't stop singing," Shell Taylor stated plainly. To Lena, he was eternally serious and when he did dare to laugh, it looked painful to do so. "So what's the deal, Lena Durant?"

"The deal?" Lena echoed, hoping he was implying what she thought.

Leaning back, Michael folded his arms. "We want to offer you a contract again. The same terms as before. And you might know, as well as discovering talent, Shell and I are also occasionally involved in producing and would like to do so with you, along with a major producer, of course. So we were sitting here thinking about which material now in our possession would do you justice." He pushed his glasses high on his thick nose.

"There's going to be a lot of work to do," Shell added. "Yet because you're under contract with Patty, we want to wait on everything until this engagement ends. We're very impressed with your talent, Lena. Time has made you even better. We're also impressed with those phenomenal reviews you've been getting. And normally we wouldn't even sign an artist who hasn't had a great deal of exposure. But your talent is rare. Like we did before, we set aside the rules for you. We want you . . . badly. Now the question is, do you want to be a recording artist just as badly?"

In awe of her spectacular fortune, Lena was momentarily speechless. Suspended in a sort of dazedness, she merely gazed down as if there were someone to thank in her lap.

"Is something wrong?" Shell asked, the furrows between his brows deepening. "Don't tell me you're thinking about passing up this opportunity *again?*"

Lena stared up into his hazel eyes, as if just realizing he was there. "Oh, no—I—I mean yes. Yes, I'm going to take it. I'm not going to pass. I'm ready to sign when you are."

"Good," Shell said, never cracking a smile. He reached into his jacket pocket and removed an appointment book. Searching through it, he inquired, "When does this engagement end?"

"August seventh," Lena answered quickly.

He scribbled beside a date, snapped the book shut, and peered up at her. "I have you down for a meeting to negotiate your contract and handle other matters on August ninth. Any problem with that?"

"That's fine." *Was she dreaming this all?*

Michael nodded. "It'll give you time to get an attorney, too. It takes time to find a good one."

Just then, Manuel returned with the drinks. He took one look at Lena's face, and his own became vivacious. He asked, "Did something happen, Lena? I recognized these gentlemen from before. This hot trio that used to perform here was signed to a recording contract with them. Did they—"

Bursting with happiness, Lena nodded. "Yes, they did, Manuel."

He bent down and hugged her. "Congratulations."

Lena's gratefulness nearly spurred teary eyes, but Shell's stern tone delayed the mawkishness.

"So you will be at my office on the morning of August ninth, at ten A.M. with your attorney, ready to negotiate a record deal?"

"Yes."

"This is no game, Lena," Michael elaborated. "We don't want to go through what we went through before with you." He shoved his glasses upward again. "A whole lot of time was wasted. Time is money. Don't be scared. Just go for it. You have it going on *big time,* so there is no need to worry about anything. You're going to be extremely happy with the results. People would give their lives for what's on your plate right now."

"I know, and I won't disappoint you. I'll be there on August ninth, bright and early."

Shell and Michael alluded to other obligations and hastily vacated Centerfields to tend to them. A short while later, Manuel was summoned by another patron. So where was Patty, Lena wondered, her scrutiny darting over every inch of the packed house. Jaw-dropping news like this was likely to explode from her if she didn't share it soon. But it was almost astonishing when, impetuously, as her head targeted behind, was an approaching vision, who for some reason, made this night far more dreamy than it already was.

"Remember me?"

Cordell Richardson towered above her charismatically, like a masterpiece from heaven, his cologne infiltrating her senses, calling to mind groves, fresh air, and emitting something uniquely his own.

"Of course, I remember you," Lena acknowledged with a laugh, not hiding her delight at seeing him. "Have a seat."

Obviously pleased at her invitation, he carefully slipped off his suit jacket and was arranging it over the back of the chair when Lena found herself transfixed. Certainly her intent was not to pay more than fleeting attention to this casual acquaintance's physique. Nevertheless, being below and before him, Lena couldn't help herself from covertly examining the massive breadth of his shoulders in that staunch white shirt, and how well his arms filled the ample sleeves.

"I had to work late Friday," Cordell informed her as he sat. He eased his chair forward. "And I had to work late Saturday also. I surely regret missing the shows."

"It's okay," she said and soon encountered skin that was powdery, but oddly shimmery, and eyes scintillating and entirely warm. The visage matched flawlessly with an unobtrusive nose and a wide mouth that appeared everlastingly tranquil and content. Like the day they chatted underneath the blazing afternoon sky, his face again reminded her of a sunset.

"Is that expression on your face because of me? Because you're that glad to see me?" He laughed that old man's laugh at himself, while his eyes dreamily traced Lena's face.

She was tickled but equally baffled at how to reply.

"I didn't see you before now," she said, gently steering the subject.

"I was around. I certainly saw you. Walked in, in the middle of your song. You blew me away as usual." Strangely with the praise there was an unforseen sadness veiling his face, and as his eyes darted briefly into the distance, Lena questioned whether it had anything to do with the song she had sung. Not only that, but as Lena sat noticing him, more and more she recognized the look. In the weeks prior to their introduction, when her gaze skimmed the audience, occasionally there was that sorrow on his face. It was always attributed to solely the mood of the ballad. Studying him now, Lena knew better.

"You took me far from the real world to a much nicer one," he added, focusing back on her.

"I'm glad you liked it. Matter of fact, you weren't the only one. I was just offered the opportunity of a lifetime."

"So that's why you're glowing like that." Again he delicately scanned her features. "I knew something was going on. I saw you talking to those two guys."

"They were record company executives."

"Don't tell me—they offered you a contract?" His voice was cool, but there was a sudden exuberance in his countenance that Lena knew rivaled her own.

"Yes, they did make me an offer, and I'm sure going to take it."

"Congratulations." And before they knew anything, each was stunned with his prompt incline across the table, topped with a swift kiss on her cheek. "I'm sorry," he apologized, seeing her staggered reaction afterward. "I had no right to do that. You hardly know me."

"It's okay." Her voice was low and supple, and Lena tried not to linger in his gaze as she was abruptly tempted to do. "I didn't mind."

"You sure?"

"Oh, you're probably just one of those people who love to see people happy and you get very expressive. There's nothing wrong with it. No harm done."

"It's true that I am happy for you. Somehow I can tell you wanted this very badly. Probably since you were a kid." His eyes lost themselves within the growing fervency of hers. "You probably locked yourself in your room because you didn't want anyone to think you were crazy for letting all that emotion out of you, when you looked in the mirror and closed your eyes and sang your heart out." He paused. "Music probably was, and is, unlike anything else for you, except . . . maybe love. I would guess that falling in love was the only thing in life you were more passionate about than music. I could tell that from the way you sing about love."

Astounded that he recreated a scene plucked straight from her childhood, complete with every puerile contemplation, Lena gawked for a second. "You're something. Very deep."

Contentment lurked on his lips, but there was intensity in his eyes. With it all, there was something about his face that appeared different to Lena. Different from all the other times she looked at it. Granted, it was still as soothing as a sunset. Yet this sunset's radiance was not merely a beautiful scene to behold. With the grace of his reflections, it had become truly alive and three dimensional, making it easily accessible to touch and be touched by.

"What you said is exactly what I used to do"—Lena spoke with wonder—"and how I feel."

"I guess I've suddenly come in touch with my intuitive side." He tugged at his perfectly aligned collar, then leaned forward and sideways, resting one elbow on his knee, while his knuckles supported his chin. "When I was a kid, I used to sometimes sense when something bad or good was going to happen. But never have I"—his compelling stare arrested her—"never have I just assumed so much about a person as I have you. Maybe those shows I've been watching lately has something to do with it."

"Shows?"

"Yes. Late at night there are these really interesting programs. They're about intuition, meditation, spirituality, and also a concept called creative visualization, which is simply imagining and focusing profoundly to obtain your objectives in life, and all of this is coupled with the higher power, of course."

Finding this fascinating and so in common with her interests, Lena was lured forward. "You know, I've been reading books about the same subjects, about intuition, spirituality, meditation and such—all centered around religion—and it's opened a whole new world to me. When I talk about it to my— my friend laughs. My friend thinks I'm starting to get crazy, except for the religion part. I've always been close to God, even though I don't often go to church, and I don't preach to people, and I can't quote scriptures. But it's there. And I think people can see it by the way I treat them. It's just like I want to be treated." Lena exhaled after her professions and felt ambivalent about having shared them. Why had she told this near stranger all this?

"Your friend shouldn't laugh at your being this way," Cordell responded, his eyes luxuriating in her. "But there is something funny—" He straightened his posture.

"What?"

"What you just told me about yourself, I kind of already knew that about you."

"You did?"

He nodded. "For some reason, I've sensed so much about you, Lena. It's one of those situations when you see or meet someone, and instantly you know you can talk to them, and they can talk to you. It's like I kind of know you, but we both know I don't. Not really."

Lena was silent a second, because as bizarre as it was, she was experiencing the same mystical feeling on her part. Something about Cordell Richardson made him so familiar and equally so easy to talk to. Without question, Lena was certain she could communicate very openly with him. But at the same time, getting to know him was mysterious, extremely exhilarating, and exceptionally unnerving—and she was starving to discover more.

"Since I've been coming here watching you, I can tell that you're very softhearted—and sometimes fans, and people in general, can mistake that for weakness and take advantage instead of cherishing you for being that way. I can also see that you have a very positive spirit."

She shook her head, staring at him. "So what else do you know about me?"

"That it's more than music and singing that you're passionate about. It's what's represented in those songs that gets to you. You're in love with a love story. I can tell you're a romantic."

It was then she braved the look again, the one that enthralled her that day beneath the afternoon sun. It was unsettling as much as nourishing and all in all so obscure. It added to that sensation of so much seemingly happening in just one night, even if Lena couldn't comprehend exactly the meaning of such a stare. Everything was all too overwhelming, but too engrossing for her to want to end.

"Maybe I am," Lena admitted. The confession made her peer into the horizon and confront the deeply bottomed ache to have a man passionately and desperately love her. A man who would do anything just to have her love—a man whose love she would do anything to have. Yet that wasn't to be, Lena had resolved, thinking of Robert.

Switching her heed back to Cordell, she strove to disguise her grief. "You're very perceptive, Mr. Richardson."

"Am I?"

"Now let me tell you about yourself," she volunteered and tensely gathered all the speculations she reasonably and unreasonably had about him. "I sense that you're a good person, maybe too good for some. I also sense that you're happy, but there's a little something about you sometimes that tells me there is a sadness, too. Someone has probably hurt you, and something is missing in your life." Like she had been waiting forever to unload the observations, her chest was heaving and she stared at him, filled with new and unexplainable emotions.

Any amusement in the slightest vanished from Cordell's face. He was returning her gaze with incredulity. "You're very perceptive, too."

There was a sudden silence and uneasy exchange of looks. Trying to break the soundless tension, Lena injected buoyantly, "Can that crystal ball in your mind tell me if I'll be a success, or am I going to be a flop once my records hit the airwaves?"

With a pensiveness coloring his features, Cordell flashed a half smile. "No crystal ball needs to tell you that. You and I both know you're going to take the world by storm. I guess now it's *your summer of life—your time to make everything happen.*"

"Oh, yes." Lena shut her eyes tight and opened them quickly, nodding with agreement. "And are you? Are you in the summer of your life?"

He speculated for several seconds, looking somewhere only his mind could see, before gazing serenely. "I could be approaching it. I think I mentioned to you before that I've broadened my horizons by taking on some new areas of law. They should give me some much needed stimulation."

"Stimulation?" She leaned closer.

"Well, I was doing corporation law and patents. But now I've expanded into several different areas, and I'm open to more. Doing the kind of law I've been doing wasn't challenging enough for me anymore—not by itself anyway."

Instantly Lena visioned those miserable days at the insurance company. As soon as possible, she was resigning. "I know what it's like doing something when your heart isn't in it."

"I'm sure you do, considering the career change you're about to make. But it's not like I didn't like specializing in the area of law I was doing. I loved it. It was just that I needed something more. Everything had become routine."

At that, a thought came to mind, making her stare at him with a smile. "Well, if you're up for all areas of law, does that mean entertainment law, too?"

His expression was beyond pleased. He reared back, bright-eyed. "Are you asking me—"

"An entertainment lawyer is exactly what I need. On August ninth, I have to bring my lawyer to the record company and negotiate my contract."

The thrilling offer hoisted his chest. "I'm your man," drifted at her sedately.

"Really? I hope you won't charge too much." She smiled.

"For you, just my million dollar fee." His lips curled, too.

"This is great. I would have had some time trying to find the right attorney. You saved my life."

"Maybe you saved mine, too."

"I did? How's that?"

"Maybe there was a reason something told me to walk in here one evening after work and hear you singing. Maybe the man above was guiding me in this place specifically to meet you, Lena—to change my life." Then his eyes traveled carefully over her features. His voice lowered to a near whisper. "Or to give me life."

There was that startling quiet again, coupled with that anxious interchanging of glances. Lightening the awkward moment this time, however, was Patty. He sauntered over and yanked Lena up from the table.

"I heard the good news! We're going in the back to celebrate with a bottle of champagne."

Lena mouthed a "goodbye" as Patty grabbed her hand. With a forced smile, Cordell nodded his parting and observed them until they were out of sight. Left to be appreciated was the cocktail he had ignored. As he raised the bubbly beverage to his lips, conversation began to replay in his head.

When Lena arrived home, she was high from a dream fulfilled. It was like Cordell Richardson was right there, too, sharing it with her, even if visibly he was nowhere around. Inside the living room, into the kitchen, and down the oblong hall, she carried the hopefulness about the future, and along with the image, the voice, the words, that man. She was beaming, picturing how her life might change, but just as unforgettable were the words spoken to her, the stares, the kiss on the cheek. Excitement leaped in her everywhere, and halfway it resulted from Cordell representing her. This guaranteed she would see him again. It had been a long time since she had found someone so interesting. Lena enjoyed their conversation; she liked the way he thought; she couldn't stop hearing his laugh; she relished his staring at her *that way*. In short, she purely loved being around him.

So when she reached the bedroom and caught sight of Robert, it was like a beautiful dream turning into a horrible nightmare. Distraught, he was fully dressed and sitting wide-legged on the side of the bed. His face seemed filled with tears, though it was dry and eyes unwatered.

"What's wrong? Where have you been?"

"I went out walking. Just walking and walking for a long time. Couldn't stop thinking. Thinking about you being a success at the club and me— I couldn't stop thinking about what happened this past week."

Frowning, Lena dropped slowly onto the bed. "What happened?"

"I didn't want to tell you. I went on some interviews. Law clerk positions since I can't practice yet. I've had them set up for weeks now, but I wanted to surprise you with good news. Yet each firm that I went to rejected me."

"Robert, I'm so sorry. You just have to keep trying."

"I know," he agreed and curtly peered over at her. "But on the other hand, I'm so lucky to have you. You're the one thing that makes my life worth living. Otherwise I might as well jump off a bridge."

"Don't say that."

"I'll try not to. But that doesn't mean I'm not thinking it."

With her frown deepening, Lena patted Robert on the shoulder. Did he really mean what he was saying? Or was it a cruel ploy to get sympathy? Thinking about leaving him was bad enough when he was down and out. Yet now that he was also suicidal, what was she going to do? Always she had feared something like this, even if she managed to push it in the back of her mind.

Four

"Hello, Patty speaking."

"How you doing, Patty?"

"Much better hearing your voice, darling. Still reeling from the good news?"

"Still reeling. I can't believe it's happening." With a flicker of the previous night in mind, Lena also couldn't believe how wonderful *he* was.

"Well, believe it. It's reality. Anyway, what can I do for you this evening? It's your night off, and I know you're not calling just to hear my voice, though that would be nice if it was true."

Lena chuckled. "Well, that's one reason. But the other is that last night when I arrived home, I had my key, but this little gold heart that's joined to it—it was gone. Must have fallen off somehow. I'm sort of attached to it, and I was hoping it wasn't lost in the street somewhere. Did anyone find anything like that at the club?"

"Hold on a minute." Patty wandered off and muffled chatter rambled in the background. When he returned, his cumbersome breathing preceded his voice. "Manuel found it in the dressing room this morning."

"Oh, great!" she sighed, relieved. "Could you tell him to put it up for me until payday?"

The receiver rapped a hard surface and she heard Patty

relaying the message to Manuel. "Said he's going to drop it by now," he stated, picking the phone back up. "You're calling from home, right?"

"He doesn't have to do that. I wouldn't want to inconvenience him. Tell him what I said."

"I won't tell him. He knows he doesn't have to bring it by. The kid's just being nice." Then Patty's tone modified when mischievously adding, "Lena, you know the kid has a thing for you. You know he would do anything to be near you. I hope your fiancé isn't home?"

Lena tittered. "Stop."

"Well, is he home?"

"No, he isn't," she responded, her light laughter cutting into her words. "And stop making trouble."

"Good, the kid will be over soon. You're in Park Slope, right?"

"Yes."

"Well, be ready for some real romancing."

"You're the troublemaker of troublemakers, Patty O'Brien," she teased.

"So some say. But tell me, this little heart must be valuable, eh?"

"I guess it has what some might call sentimental value," Lena said, thinking of its prophecy, which promised true love. Even though Robert's unpredictable behavior made that prospect very unlikely with him, it was still in her nature to dream. And since last night at the club, dreaming is something she did plenty of, dreaming about . . .

Approximately twenty minutes later, Lena opened the door to greet Manuel's grand, paper-white smile. "Lena, this is too nice to just leave around." He presented the charm between willowy fingers.

"Thanks, Manuel." Eagerly Lena accepted the other half of her key chain and widened the doorway for his entry. "Come on in. I really appreciate this."

"It was my pleasure." He strode in and settled on her love seat. After looking around, "Nice place." He patted the plump white pillows of the couch. "Expensive, too."

"Thanks. It wasn't that extravagant. A Seaman's sale."

"Oh, yeah." He nodded, flaunting his flirtatious eye.

"Yes," she drawled and couldn't help grinning. "You're funny, Manuel. Really funny. Stop looking at me like that."

"Am I cute?"

She laughed. "Stop it, mister."

"But you look so good to me."

Lena was blushing. "You're sweet."

"Like candy, I hope." He brandished that enormous grin again. "And it was no problem coming over. I was on my way home anyway, and I'm not far from you."

They prattled about Centerfields, her forthcoming success, and eventually drifted onto the subject of other musical artists. Manuel and Lena revered the same singers and worshipped oldies but goodies, too. When she put on their mutual favorite fast tune of all time, "Hold On," by En Vogue, it was too funky for them to resist. Giggling, they started showing off their swiftest moves to each other.

They were having so much fun, laughing, dancing—and the uptempo number was so deafening, they didn't hear Robert unlocking the apartment door and treading toward the living room. When he did appear, their sight fell on him with surprise. His eyes lunged on them with anger.

Instantaneously Lena turned down the volume button

on the CD player. Praying for his civility, she inched toward Robert, inquiring, "You remember Manuel from the club, don't you?"

"Hey, man," Manuel said, walking over to Robert, extending his hand. "I just brought your lady her charm that she lost at the club and we were enjoying some jams. This one here was my record," he mentioned enthusiastically.

Robert's hands remained down at his sides. From Manuel to Lena he glared and glared and finally roared, *"What the hell is this! What!"*

"Hold on, Robert," Lena protested. "Don't get—"

"What the hell is this? And what do I look like to you? A moron? I know what's going on here! I'm not the dumb one. You two are! Not me! You're the idiots!"

Lena was so mortified her head throbbed, her blood churned, and when her vision caught Manuel, his pale white skin was the darkest red, complemented with eyes that had quadrupled their usual diminutive size. Judging from her pal's disconcerted state, Lena surmised he was about to collapse. Despite it, he managed to utter, "I didn't mean you any harm." He sounded feeble and petrified. "We were just dancing. I came to return her charm. I mean you no disrespect. Your lady is beautiful and any man would love her, but I mean you no—"

Robert swung. Manuel ducked. Robert attempted a blow again, but this time Manuel elected to battle the best way he could. Like a rabbit, he hopped onto Robert's back and stuck there. Round and round and round in a circle Robert went, struggling to hurl off Manuel and wrestle him to the floor. Yet tenaciously the fearful man endured in the position—grasping, sweating, wheezing, hollering—until Lena was able to pry them apart. As

soon as Manuel's feet tapped the floor, there was a blur
fleeing the apartment. It provoked a glower, which Lena
caught before she went to check on her friend.

She dashed to the door and leaned out of the apartment
yelling, "Manuel, I'm so sorry about this." But solely
the hollowness of a hall resounded back.

Furious, Lena stormed back in the house, shaking her
head at Robert. "That was so wrong! So damn unnec-
essary. Now you know that boy is my friend. You saw
him talk to me at the club. I've even told you about him
and his little crush. You know damn well he's harmless.
We were just dancing. Dancing just like you were here
in front of us."

Immediately Robert stirred around aimlessly, rubbing
the back of his neck. "Okay, I'm sorry. I just get crazy
when I know another man wants you." He stopped moving and faced her. "But don't tell me that kid wouldn't
take you to bed in a New York minute if he had a
chance."

"Oh, please. Like I would have no say in the matter."

Cunningiy his eyes narrowed. "But maybe you have
been saying in the matter. Because you *sure* haven't been
giving it to me."

Anguish racking her insides, Lena leered for a moment. "How dare you! How dare you say that to me!
You know me and why I can't respond to you. As cruel
as you've been to me, you've made it impossible. Lovemaking starts outside the bedroom. It starts with how
you treat a person." If he couldn't understand this, then
it would be the perfect excuse to tell him it was over.

Except Robert refused to let her have an excuse for
long. He dared making amends with, "I'm sorry. I was

just going off at the mouth." Coming nearer, he stressed, "I don't believe you're being unfaithful."

Instinctively Lena eased several inches away.

"Now what? You don't want to be near me now."

"Just leave me alone, Robert. I'm too tired for this."

"You weren't too tired to dance with that kid."

"I didn't say my body is tired. I'm saying I'm tired of your nonsense. All of it! I can't live like this anymore!"

"What are you saying?" Alarm thinned his rage to a murmur.

"Robert, I'm saying I want out—"

"I don't want to be away from you." He slid closer. "I'm really sorry. I guess I'm scared. You're about to sign a record contract, and I'm still struggling and not knowing what I'm going to do with my life. I'm scared of other men that are in—or going to be in—your life, trying to steal you. And . . . and you might be thinking that you want someone who has it more together, because you're about to be a star now."

"Do you honestly think I'm like that? I've always been there for you, through the good times and the bad. But now I'm tired of you taking out your frustration on me! I feel we should—"

"If I've made you feel that way, I'm real sorry." The alarm that had plagued his voice piqued in his face. "It will never happen again."

"Why don't I believe that?"

"I'll prove it to you." He cleared his throat. "I will. But we both have to prove things to each other. And . . . and it's hard since we're going off . . . off in directions that are so far apart. So we have to make time for each other. We both have to compromise. And you can't do it if you're spending all your time on the music. Matter of fact, I have reservations about this career choice of yours."

"Reservations?" She eyed him skeptically. "Haven't you been throwing it down my throat that I let my father rob me of my dream? Now that I'm going for it, you have reservations? I don't get it, Robert."

"It's simple," he claimed, his voice gaining command. "I don't think you should give up your regular job for this. It's not a sure thing. Maybe you were right in not pursuing it in the past after all."

She blinked, then gawked at him.

"Plus," he went on, "it would take so much from us. With you singing at the club, it's hard enough to see you as it is. So what's more important to you—marrying me, having a life with me, or your dream?"

In awe of what she was hearing, Lena had no choice but to give one answer.

"Robert, I can't marry you."

"Don't say that." He began looking everywhere but at her. "You don't mean that."

"I do. I've been trying to tell you."

"And I won't listen. You don't mean that. Besides, you couldn't hurt me that way. I know I've been a little mean to you, but I'm not myself. Hell, if you had all this crap happening to you, you wouldn't be yourself, either. I'm— I'm going to make everything better. I will. Just please don't leave. I need you. Without you, I'll die. I won't want to live, Lena. And without you, what else do I have to live for?"

"Yourself, Robert. And all the happiness you can make happen in your life."

"I can't see it. I can't see a future and a life without

you. Really, I mean it, Lena. Don't leave me. We'll both be sorry. Give us another chance."

She gaped at Robert, then went into their bedroom and lightly closed the door. She was going to put on her nightgown and go to bed. Yet before taking off anything, she slid off her pear-shaped diamond engagement ring. Once she loved to marvel at its design and twirl it around in the light. Now Lena slung it in her top dresser drawer. She wasn't wearing it anymore.

They had quarreled about her signing the contract, Manuel, the club, and too many other issues by the time Friday and showtime rolled around. Not surprisingly Centerfields that evening was a haven, especially Cordell's presence, his face as magical to her as a baby's smile, the dusk, waterfalls, the fragrance of strawberries, and the ecstasy of falling in love—all chaste pleasures of life she treasured.

He was all the beauty in the world when Lena beheld him in the audience, watching her like she was a breathtaking jewel never before discovered. Feeling every bit a priceless gem underneath his steadfast scrutiny, she couldn't wait until her first set concluded so she could be near him, to talk, to lose herself in his gaze and be warmly bathed within the inmost depths of his passionate soul.

Beneath all this, nevertheless, Lena was perplexed at herself. Imparting someone she recently met so much importance, so much power, was unlike her even prior to meeting Robert. Yet since she was still with Robert in a sense, the growing interest made Lena feel adulterous and silly. In the past, she had always prided herself on telling admirers she was spoken for. Then again, what was she presuming? By merely being cordial, commending her talent, consistently attending her shows, and granting her an enigmatic look, was this man indicating an attraction in the short span of time they knew each other? Lena cringed at her own nerve. What was she thinking, and was it in fact wishful thinking?

"You were as good as it gets," Cordell said, pulling out a chair for her. "You were even better than last week, and I thought that was impossible."

Lena situated herself opposite him at the intimate table. "And as always, I'm glad you enjoyed it." She gingerly shook a swath of hair from her eye while tilting slightly forward. "I missed . . . I missed talking to you. I liked our conversation last week. It's nice to talk to someone who understands you. I'm really glad you're here tonight. It's so nice to see your face."

With her professions, shock bloomed with Cordell's pleased expression. It rivaled Lena's own astonishment at letting her feelings escape.

He was more invigorated. "Must be my lucky night. I come here thinking just seeing you makes me feel good enough, then you say something like that. You can really make this man feel good. And it truly was nice talking last week. I couldn't wait to come back and see you, too."

Trailing his last sentence, an admirer of her vocal style stopped at the table, introduced herself and engaged Lena in conversation. Cordell didn't mind. Absorbing the fact that she looked forward to seeing him was still sinking in. Her attraction to him—all that he was beginning to feel from her—wasn't in his imagination like he repeatedly reminded himself it was.

And as he observed her chatting so easily with this fan, conversing with this stranger like they were old friends, showing a genuine interest in this individual, authentically caring about the woman's life, Cordell confirmed what was spinning in his head for days: Lena Durant was special; so special she longed to make everyone else know that they were, too, and that elusive quality had extended most definitely to him.

It was more than Lena Durant's voice or the tunes she sang that affected him, Cordell had come to realize. From what he had seen, what he knew, and what he was learning, Cordell felt what had to be a boyish infatuation thriving.

"She loved the last song," Lena related after the woman left. "It reminded her of her lover. Since Patty told the whole world that I'm about to cut an album, she asked if I was going to record that song on it"

"Are you?" He leaned forward, his arms folded on the table. "It was a great song, and I've never heard it before."

"That's because this songwriter that helped me with a demo wrote it. First, I would have to pitch the idea to Shell and Michael. If it's okay with them, then I would have to get permissions . . . well, I would have to have my attorney speak to the songwriter about it." Scouring his face for a reaction, her own was humored.

Cordell laughed. "Again thank you for the opportunity. I'm very happy to be your attorney."

"No, thank you."

"And we will contact him. After all, it is a great song. You must really like it, too. I noticed you closed your eyes on that one, and you didn't on the others. Now why

is that?" He tugged at his tie. "What were you feeling
and seeing as you sang that one?"

Lena resisted the yearning to be honest and brazen,
so she could have discovered his heart's desire, too. Yes,
she could have revealed the truth—that oddly enough,
ever since they met she was thinking about *him*—a near
stranger, because he was the most amazing and sweetest
thing in her life to think about. Nonetheless, Lena rejected that notion.

"I guess I sometimes sing with my eyes closed because I can see a situation and feel it better, and in turn
perform it better. Then other times, I can look out into
the audience and still feel deeply and sing the words
from my heart. I guess it's my mood. Whatever the spirit
moves me to do, I do."

Lena smiled, but only because she was uncomfortable
with a sudden seriousness that washed over Cordell,
drawing her eyes to his. The mysterious look was there
again. Watching him study her that way once more, Lena
had to force herself to shake off whatever mist the gaze
exuded.

"It's sure getting crowded in here," she spoke san-
guinely, attempting to alleviate the tension. Lena scanned
around the room, expecting him to follow her lead.

"Yes, it is getting there," he responded, his voice now
husky and low, his heed not budging from her. "But I
was thinking about what you said before, much earlier,
before the lady came by. About being happy to see me,
just like I'm very happy to see you. I sense we're going
to be great friends, Lena."

"I hope so."

There was the quiet again, dramatic and strained as
the vibrations Lena felt holding her eyes inside his again.

Why was she looking at another man this way? And why was it that whenever Cordell stared at her, it felt as un-utterably wonderful as when she was singing? Sometimes it felt even better. The silence was too powerful. The gazes were overwhelming. The room was getting warmer by the second, and with its increase in temperature Lena became more and more aware of her heart. It was beating so abnormally fast, but now that she thought about it, it always did this lately . . . lately around this man.

"So have you thought about me, Lena?" His voice tremored with a whisper. It invaded and intensified the visual interchange.

Trembling lips parted, but Manuel tapping Lena's shoulder interfered with the response.

"Is it time?" she asked, her chest heaving with relief, her attention fastened to the slender figure looming above. If only Manuel knew how he saved her from di-vulging a desire she would have regretted revealing. "My break is up so quick?"

"Showtime again," Manuel affirmed. "Patty sent me over."

Lena gazed at Cordell. "I guess I'll be seeing you."

Cordell half smiled, peering at her intently. "Go do your thing."

As she stood, he noticed how the snow-white knit mini clung to her figure, accentuating caramel-hued skin that lusciously encased softly sloped legs and healthy cleav-age. A long, slim waist, the roundest backside, and gentle curved hips were additionally taken in as her limbs swayed farther and farther away, and Cordell heard him-self call, "Lena?"

She turned around, hair uncurled by her eye again. "Yes, Cordell?" Breathiness laced her voice.

He stared for a second, couldn't help staring, a smile nowhere on his face. "I want to see you after the show."
She nodded, then walked onstage.

Outside the club, they began strolling. There was no direction, merely wandering and sharing whatever excitement, poignancy, or reflection the moment inspired. New York was still very much awake at a quarter past three A.M. Cars were honking, playing music, cruising and rushing. Many nighthawks were exploring the restaurants, the avenues, the parks, and entertainment spots. The remainder of the folks occupying the street were either going in or coming out of stores that stayed open twenty-four hours.

Laughing, joking, teasing, roaming, sometimes baring her soul, Lena didn't really mind the humidity in the air. In his own atmosphere, Cordell had already swept her. She hung on his every utterance, his every gesture, discovering a new world, his world filled with his intelligence, his sensitivity, his positivity, his openness—all this wrapped in a sensuality that was assailing her with every second that ticked by. Lena knew she should have gone home to Robert. He needed her. Even so she couldn't detach herself from this dream of a man, who with each breath of his existence was making her extraordinarily glad to be alive.

They came upon an ice-cream parlor.

"You like ice cream, Lena?"

"Can't go to bed without some."

"I knew you liked sweets."

Noticing a girlish zealousness brightening her face,

Cordell escorted her inside. She left with a peach cone. He had a cup of rum raisin.

"This is good," he admitted after tasting a spoonful. "Would you like a taste?"

To her, his eyes sparkled as he asked that. During their outing, Lena had discreetly avoided them, the breathtaking brown crystals, modest, but at the same time possessing a beauty, a provocativeness, a puissance so astonishing her eyes craved to delight in them again and again.

Bedazzled by him this way, it was hard addressing his question. Finally, she managed to let her eyes drop elsewhere. "If I sample your rum raisin, it'll make my peach less tasty."

"You think so?"

"It might. This peach is sure scrumptious." Hungrily Lena licked around the edges of the cold ball, but became self-conscious when she caught him gaping. Not a trace of humor shone on his face. "You want some? You can have some if you like. Not that you would want some with me slobbering over it like I did."

"You weren't slobbering. I just liked watching you tear it up. It seems like everything you do, just turns me—" Cordell stopped and for a fleeting moment looked off, recapturing that sullenness about him, which she had seen before. A second later, sorrow was replaced with something extremely warm. The warmth showered Lena.

"What I was trying to say is that you really enjoy things. You get all the little pleasures out of your life, your music and everything else. I've noticed this about you. Every second of your life, you want to savor all the joy you can get, all the passion. Every part of it. I like that. I'm that way, too."

There was a hush after that revelation, and afraid of the ambience that silence always enticed them to, Lena steered their conversation by asking, "Now what were we talking about before we went in Baskin Robbins? Oh, I know, we were talking about the music and the signing on the ninth."

"Right." He swallowed a hefty scoop of rum raisin. "I know you can't wait. I can't, either."

Lena shook her head. "It's so unbelievable. I keep thinking I'm going to wake up from some dream."

"That's how I feel sometimes lately."

He abruptly stared at her. He ceased to eat more of his treat and slowed his pace. Lena stared back, her steps languishing, too, her delicacy merely idle in front of her. It was only a blaring car horn that startled them out of the dangerous space they were entering. The horn was their signal. Cordell continued eating ice cream. Lena gazed straight ahead.

"I wish I could have told my father my good news before he left the country," she shared with him. "He's on a trip."

He looked surprised. "But you have told your mother?"

"No, she's passed on. When I was a child."

"I'm sorry, Lena. I wouldn't have even asked—"

"It's okay. Right now, what pains me is my father." She looked down, then ahead. "I've been down this road before with him. He believes in solid jobs, professional jobs. He believes this music thing is too much of a gamble, even though he points out that I'm talented. My aunt had the same dream, even had a contract, but it didn't work out. She killed herself."

He frowned. "I'm so sorry."

"Me, too." Pausing, she shook her head. "Plus he's seen too many people with the same dream whose lives have turned into nothing. It's so hard. If he knew what I was about to do, he would be positive that I'm screwing up my life. But I'm not!"

Listening to this, seeing how much it hurt her, Cordell couldn't help halting his footsteps and facing Lena. All the while, the urge was suppressed to smother her in the sanctuary of his arms.

"I'm really sorry to hear this," he said, his candor drawing lines between his brows. "But your father is like that only because he loves you so much. Love is what makes him think that way. He doesn't want you to get hurt. He just wants to shield you from all this pain he thinks might come up and hit you. It's not so much that he doesn't believe in you. I don't think that's it at all."

Her lips formed a warped smile. "Sometimes you say the most perfect things."

"I'm glad you feel that way. I guess your situation with your father compares to when a man loves a woman and woman loves a man. They'll do anything to protect what they love from harm. Even die. On the other hand, though, you have to do what you have to do. It's your life. You are the only one who knows what's in your heart and what fills it. Clearly you know it's not the position at the insurance company. You're lucky that you do know what it is. So go for it. If you don't ever try, you'll die wondering. You'll wake up every day trying to feel good, but deep inside you'll know that feeling good is impossible. Impossible because you were too afraid to strive for the best for yourself. You'll love yourself much more when you just try, Lena. Just try that's all. And with what you have going for you, I would bet my life that you won't lose." They started strolling again.

"You explain everything so perfectly. You see things as they should be seen. And all that ego boosting you give me—"

"You're going to do it, too. I can feel it. I hope I can be right there . . . to cheer you on, I mean."

"I think I'll listen to you, Mr. Richardson. You seem to be a very smart man."

"And you're a very beautiful woman," befell across her ears. With it, she was devoured with that unforgettable look. Yet this time, Lena had no trouble interpreting its message. Her heart was eternally out of control around him, but at this moment it had broken its own record for speed and strength. Lena could feel it all over and through her, just as she could feel the heat from his eyes, just as she knew he could feel hers.

They had come to a standstill, and it almost seemed to Lena that she had stopped breathing. Not even his whisper could break the desirous spell.

"Lena, are you sure you wouldn't like some of my ice cream?"

She glimpsed the scanty amount of ice cream and afterward raised her uptilted—eyes back to him. Her lips separated, but no sound escaped. She merely watched him coming closer.

"Lena would you like to taste some . . . from me?"

She persisted in staring at him, watching and watching until Cordell placed the last scoop in his mouth. Scrupulously Lena explored his lips, his sensuous open mouth, the titillating motion of his tongue savoring the taste of the delectable cream. All came nearer, so near his skin's scent invaded her pores. Her senses inflamed.

Whether it was the smell of him or some alluring, rare cologne or both, the essence invited her nearer. And when it was almost too late for Lena to be an angel, heaven helped her: conscience backed her away.

"I have to tell you something, Cordell," she announced breathlessly. "It's important." She retreated a step more.

"There's something I have to tell you, too."

"I don't know if I can tell you now. I don't want to ruin this. There's problems . . . there's . . ."

"There's problems with me, too. Incredible circumstances. I want to tell you all about it, Lena. And I will. It's just not the right time now."

Dazedly Lena nodded.

"I'm going on a trip."

"A trip!" She almost yelled it out. "You are? Where? Why?" Lena knew she had no right to ask such things of someone she was hardly acquainted with, in respect to time—but at that instant her emotions had a will of their own. "I'm sorry. What I mean is, will you be back . . . I mean in time . . . time for the meeting?"

"Of course," he assured her. "I wouldn't leave you in a bind like that. I can't wait to get in there and wheel and deal for you. I'm looking forward to it. But this is a . . ." He paused. "An important matter, too."

"Oh."

"But I will be back on the seventh. Can I have your number so I can call you while I'm away?"

I would love you calling me every second of the day, Lena's mind rang. "Can you call me at the club?"

"Sure. I have the number."

"You can also call me at the office." Haziness still swirling about, she reached into her purse and took out a paper and pen. Scribbling her number, "You can reach me there during the daytime until Wednesday."

Accepting it between long, bare fingers, Cordell recalled, "Oh, yes, that's right. You gave in your resignation. Your last day is Wednesday."

"That's it. It's over," she mouthed blankly, halfway alert of the last statement, because fully she was feeling the wind of forlornness blowing, bringing with it truths about this dreamy creature, which Lena didn't want to know. On the bright side, however, she had a new friend, mysterious, but an equally precious gentleman, and scrutinizing him fumbling in his pockets Lena somehow perked up.

"I'm looking for my business card," he said. "It not only has my office number but also my beeper and answering service, too. You can reach me through the service while I'm away. I would love for you to call me if you can."

But no home phone number, Lena was telling herself. No home phone number spelled out so much. At the same time, however, there was no ring on his finger. No ring meant something, too. So the sweeter thought is what she chose to believe. He couldn't be— She couldn't bear him being—

Five

On a pale pink-sanded beach, where women donned colorful bikinis and men flaunted shimmering golden limbs, and the grainy feet of boys and girls kicked balls ornamented with popular animated characters, and the Acapulco sky bared a striking reflection of its rippling waters, Cordell strode slowly, holding the soft hand of a beautiful, dark woman. She was thin built, her countenance exotic and entirely African. Her black hair was shoulder-length and brushed back. A clip made of pearls gathered it together in a shining bun. She wore a green, yellow, red and white flowered sundress, with flat sandals. The outfit harmonized well with Cordell's white shorts, matching open vest, tube socks, and sneakers.

The couple appeared to be on vacation sightseeing, or, some suspected, on a honeymoon. As they traveled farther and into the bustling district of what appeared as paradise, he was purchasing her gifts: flowers, balloons, stuffed animals, souvenirs, jewelry, a bathing suit, slacks, and some dresses.

Clutching her hand, he was showing her utopian scenery. He was jesting with her about humorous events. He was explaining the language to her. He was also conversing with the Mexicans, and venturing to relax her into doing the same.

She was carrying the lighter packages. She was eating tiny portions of the exotic foods. She was looking when he pointed out something interesting. She was gazing at the children more intently than anyone else. However, this woman was not smiling.

When they entered their hotel suite after the leisurely jaunt, she rested her bags on the chaise longue, slipped off her sandals and lay across the bed. Similarly Cordell relieved his hands of packages but afterward headed into the bathroom. Since he liked the air very steamy before showering, he turned on the water, then reappeared in the room where she was.

The television was playing. Featured was an old movie starring Bette Davis. Bold captions loomed at the bottom of the screen, translating the film into Spanish.

"I can take out the words for you," he suggested and started to adjust the picture.

Nevertheless, "That's okay," halted his steps.

"Do you want me to run out and get anything before I get in the shower? I might be a while. Feel like meditating."

"No," she replied, her eyes on the set, her voice as listless as her entire manner.

"The maid told me they make the greatest popcorn in that novelty shop in the lobby," he went on.

"I don't want any."

"You sure?"

"Yes."

"It won't be any trouble. Hope, if there's anything you need, you know I don't mind going to get it. It's no bother for me to run out."

"I don't need anything."

"All right. Just give a yell if you change your mind."

Cordell walked back into the bathroom. It was overly steamy, exactly how he liked it. He disrobed and surrendered himself underneath the stream of flowing heat. The door was left ajar. At the last minute Hope might have thought of something she needed.

Cordell sudsed up his hair first, his face after, then rubbed the soap over the expanse of hairy chest and in circular motions over his slick, firm stomach, before prudently soaking his private areas. In his mind, though, he had already been stroked all over—by her. His eyes were closed.

Just then, a muffled sound from the other room grasped his attention. Briskly he shut off the faucet and called, "Hope, are you all right?"

No answer.

"Hope, are you okay in there?"

"Yes, I'm okay," he heard her say, a hint higher than she normally spoke and with annoyance. "I coughed. I just had something in my throat."

"Just checking."

The water downpoured again, and with its onrushing came his guilt. Slowly he pivoted around, rearing his head back, feeling the heated torrent rushing down his sensitive flesh and remembering what had recently been so easy to forget.

Cordell had married Hope Deidre Bellworth nine years ago. Three weeks prior had made nine years. They met in Atlanta at a barbecue. It was hosted by the head of the esteemed law firm where Cordell practiced at the time. The gathering was to celebrate Cordell's promotion among the hallowed legal halls.

Hope was a friend of an invited colleague, one of the female attorneys. As she circled around the festivity being introduced to everyone, Cordell noted a shyness in the attractive young woman. Innately one to rescue, he initiated easy conversation with her. From it, he discerned she was introverted, sweet, but exceptionally dignified.

They began dating. Becoming acquainted, he learned she lived in an orphanage until she was eleven years old. At that point, Hope was adopted by an affluent family. Entrepreneurs with various types of corporations, they were regularly listed in *Black Enterprises* top one hundred businesses. Cordell admired the family's ambition and success and was impressed with Hope's nonchalance about her wealth. Kind, giving, gentle described her temperament. Much the same, her hopes were modest, and there was one that far outshone all the rest: children.

At first Cordell glorified her monumental love for them. After all, he cherished them, too. But Hope could see a child anywhere, and regardless of what she was engaged in, she was magnetized to the youngster. Wherever the little people were was where Hope had to be, to talk, listen, cuddle, do for them, give them a present. For hours and hours, she gushed about them with Cordell. Children mesmerized her more than all else. A career or her own aspirations were never discussed; motherhood consistently was. Kids became so prevalent in their lives, Cordell started sensing something slightly awry. He couldn't fathom why Hope frequently declined lavish dates with him to babysit a friend's toddler. On the other hand, he considered his selfishness and possible jealousy.

Without a doubt, Cordell loved Hope. Therefore when she became pregnant six months into the relationship, there wasn't any indecision about marriage. His upbringing stressed responsibility.

Reared in a Christian family, his mother earned a living as a licensed practical nurse; his father had been a sergeant, and the victim of a bomb attack in the Vietnam war. The Richardsons weren't too bad off financially since they were savers. Aside from that, Winston Richardson's demise provided a generous insurance policy that afforded his wife, son, and two daughters a decent home and other comforts.

Marrying Hope meant his child wouldn't have those mourning, fatherless days that he suffered after age nine. Cordell would be there for every adolescent problem, every Boy Scout outing, every baseball game his child didn't win, and every overlong graduation. What he didn't count on was a miscarriage.

Hope was frantic and as gravely depressed as Cordell was. He disguised his torment with smiles and shoulders for her whimpers, whereas she sank deeper and deeper into the hurt. Yet after realizing the bereavement would be eternal if she didn't allow some new radiance into her darkened world, Hope was determined to try again. They did, but unfortunately there was another miscarriage, and another, and yet another. All in the fifth month, all after they had planned, dreamed, hoped, and even viewed the baby on a monitor. Worse, ultimately there were the uterine tumors that devastated her mind far more than they did her body. Because of them, there was the utmost misfortune to a woman whose entire existence depended upon a child; it was a hysterectomy.

After the second miscarriage, Cordell felt his function was a baby machine. Communication, touching, tenderness, kisses, hugs, sharing plans, sharing dreams, were no more. All there was, was procreation. After Hope was pregnant, she didn't covet intimacy. Quite the opposite, Cordell did desire it, in every way and more than ever amid his grief. They were his children, too, that perished, the greatest splendor of his soul, whom he would never know. The tears of a weeping heart and bottomless pain longed to be soothed away.

Hope swallowed a bottle of pills after the hysterectomy. Luckily Cordell arrived home from some legal proceedings precisely in time. In shock he dialed the ambulance and attempted to revive his unconscious wife.

After she was hospitalized and her stomach pumped, the doctors assured Cordell that Hope would recover. Very late he returned home that night. It was then he discovered something he hadn't noticed when discovering Hope earlier. Lying on the floor were letters. Letters addressed to him and Hope's mother.

Painstakingly he pored over her goodbye to him, and there were no surprises. However, when curiosity guided him to open the sealed note addressed to her mother, bared was the greatest fear of a man or woman deeply in love: unrequited love. The letter read:

Dear Mother,

You've been so wonderful to me, just like you were the one who gave me life. But still I couldn't help wondering why my parents didn't want me. Why didn't they love me? Maybe they inherently knew I was nothing—nothing as I feel right now with nothing to look forward to in life. The hysterectomy was my punishment for everything wrong I did, especially the horrendous atrocity of marrying a man I never loved. That's right, I only wanted Cordell be-

*cause physically he was so beautiful, and I knew he
would make beautiful babies. If I ever could love a
man, it would probably be him. His heart is good
enough, but in this lifetime the love in my heart for
him just wasn't so. Wonder what would he say if he
knew I felt no love for him? None.*

The farewell continued lengthily, but after that heartbreaking bombshell, Cordell couldn't read anymore. He
couldn't think anymore. Weightlessly the paper fluttered
to the floor as a nightmarish haze swept over him. At
that moment, he felt himself slowly dying. A tempestuous
storm of agony somersaulted inside him, imprisoning
grief so prodigious it settled right beside that grief he
held for the babies that never were.

When Hope was transferred from the hospital to a
mental health facility, Cordell never disclosed knowing
her true feelings. By then she required extensive psychiatric help. In and out of sanitariums became her way of
life, and his, since he stood by her. During all the therapy,
they determined her troubles didn't solely stem from the
miscarriages. Each doctor maintained her problems de-
rived from a combination of difficulties, mainly being
deserted at birth by her natural parents, and not being
wanted until she was approaching pubescence.

Hence it wasn't in Cordell's nature to abandon anyone
helpless, not even someone who had indisputably used
him, taken him for granted, and loved him no more than
they did a stranger in the street. They hadn't lived together in three years. The last time she entered the in-
stitution, she was so ill the admittance was on a
long-term basis. Upon her release, physicians recom-
mended they make this trip. A fun-filled vacation is what

they suggested to Cordell. Though she had improved
markedly and enough to be released, she needed some
positive stimulation. There were still some problems.

She was sedentary. She was living on television. She
was living in near silence. There were additional bad
signs: outbursts of crying, the trances, and the attachment
to those sonogram pictures. Most peculiar, she had to be
talked into venturing outside the door.

The club had merely been a whim one evening after
too much office politics. Often Cordell passed Centerfields and proceeded on by. Yet something was tempting
him inside one particular Thursday night. He acquiesced
to the unexplainable urge and that's when he saw *her.*
Standing there swaying her round hips so sensuously in
that soft yellow dress was a woman so beautiful his wildest fantasies couldn't create her. Adding to her enchantment was a voice that jerked him down in the first seat
he came to. Motionless he sat at the table, so motionless
he couldn't move if someone were killing him.

Now picturing how it all started, and thinking how easily a moment weeks ago had changed his life, Cordell
cut off the water and stepped out of the shower. Drying
himself, he kept promising that he wouldn't think of
Lena. He wouldn't even try to telephone her anymore.
Since landing in Acapulco, there had been several at-
tempts. Credited to his bad timing, she was never at Centerfields or the insurance company when he phoned.

Some men would have felt justified in desiring another
woman. After all, the letter and everything Hope did
proved she didn't love him. On top of that, they hadn't
lived together in three years. However, Cordell had never
considered himself average. What he felt for Lena bothered him. Constantly he could hear the minister reciting

his wedding vows. But what did they mean, when he had already broken them in his mind? He had vowed to love and honor Hope *for better or for worse.*

For years he had survived without affection. In fact there were times he sympathized with Hope not granting it. Long before the psychiatrists diagnosed her, long before he read that catastrophic note, it became apparent to Cordell that there was too much heartache inside her and between them. When she gazed at him, he knew all she saw was their angelic babies and nothing else. The truth was in her eyes. Truth is in anyone's eyes, he thought, suddenly feeling invigorated by the sultry image of Lena. It made him feel extraordinarily good recreating how she stared at him.

Cordell wrapped a burgundy towel around his hips and tracked damp footprints onto the beige carpet outside the bathroom door. With the air conditioner's frost prickling over his flushed skin, he observed the television was still going. A new movie played. Hope was asleep. He strolled over, cut off the set, and that's when he saw a sight that troubled him so he didn't move for a minute. Cordell just stared and stared, and studied them and her. It was those pictures. Scattered on the blanket by Hope's stomach and left hand were four sonogram pictures.

He began dressing. Underpants, jeans, a black polo shirt, black sneakers were thrown on and he hurried out the door. There was no way he could stand it tonight. Why did she have to bring them along?

Within moments, Cordell's heed divided between the obsidian sky to his darkly cloaked feet, the footwear dipping deep into the sand amid the shore. It was much cooler than earlier. In contrast to daylight, few were lounging about. Cordell located a spot close to the edge of the ocean and was grateful that those populating the area didn't hinder his view. For this moment, he needed the seascape just for himself.

A craving overcame him to smoke, and Cordell recalled leaving the cigarettes he bought at noon back in the hotel. He was with Hope when he purchased them. Never knowing him to smoke, she had looked at him oddly but didn't say anything. Strangely enough, Cordell hadn't lit up since he was an undergraduate at Moorehouse. In those days, when he did indulge, it resulted from pressures that were overbearing.

Pressures were overbearing now. He wanted a divorce, had wanted one for years. Yet Hope was always too ill to put her through it. Now he felt the urgency more than ever. He wanted to see that she was well taken care of and provided for, but at the same time, he wanted to live. He starved to be happy. He ached to love and be loved. So perusing the water, black from the night shadowing the sea's blue and the moon's reflection entangling through it all, Cordell confronted his anxiety.

Did wanting an exciting woman while married to a disturbed one who needed you to survive make you a jerk or what? Was it wickedness to throw someone with the most fragile heart away for someone you hardly knew in terms of time, but who you had always known in your soul, but had never met in the universe? Was it sinful to tremble at the fantasy of making love to that woman? Was it so immoral to desire to be near her and see her beautiful eyes look at you like you were her world, and see her smile, which made waves jump in your stomach, and hear the alluring timbre of her voice and hear the fascinating things that came from her mind? Was it indecent to feel her right there when you closed your eyes, and you felt so indescribably good—so good like she made you feel when she was right there in front of you, with that something beaming from her, making your body turn to stone—but you knew that in actuality nothing compared to her being in front of you, when her presence gripped your body and made it feel like something you'd never known or would know again? Why did he feel this way? If he could pinpoint the source, Cordell could have had his life back the way it was, as dispassionate as it was. Yet the source was as unknown as the future, as unknown as the questions that led to the beginning of civilization. Why did any man feel this way for a woman? At heart, he knew there was no absolute answer for any instance. There was only what he felt: emotions—emotions that made Cordell face an unescapable fact: he was falling in love.

A pebble was tossed into an incoming tide. When it splashed, Cordell was certain of something. Lena was involved with someone. That he was convinced of when she gave him her business phone numbers. He even thought he saw a diamond on her hand once—one like an engagement ring. What's more, her mentioning a problem, but foremostly intuition, guaranteed there was an undeserving lover lurking. In spite of it all, Cordell knew one thing more: it was too late to care.

Sprawling lazily atop silken sheets, Lena thumbed through *Essence* magazine, contemplating if success would one day grant her the privilege of gracing pages between its covers. Page after page, Lena imagined sharing an inspirational story with an aspiring singer, but soon lost the resplendent illusions when they were su-

perseded with that which she viewed everywhere she
looked: her beloved sunset and all the seductiveness that
adorned below it. Whatever she was thinking lately, the
magnificent vision was always right beside it and eventually faded the other ponderings away. Cordell's striking
presence was embedded inside her system so deeply,
Lena could close her eyes anywhere and create him with
precise detail as if he were directly in front of her.

God knows he was constantly on her mind while he
was away. Closing her eyes then, Lena rekindled the
charm, the laugh, the beautiful thoughts—and bodily, the
reddish brown skin embellished with the simple lips and
an even simpler nose and the mouth that was simple,
too, except it always looked poised for something succulent and always appeared ready to be succulent. Lena
had thought and thought about the sunset. Although if
she dared down lower to where his shoulders spread so
vast, and to where arms were massive and hips narrow,
and to where her imagination enticed her, to legs that
were concrete hard as his forbidden splendor, Lena knew
she wouldn't see another sunset, but an erupting volcano.

"What are you thinking about?" Robert's voice startled her eyes open.

"Oh, good, you're home," she remarked nervously.

"What's good about it?" Incensed about something,
he made heavy steps throughout the bedroom. "You
looked silly. What were you doing, fantasizing again
about being onstage? Please. Give me a break." Slinging
off his suit jacket, he shuffled restlessly about the room,
radiating an energy Lena didn't want to deal with. Other
articles of clothing flew off.

"How was your day at the job?" Striving to be upbeat,
Lena sat up, knees updrawn to her chest. "You've been

there a whole week, and I haven't heard one complaint when you come home. Maybe you were right, the stock market is for you?"

He flung off his tie and dropped hard on the side of the bed. "I quit! That crap isn't for me."

"You quit!" Lena blinked and stared in disbelief. "You quit today?"

"Don't look at me like that."

Promptly she moved her eyes away. "I'm sorry. You shouldn't be anywhere where you aren't happy. I, above anyone else, know that. But maybe this is a sign you should start studying for the bar again." With empathy she found his eyes again. "I'll help you study. I don't want you to forget your dream, Robert."

"Oh, you don't want anything!" he snapped, "but something for yourself!"

"What?" Her knees unfolded. She sat up straight, frowning and bewildered.

"You heard what I said."

"Please, let's have a nice evening."

"Easy for you to say. You're signing that so-called record contract. You can sit back and relax. But what about me?"

"You know that if there is any way I can help you, I will. I told you I'll help you study for the bar. I don't care how involved I am with recording the album, I will make time for you. You're important to me, Robert. I care what happens in your life. I want you to be fulfilled and feel purposeful like I do. You know that."

He was silent, his large eyes squinted and peering around the room, until they reached hers again. "If you want to help me so bad, I know a way that you can."

"Sure, anything."

"Okay," he said, nodding. "I want to be your manager. And I want you to set everything up as soon as possible. Who else is better to manage a woman's career and finances than her man and her husband-to-be one day? I've given this some thought, too. It just didn't come about today."

Lena didn't respond immediately. Her head was too busy spinning. Now this was something, Robert wanting to be her manager. Thankfully that role was reserved for someone else. In phone conversations with Shell and Michael, they proposed that her lawyer could assume the second position as her manager. Enthusiastically Lena agreed with them. Not only had Cordell shared some fantastic ideas about building her career, but he was also highly successful with investments. When it came to projects where her possible royalties could be invested, she believed he would be ideal. Lena couldn't wait to approach him with the proposition of being lawyer/manager. She couldn't wait to see him for many reasons.

"Robert, your being my manager is not a good idea."

"Why not!"

"Shell and Michael said that it's good if you can get an attorney who will function as both. And I agree with them. Plus I feel we should pursue our separate interests. You haven't been the easiest person to live with lately, and I don't want my career to be affected if we have problems."

He stood up and began pacing. "I don't like this. I don't like this whole thing. And I want it to stop." His arms gestured wildly. "If we're separated when you're working those long hours, our relationship could fall apart. Plus I just don't want you to do this, getting involved with all these people and all this nonsense, and for what? This album isn't going to go. I know it's not if I'm not involved in it. People will rip you off." Harshly he rubbed the back of his neck. "You're too soft for the cutthroat music business.

"Shell, Michael, this lawyer—all of them will use you and throw you away. Like Angus once told you, it won't work. Maybe the old dude was right about something. And what if—what if people don't like your sound. What if they don't think your voice is so hot? You can't handle that rejection, Lena."

Too aggravated to look at Robert, Lena was shaking her head. "Please, don't do this."

"Do what?"

"Don't try to make me doubt myself or hold me back. This is my chance. First it was my father trying to stop me, but now don't let it be you for a far more horrible reason. This is my time—my summer of life," she said, recalling what Cordell told her.

"Without me?" he asked and stopped pacing, stood still. "You're going to do this, forgetting about me?"

"Don't be selfish. And just really look at the situation. If I have, you will have. Doesn't that sound good?"

"No! Hell, no! What the hell am I supposed to do? What about my damn life? It's going to be in limbo while you're out there. Well, you'll only be thinking you're having the time of your life, but really you're screwing up big time and don't even know it!"

"Stop it. I don't want to hear this. You're jealous!"

"Don't make me laugh. Jealous of what? Jealous of a fool who's going to fall right on her face."

"No way I'm going to fall on my face! Especially when I don't have someone like you dragging me down in my life!"

His eyes stretched.

"Why don't you go somewhere, and find yourself!" she ranted on. "Find yourself! And stop trying to hurt me! Focus and get in touch with your spiritual side. Get in touch with God. Meditate about your future! Do something constructive rather than trying to hurt someone who's trying to help you!"

"Find yourself! Meditate!" he repeated in mockery. "Get in touch with your spiritual side. Do only constructive things with yourself. That's all I hear. *Well, I thought I was trying to do something with myself!* I asked you could I be your manager! We could have been a team! A *team,* Lena, do you know what that means? You can't do it without me!"

"I don't care what you say! I'm signing that contract, and I'm going forward with my life."

He smirked and nodded faintly. "So you are. You're going to go in there with your lawyer and think you're going to get the deal of a lifetime?"

"I'm hoping so."

"Bull! You're going to screw up everything without me. No way you can do it without me. You'll fall on your damn face. You're too scared. You're not hungry enough. You'll cop out because of your dad! You're going to be a screwup!"

His stabbing words still wounding her, she stood tall on the floor. "You're wrong. I'm going to be a success. I have my talent, and I have people on my side who believe in me. They are so supportive, unlike you."

"Who, Shell and Michael?" He laughed wryly. "They want record sales so they can swindle you." Then he lifted one brow and ogled her up and down. "But then again, you are fine now. They might want something else, too. And I can vouch, it is good."

"You are so disgusting sometimes. You make me sick!"

"So that's why?"

"That's why what?"

"That's why we haven't been hitting it?"

"Robert, you know why I can't stand for you to touch me. Look at how you talk to me lately. Look how you've talked to me these few minutes. I can't erase it from my memory. Lovemaking is not just physical; it's very much emotional."

"Well, maybe I ought to remind you to remember how good it was between us, and we can see how emotional we both can be."

There was a hush, and a ferociousness in his eyes that Lena had never seen before. It terrified her. It compounded with all the verbal abuse, making it hard to believe she actually agreed to pledge a lifelong commitment to someone like this. He was never focused and confident, but there were always attributes about him that warranted loving. Tender, kind, and loving at one time—now he was insinuating violence.

Lena couldn't take it, and she wasn't foolish enough to wait for what happened next. Alarm welling inside her, she dashed into their extra bedroom, apologies flying against her back, the breeze of the door slamming whipping against it, too. Once inside, she locked herself in the room and looked toward the closet. Luggage was inside.

Tears were trickling down her flushed cheeks. She wiped them continuously, but it did no good. The torment just experienced made it impossible for the sobbing to cease, even if there were something beautiful to lift her spirit as they flowed. Yanking open the first suitcase and gathering whatever belongings were tucked in the dressers of this room, Lena mentally sorted which hotel could she go to. After a few phone calls and a place was settled on, she sat on the bed for a moment to calm herself. There and then she pictured Cordell. She thought of him—like she thought of him while arguing with Robert, like while attending her last day of work, like while performing at the club. She thought of him like she thought of him while doing anything and everything, at any moment, at all times. Shaking from the wild thumping of her heart, Lena envisioned him kissing her and taking her far away. Amid all this, she counted the days, the minutes, the seconds before she saw him again. She had counted time the instant he was out of her sight.

Six

Lena trailed nervously behind Shell Taylor's secretary as the petite, lean blonde escorted her to a conference room at the end of a long hall. Heels clicking rapidly against the glossy tiles, the floor's slickness nearly tripped her twice—although colliding with the dense surface probably wouldn't have fazed Lena too much. She was too overwrought. In the rush, a button even popped off her suit, but she didn't budge an eye to see where it rolled. Lena was late. The alarm clock hadn't awakened her.

A huge paneled door opened. Seated around an oblong oak table were two unfamiliar middle-aged men, Shell, Michael, and Cordell and something inside her revived seeing him again. Apologizing for her tardiness, Lena's moist hands ushered her skirt underneath her buttocks, letting her settle comfortably into a red velvet, thickly cushioned seat. Straightaway she traded glances with Cordell, the warmth in his eyes easing her, but somehow eliciting incredible excitement, as did the magnetism of his smile.

The jesting of one of the older gentlemen assured Lena the executives weren't miffed about her lateness, and then there was Shell. Looking like he was biting thorns, he was actually smiling and joking. "Lena, we thought you had skipped out on us again. I was about to give birth."

The banter wasn't funny, but Shell's unusually amused expression made everyone laugh.

After a detailed discussion about the contract, there were handshakes, congratulations, and a schedule for another meeting with solely Lena, Cordell, Shell, Michael, and the executive producer. Other than a few revisions Cordell decided to make, the terms offered Lena were generous and solid. Yet it was because of important artistic affairs that a new meeting was arranged. The most significant business negotiations fortuitously had been mutually agreed upon.

As everyone filed out of the conference room, Lena procrastinated as did Cordell. When all had left, dispersing into the hallway off to their individual destinations, he sauntered around the table to where Lena was. A smile was bright on his face. It rivaled hers.

"You are some wheeler-dealer!" she raved. "My God, I didn't know what a dynamo I had on my side! Now I'm sure I want you to be my manager, too!"

"Well, you heard how the offer was immediately accepted when you proposed it at the meeting." He laughed heartily, again sounding much older than he was, infecting Lena so she joined him in the enjoyment. "How long did it take me? A second to say yes. As you can see, I'm easy."

"Great! This is great! Everything is great."

"So how do you feel?" But the glow on her face that held him captive already spoke volumes.

"Wonderful. Just wonderful." She outstretched her arms, raised them, while throwing her head back. "Thank you, God!" She then gazed at Cordell. "And thank you,

Mr. Richardson. How can I ever thank you?" The question was nearly whispered.

Cordell shot her a sly look. "Whoa, that can be a dangerous question."

"I know," she said, and just looked at him, her eyes traveling over his eyes, his lips, his skin, and descending across his shoulders and winding down to the rest of him. She felt unlike herself behaving this way, being bold, enticing almost, making him aware of what she desired. "I like being dangerous sometimes," she proclaimed softly. "It's good sometimes. Makes life exciting."

A glimmer sparked in his eyes. "I missed you, Lena. You have no idea how much." He paused and stared. "Is my saying that all right with you? Or does it make you uncomfortable?"

"It makes me happy. I missed you, too. If only you knew—"

Strangers began entering the room. Obviously another meeting was about to take place. Lena and Cordell started walking in the hall, toward the elevators.

"How was your trip?" she asked, still feeling unlike herself.

"Fine. Just fine."

"Did you get in any swimming or sailing or anything fun?"

Cordell chuckled uneasily and hesitated. After a moment of contemplation, he conceded, "I did some swimming. I sailed once." He pressed the elevator down button. "The weather was good. But the best time I had was in my mind."

"Your mind? The best time you had was in your mind?" Lena prepared to hear something fascinating.

"Yes. That's because I was always thinking of you."

There was a hush after that. Cordell hadn't intended to move so fast. He didn't want to scare her off. Yet what he was feeling was so overpowering, it leaped out before he realized it. That was totally unlike him. He was a thinker, then a doer.

"What you just said," Lena heard herself saying, "made me even happier than getting a record contract and that's a lot. All I did was think about you, too." *There, it was finally out, Lena thought.*

His eyes smiled more than his lips. "So you thought about me?"

"Constantly."

At that his gaze cut into her deeply, drawing hers further and further into his.

The elevator opening dragged their attention away from each other. Naturally she stepped on first, maneuvering and wedging in a spot amid the crowd. Cordell followed. They rode swapping stares in the silence of the packed space. When finally the two reached the lobby, they walked together speechlessly, absorbing all that was new, beautiful, and awesome until they arrived at a less occupied section of the building. Cordell tenderly entwined his fingers with hers, and Lena felt something overwhelming from that. It made her heart race, her ears pound, her blood scurry crazily.

He guided her to a beige marble wall. She leaned against it, looking up at him before her. Returning the scrutiny, he tilted forward, propping one hand on the sleek wall, while his chest rose and fell dramatically before her.

"Lena, I have to share something else with you. It's serious."

That made her stomach knot inside. "I have something serious to tell you, too."

He looked off, seemingly grappling with whatever overtook his mind. Finally his eyes pensively came back to her. "First of all, I know we've known each other only a short time, but believe me, it feels like I've known you forever inside here. . . ." Delicately he lifted her warm palm and placed it against his madly beating heart. Merely touching his hard chest aroused Lena to no end. Adding to it was the savage pounding. It matched the insane rhythm of her own heart, and Lena believed she could die from feeling so much, but instead something spared her. It let her retrieve her trembling hand to push aside hair that spilled over her eye.

"Lena, there are other moments that I find everything, every new thing I learn about you so exciting." He loosened his tie. "And I get excited knowing that there is so much more that I could learn about you, so much more that turns me on and on." The tie came off; buttons were undone and just enough hairy chest showed to make Lena swallow hard. "I could never get enough of being with you, around you."

"Wow . . . I . . ." Lena could feel his depth of emotion, but was so shocked to hear it, she dropped her head. After a few moments of her heart rocking her entire body, "Wow."

As though the beautiful facial bones before him were fragile crystal, Cordell cupped her chin and raised it. An overpowering sensation ran all over her, compelling Lena to hold his hands to her face. She didn't want him to stop touching her. She only wanted more.

"I know what I'm saying is heavy. I know it's so quick, but you felt how my heart is beating. It doesn't just beat like that so I can exist. It's beating like that because of you and only you, Lena."

Her eyes locked in his. "Everything you said, Cordell, is exactly how I feel." She couldn't believe she was saying this to another man, a man who wasn't Robert, a near stranger, but Lena couldn't help it. The growing emotions for Cordell were consuming her. It was doing her talking, causing her to feel so alive.

"I knew it," he whispered. "I just knew it." Cordell shook his head. "We have to go somewhere else to talk about this more . . . to talk about other things, too."

"Can we go back to your office? Can we have total privacy there?"

He was biting his bottom lip, something Lena had never seen him do. For some reason, it appeared provocative to her. What else could he bite so sensually, she pondered. How she loved his mouth and lips.

"No, not the office," he said. "Too many interruptions. What about lunch? I know a very cozy place."

"Perfect."

The jazz pianist was barely noticed at the restaurant. Neither was the lush decor: the numerous chandeliers, the crushing-thick carpeting, the raspberry-scented candles, the glass tables with the floral arrangements embedded inside. Neither were the entrees. Lena ordered a seafood platter. Cordell liked ribs, corn bread, collard greens, and macaroni. A pitcher of piña colada perched in the center of the table. The drink, void of alcohol, filled their lofty glasses, too. Yet all this was irrelevant when Cordell inclined toward Lena. Her entire body appeared paralyzed as she braced herself to hear the news that she prayed wasn't true. Her heart was running the race of its life. She knew it wouldn't settle down until she heard it.

"I'm married," he announced and waited for her reaction.

Lena peered downward in her lap a second, weighing his confession, then stared back up at him. "Deep down I knew, Cordell, but I tried to convince myself otherwise."

"When did you know?" Lines creased between his brows.

"When you didn't give me your home phone number." She paused to stare at him. "I don't understand something, though. Why don't you wear your ring? And why have you been . . ." She was praying he would have a sensible answer, a decent answer. But which one could there be? He was married, and that was all there was to it.

"I don't wear it because I read something in a note once. A note that my wife wrote." Stern faced, he looked off, then returned to her searching eyes. "It made me so angry I tossed my wedding band out the window."

"She must have really hurt you."

He chuckled sadly. "Hurt doesn't even begin to describe it." He took a deep breath. "My situation is a . . . complicated. Is yours?"

She was surprised. "How—"

"The problems you mentioned before I left told me there was someone in your life. I know not a husband, since there was no ring on your finger. But something told me there was a significant other. And somehow I even sensed something is awry in your situation as it is in mine. Because you're not the type of woman to just step out on her man. You have a heart that is determined to do the right thing. Instinctively I know that. But I told myself I had to back off. I had to have respect for my wife and your relationship if you valued it. And your hiding it somehow meant that you did."

He told her about Hope, their lives together, her obsession with children, the miscarriages, the lack of love, the lack of lovemaking, the horrible letter, the pain, the loneliness, her coming and going into sanitariums, and their being apart for three years. She shared with him her life with Robert, the way he was once compared to the way he was now. Cordell abhorred him, wanted to kill him, especially when she revealed the events of the other night. However, there was something positive that resulted: it was a turning point in the relationship. For then, more than ever, she realized she wasn't in love with Robert anymore.

Being a woman, Lena felt bad about Hope's suffering. More so though, Lena understood Cordell's anguish, too. She felt touched by the loss of his children and applauded the sacrifices he endured for Hope. Hope's well-being and sanity was his only concern. Never were his feelings considered. She cherished him for that, as much as Cordell cherished her unselfishness. Oddly enough, both of them had shared the same trying circumstance of preserving the sanity of another human being.

"And believe me, Lena, I've never done this before. I—I mean let another woman know I was very interested in her. Sure, since my wife showed a lack of interest in me, I've been attracted to other women. But never had I acted on those attractions. Not once even in those three years apart. The feelings passed, too. But Lena, what I feel for you is different. You have no idea."

Lena smiled. "I do have an idea. Everything you feel, I feel. I've never done this before, either. Like yourself, when Robert and I began growing apart, I was attracted to other people also. But never did I act on it. It would have been immature. It also would have been wrong. So it passed as easily as it came. But this is different, Cordell. And now I've left him. Left him because he mistreated me so horribly I couldn't take it anymore.

"And now you're here, and I've never felt this way before. I know I never will again, either. It's overwhelming and all so wonderful. I don't even feel like myself. I feel like I'm watching this woman moving and moving farther into something that's making her feel better and better the farther she moves."

"Lena, we can't leave it like this."

"What do you mean?"

"I mean I can't just go on seeing you so casually."

"But the fact remains you're married."

"I'm going to tell Hope."

"Tell her what?"

"I want to see you. See you in the right way. So delicately I will tell her that I know she doesn't love me, that I've known for a while. I'll assure her that I will take care of her and give her the ultimate respect, but I can no longer play this charade. I'll begin divorce proceedings as soon as she comes back from her folks. She's out West, visiting. But this divorce will be best for us both. We both have only one life to live, and for the first time in a long time, I feel like I'm alive living it. You caused that, Lena."

They stared at each other for a moment before Lena broke the silence.

"Cordell, you really have to think about what you're

doing. That woman is very sick. She's been through a lot, too." Then she paused, appearing in deep thought. "Then again, so have you. You've been through so much."

"I have thought about it. I've thought about it not just today or recently, but for years. The time has come to act now. In the meantime, I want to get to know you even better. But I also have to respect Hope. I'm well known around New York. I can't really wine you and dine you until it's out in the open that Hope and I are divorcing. I don't want to make you or her look foolish, and I don't want someone to tell her something that might hurt her. That being the case, I would like to spend some time with you in my home in the Cliffs. You can stay in the guest room, of course."

Lena didn't know if she should be surprised, insulted, or flattered. Even so, the idea of being away with him was so enticing. "The Cliffs in Jersey?"

"You've been there?"

"No, I've heard about it. I hear it's beautiful. But . . ." Grappling with her discomfort, her gaze scattered downward.

"But what?"

Her eyes reached back into his. "What about—"

"Hope? As I said, she's visiting her family out West. When she returns, I'll approach her with the divorce."

Lena nodded. "I guess you're very serious about this."

"I am."

"I'm glad—not glad about your divorcing someone you were married to for so long. But glad that you know that this is best for everyone."

"That I do know. Hope will see it my way, too. But enough about that. Let's just concentrate on us—us being far away from here. The Cliffs will take your breath away, and I will, too, if you let me."

Suddenly he was looking, perusing lips, eyes, skin, neck, breasts, down to as far as he could see of a dangerous depth.

Lena's lower stomach welled with pleasing sensations. They assured her wherever he desired her to go, she had to be there. "When can we go?" she stunned herself by asking.

"I'll make a few calls to my office. They knew I was with a new entertainment client, and I'll just say that I'm going to work on the case at my home in the Cliffs until I'm finished. If they need me there, they can page me. What I want you to do is go pack, and I'll pick you up at the hotel in the morning . . . say around nine. I would love to say this afternoon, but I'm expected back at the office and have to finish up a project. So how does tomorrow morning sound?"

"This all sounds too good to even imagine it."

"It will be good." Good was moaned, stirring something down inside Lena, rousing warmth that satiated at the base of her stomach, which throbbed, aroused, tingled, made her ache with desire.

The sweet wind of ecstasy moved through Lena like it never had before while she packed. All types of items were tossed into the suitcase. There was no consideration to what she chose. Lena was too filled with feeling. New feelings. Breathless feelings. Unreal feelings. Dreamy feelings. Desirous feelings. The mist of her exhilaration wasn't even pierced by the realities of what she tossed onto the bed.

There were nine messages from Robert. Upon entering
the lobby, the desk clerk handed them to Lena. The young
woman stressed the party relayed that all the messages
were urgent. Packing, Lena rolled her eyes at the papers,
her gaze catching them between the slips, dresses, panty-
hose, panties, sandals, blouses, and other garments that
flattened in the luggage. Robert didn't want anything
more than he did the other night when he visited unexpectedly. Sorry, sorry, sorry was coming out of his backside. There was no true intention behind the words, and
Lena was immune now. That she knew for certain when
she snapped the suitcase shut.

Later she pampered herself with R. Kelly's latest CD.
She liked each one of the songs on this newest release
and listened as she showered, powdered, oiled, bathed,
and lay down. All the ballads were played at least four
times by the time she closed her eyes. Within the darkness, Lena saw her own possible musical achievement.
Fantasies of how wonderful everything would be made
her shiver with anticipation. Yet it wasn't solely the possible triumphs that made her quiver. In the images, Cordell was next to her, just as he would be next to her in
merely hours, hopefully in ways she had dreamed of but
never believed would actually come true. Her breath
caught in her throat, thinking of him. Lena tossed, turned,
clutched her pillow, and didn't know where to throw her
legs to be more comfortable. It was going to be a lingering, scorching summer night. It didn't matter if the
air conditioner was on full blast. And if tomorrow wasn't
the beginning of the true summer of her life, there wasn't
such a season.

* * *

Shortly after sunrise the next morning, Cordell was folding items and placing them in the suitcase. The articles were belongings he hadn't used in a long time. There was that particular brand of Pierre Cardin cologne he wore for special occasions, the last time being his sister's wedding three years ago. There was also the black silk bathrobe, right beside his barely-there underwear. When all was packed and Cordell was almost ready to head out the door, he gazed at the empty spot where Hope had slept before she left. Motionlessness seized him for a while. He felt odd. Not just about his impending unfaithfulness, but simply about Hope.

Something was different about her since she left the hospital. Something other than her staring at him like she did sometimes. Her entire demeanor appeared altered, somehow more enlivened. Possibly she was getting better; Cordell prayed that was true.

Seven

Everything had entranced them as they traveled the streets, boulevards, roads, and highways. If they weren't bent over, hysterically amused about embarrassing, comical incidents each had experienced, they were swapping tragedies, triumphs, and all those occurrences that were significant and inconsequential but had influenced their lives. Because they communicated so well, profoundly understanding each other, knowing the deepest feelings, thoughts, passions of the other all without reason, the drive was electrifying. Time passed in a twinkling. So fascinated they were, they craved more of this magical ambience they had discovered. Never had it been found in anyone else, and they were convinced it wouldn't be encountered ever again. They were compelled to go further.

Hours later, Lena was momentarily distracted from her favorite sunset. Gaping out of the car window, house 333 stood breathtaking. Tremendously sized, colonial designed, displaying a manicured lawn and burgeoning, exotic flowers, its three stories were among a line of enormous houses separated by grounds that extended approximately the width of three parallel cars. Adding to it all, a sun-brushed ocean billowing behind the backyard could be viewed from the sides of the house. All the homes were perched on a high altitude of land that folk-lore had exaggerated into a cliff.

"This is some gorgeous home," Lena observed. "I don't see why you stay here just once in a blue moon. If it was mine, I would be here all the time. I'd live and die here."

A response, Lena expected, but no sooner than she spoke fingertips grazed her chin, inducing her back to the eyes, the lips, the skin, the sunset, which was him. Such an innocent gesture allured the heat from her senses, making her relish the lust-rousing touch of his large probing hands and hope for so much more.

Staring at the slanted eyes that always spellbound him, Cordell cared less about her opinion of his second home. His interest was maneuvering in order to attain what he desired feverishly, needed desperately, and had dreamed about a million times.

"There's something I have to have," whispered hotly across her ear. "I've been wanting to do this for too long and a whole lot more."

Blazing hands caressed the silken skin of her face. So joy rousing it was, it summoned blood to her head, leaving Lena immobilized by his sensuality. It was only after he urgently came forward, his massive arms immuring her, their bodies pressing, that she stirred. With her frantically pulsing heart synchronizing with his own, Lena was dazed by his face coming nearer and nearer and soon surrendered to the inconceivable lusciousness of his mouth devouring her own.

Oh, God, what a feeling, her body cried.

With an untamed hunger raging through him, the pressure of his lips opened hers more. Winding, dipping, tugging his tongue amid the sweet nectar inside her mouth and that which dusted her lips, he knew of nothing that had brought him such pleasure. Bolder and fiercer he became, filling her with more of what her moans and body rhythms screamed for, but equally satisfying himself, increasingly swaying toward that brink beyond his control.

Cradling her head in the crook of his arm, he claimed her succulence with all the fire and passion he had harbored for this woman for so long. Never could he get enough of her.

Lena had known nothing else like what was happening between them. Sultrily swirling his tongue in her mouth, erotically using it to inflame rapture more potent than she fantasized about, she felt every fiber of her awakened to ecstasy she had never known. Each thread of her being surged with longing. Desire swarmed acutely in her femininity. For no man had ever kissed her like this. Lena wanted Cordell—*badly*. There was never too much of this delirium to feel—of him to feel, the man who possessed her.

During the heat of their frenzy, though, there was that noise. Every now and then, a horn honked. They had merely tuned it out like an insect buzzing in the distance, until it came closer and was so annoying it couldn't be ignored. Unwillingly Lena and Cordell looked up and saw a woman inside a Mercedes Benz, trying to get their attention. She was the shade of light caramel and wore her hair in a fade haircut short as any man's. Her motions indicated that Cordell's Jaguar was blocking her driveway. From the ear to ear grin on her face, Lena surmised that she knew Cordell well.

"That's my neighbor," he said and steered out of her path. The woman drove into the driveway of the house to the right of Cordell's. In turn, he parked in his drive-way.

Watching Cordell get out of their love nest, Lena felt bittersweetness about the interruption. For those steamy minutes, she was ravenous for him, in broad daylight, in early afternoon, possibly in front of all his neighbors. Suddenly self-conscious, she neatened her tousled hair and appeared composed by the time Cordell opened her door.

The intruder, a big-boned, medium-height woman, wearing lots of jewelry, was approaching him.

"How are you doing, handsome?" She greeted him with a hug and afterward peered at his companion. "And who is this fox you have here?"

Both Lena and Cordell smiled, but his appeared a little off. Never had he brought another woman to his home, and it made him somewhat awkward. Despite the shame, though, he eventually stared Tobia in the eyes. "Tobia, this is a very special person in my life, a very precious young lady, Lena. Lena, this is Tobia, my neighbor and—"

"A client." Tobia completed his sentence. "Lord, girl, this is a smart man next to you. This here sharp attorney saved me a whole lot of money. I had this customer who was trying to sue me about falling in my lingerie shop, and she almost had me big in the pocket, too. Deep—you know what I mean? Anyway, then I come to find out my neighbor was a lawyer, and I mean a good one, too. This here man saved me a whole lot of money. Many, many, many thousands. Cordell did his homework on this woman and came to find out that the back injury she claimed she received in my shop, she had received sev-enteen years ago from a car accident. I tell you, I was so mad I brought a frying pan to court with me that

morning the judge handed down his decision. I was going
to clop her right on the head with it, too."

Lena was cracking up. "No, you're joking, right?"

"Uh-uh." Tobia glanced up at Cordell. "I'm telling the
truth, you know that?"

Nodding, he was too tickled. "She's telling the truth."

"But this man here saved me, thank God. On all accounts. She could have pressed charges if I had clopped
her on the head."

Thoroughly entertained, Lena couldn't help staring up
at the hero. "He's something, isn't he?"

"Girl, who are you telling! My husband loves him,
too, and my husband don't love nobody. He just works
himself to death and sleeps. Sleeps anywhere, even
standing up. It doesn't matter."

All of them snickered, but Cordell turned sober, his
eyes lingering on Lena. "Lena here isn't too bad of a
professional herself," he volunteered.

"Yeah? She's a lawyer, too?"

Cordell was still staring. Lena was blushing.

"She's a singer. She—"

"She's a singer!" Tobia boomed, her hand slapped
against her chest. "What records you recorded, girl? I'm
a music connoisseur. Lord knows, I love me some good
R&B music. Especially slow jams."

"Slow jams are her specialty!" Cordell declared enthusiastically. "She can tear up a song, rip up a note,
twist around a lyric, have you crying and screaming and
praying and wanting to make love and everything! You've
never heard a woman blow like this one. I'm not exaggerating."

"Oh, stop!" Tobia teased. "I'm sold. I'll buy all her

records, but you're embarrassing this woman." She gawked at Lena. "But can you really sing like that?"

"I'm okay, I guess."

Cordell shook his head. "She's not *okay,* she's great! Spectacular. A diva unlike any you've ever heard."

Lena blushed some more. "I've been blessed enough to have recently been offered a recording contract with a major label, and I'll be recording an album in about a month. I'll be glad to give you a complimentary copy when it's ready. Cordell is representing me, and he's my manager. A . . . actually that's why I'm here with him. We have some contract matters to go over . . . and other business stuff . . . you know . . ."

"Yeah?" Skeptically Tobia's eyes shifted from Cordell to Lena. "Well, good luck, girl. You seem like a nice person, and if your voice is good as he says, you're going to make it. Just believe in yourself, and follow what's in your heart. That's what I did with my shop. It's doing more than good, too. Don't let others discourage you, either. There's a lot of that out there. And give me a call sometimes. Cordell knows the number. And here's my card, too." She rummaged in her bag, removed a hot pink business card, and handed it to Lena between multicolored nails. "Come by the shop and get a baby doll or something, too. You'd look good in everything in there."

"Ooh, yes," Cordell agreed.

"I'll drop by. I'll do that."

"Good. Let me get in the house to Reuben. I bet you he's sleeping and snoring."

Tobia rushed up the beige stone pathway leading to her front door. As she did, Lena and Cordell gathered their luggage, then strolled up toward his house.

"She's nice," Lena remarked. "Real down to earth."

"That she is. Crazy, too."

Lena looked at him, her eyes smiling. They both chuckled, while in the background Tobia's front door slammed hard. Yet it was a wonder they heard the harsh sound above the boisterous children playing in the next yard. When they reached Cordell's door, they gazed over at the kids scurrying about and afterward noticed their parents reposing on the porch.

A middle-aged, saggy-cheeked man looked at them. His much younger, thin wife was scowling.

"How you all doing?" Cordell yelled over, feeling awkward again. Both were staring from him to Lena. He tried to overlook it by fumbling for his keys.

"Fine, and you?" the couple asked in near unison.

The woman even stopped frowning and flashed her gap at Cordell. "Your rosebush has been growing like wildfire," she commented.

"I see," he said, finally pulling out his key. Sticking it in the lock, he shouted across the porches, "I have a great gardener to thank for that. No doing of my own."

"Yours is some sight, too," Lena added. However, oddly enough, the woman's grimace returned. The gap vanished, and hostility reeked in the air. The leer was so discomforting, Lena debated if the woman misunderstood her meaning and promptly thought of something nicer, but truthful, to say. "Your children are beautiful. How old are they?" She looked directly at the woman.

Like any ordinary human being, Lena expected a civil reply from this person. Not so lucky. There were more glowering, balled-up lips and a harsh rolling of eyes. Nevertheless, the man, seeing his wife's rudeness, lightened the air, replying, "Thank you, and they are three, seven, eight, and eleven."

"You're lucky," Lena complimented him.

But still his wife's behavior bothered Lena so much she whispered into Cordell's ear, "I don't think your neighbor likes me. The woman."

"Darlene?" he murmured back. He was having trouble with the lock.

"Whoever she is."

Cordell glanced up at Lena, smiled, then concentrated on what he was doing again. "Well, I sure like you. Very, very much."

Of course, she wanted to smile. Try as she did, though, Lena couldn't. Questions were suddenly nagging and circling her mind.

"Is it Hope?" she asked. "Is that why she's giving me the cold shoulder? Is she a friend of hers, and she suspects about us?"

A tinge of guilt came over Cordell. In spite of it, he shook his head. "No way. Hope was here only three times. They probably don't even remember her. She never wanted to come out here. But let's not think about that. There's just you and me and what we feel for each other."

Like a magic elixir, those words transported her back to that euphoric mist showering them in the car, the emotions, the feelings. She couldn't wait to be alone with him.

Once the door was unlocked, Lena proceeded carefully, scrupulously assessing her surroundings, amazed at the luxury of the home. The furnishings were soft gold and white, even the numerous ornaments. There were a few antiques, but overall the style was a potpourri of modern and traditional.

"Who decorated? It's so lovely and cozy at the same

time." She was whirling around and around, still examining. "Who did this?"

"My mother," he answered, staring at her like he had in the car. "She's beautiful, too."

Knowing the intent of his gaze, Lena tried to stay grounded, continuing to delight in the lavishness of the interior design. But in a whirl, her expressions were cut off by the hardness of his chest shuddering against her. Hazily she found herself melting on the sofa and Cordell reclaiming her lips. Desire mounted in her so unbearably, her hands had to christen him, everywhere—but not the place she restrained from seeking. Cordell savored every tantalizing stroke of his limbs, every lustful whimper that escaped, every seductive mingle of their tongues and lips, but it was the unsteady breaths that encouraged Lena to that most intimate part of him.

"Oh, yes," he moaned when her palms roamed over the fabric of his slacks, causing his body to turn to stone a billion times over. He embraced her like breakable glass as much as he enthralled her tempestuously. At times he kissed her so severely, Lena throbbed, biting her lips because the strain of withholding all she craved to do was so extreme.

Amid their seductive flight, though, she could feel his restraint. She could feel his struggle to be the gentleman he believed she yearned for. However, all that was overwhelming Lena guided his hands to touch her all over.

Cordell needed no more encouragement. His tongue bursting, delving, slow dancing provocatively throughout her mouth was no match for his fingers painstakingly enthralling her flesh. Quivers overtook her. The anticipation was unbearable, and between the flame of his lips and hers, Lena could hear him groaning, "Let's go upstairs."

Lena wanted to. Her body, heart, soul, everything within her screeched to follow him up the road to paradise, let him undress her and deliver her to a dimension beyond the universe. If his kisses and caresses were driving her out of her mind, what would making complete love to him do for her?

Except Lena was hesitant. Being literally in his house made certain realities rise closer to the surface.

"Were you with Hope . . . upstairs?" she asked, rearing back to take a breath.

Staring as if he were intoxicated, Cordell picked up her hand. With his thumb feather-stroking its satin feel, he thought for a moment.

The delay in responding sank Lena's heart. "So you did make love to her up there? No, this is not right."

"No!" he denied adamantly. "I was just thinking of how I could explain it. We weren't up in the bedroom in the way that you think. As I told you, Lena, it's been a long, long time with her and never in this house. Yes, we slept in the same bed upstairs, but we just slept. We never touched."

Lena frowned. Not only did the image crush her, but she wondered if he was telling the truth. A great part of her believed he was. A smaller part held some suspicion.

"Lena, there is more than one bedroom upstairs," he assured her. "We won't be in the same one Hope and I were in. And also if you're wondering, to be totally honest, when we were here I did want Hope. Even when I knew she didn't love me, I felt desire for her from time to time. I'm human. But this time when I saw her, and lay next to her, strangely enough, there was nothing. And

since I met you, I know there will never be anything
with her again. Believe me, Lena. I mean it with all my
heart and soul."

"You didn't have to tell me that you had wanted her.
You could have lied. That tells me so much about you.
And if any other man was telling me that since he met
me, there would be nothing else with her, I would think
they were lying just to get me in bed. But something
tells me not you."

He exhaled. "I'm so relieved."

"I'm starting to believe in you more and more." She
relaxed back on the lush cushions, her eyes searching
the ground, but her mind seeing another view. "But what
I can't believe is that I'm here."

"I can't believe you are, either. Are you having doubts
about coming? I don't want to force you to be somewhere, or do something, you don't feel right about doing."

"I would be lying if I said that I'm very comfortable
with everything. After all, as terrible as Robert was, I
just broke up with him."

"And you're feeling guilty?"

"Some."

"Me, too, but I—" He looked off, then back at her.
"I'll tell you what. Let's do something that's not so"—he
sought the appropriate word—"so *stressful*. Let's go
horseback riding, and walking along the beach, then eat
something delicious—and also there's a rodeo in town.
Let's just have some simple fun."

"What about swimming?"

"No." His eyes scattered over her body. "No way. Now
that would be *stressful* seeing you in a bathing suit and
trying not to touch you. I might have a heart attack."

"I couldn't take seeing you that way, either," she admitted with a giggle. "Just simple fun sounds good. I need time, Cordell, and maybe you do, too. We can think all during the day."

"Yes, we can think and by . . . by night we'll know . . . what's right and what's wrong."

Inside a powder blue bedroom, Lena dressed in dungarees, a yellow tank top, and high-top Nike sneakers. She brushed out a cute side bang, hot curled it under, and pulled the rest of her hair in a loose ponytail. All the while her heart was beating as emphatically as her mind was working. Was she doing the right thing? It wasn't too late to go to the hotel, or go home, or return to Robert. Was she being a tramp, a whore, a mistreated girlfriend looking for some new action? Outstanding above all this, too, Cordell was another woman's husband. Granted, Hope had treated him horrendously, but still she was a sick woman. A helpless one.

Loathing is what Lena had always felt for women who went with other women's husbands. She had berated them among discussions at lunch with her co-workers. They were always despised when they were characters on soap operas. They shattered families, made children fatherless, and caused loving, devoted women to go mad. There was a hysteria to what was happening as there was guilt immeasurable in Lena's soul. Mistresses had the power to transform someone's fairy-tale existence into an unbelievable nightmare, and for that reason many women longed for their slow, painful deaths—the slow painful deaths of that woman—the other woman. Hence, how could Lena now be that other woman, even if she in no way felt like her? Because she wasn't. These circumstances were well beyond the ordinary. Because of

Hope's institutionalization, they lived apart for three years. Not only that, but ill or not ill, Hope had married Cordell under false pretenses. She admitted that she didn't love him and probably never would. How he lived with that knowledge, never divorcing her before, was beyond Lena's comprehension. Except now he was asking for a divorce. He was asking, because like anyone wanted, he wanted to be with someone who was in love with him. Like anyone who always tried to do the right thing, wasn't he deserving of that simple human need?

Cordell was someone, an individual, a man with a past, future, present, one of God's children trying to pass through this world and obtain some joy. All he had ever done was behave as a loving, devoted husband to a woman who felt nothing for him. She had even used him. Everything he did for her was at the expense of his own happiness. Severing the ties was the sole way to seek peace for either of them. With Hope having no feelings for him, surely she would agree. Wasn't it long overdue for Cordell to receive just a little sunshine out of this old world? When Lena allowed herself to think about this, an ache dwelled deep inside. She could feel his pain. She ached to soothe it. She had to be his sun.

In another room on the same floor, the same side of the hall, Cordell dressed and reflected, too. Denim beige shorts, a beige tank top, and white sneakers were thrown on and he was ready to go. Nonetheless it was his mind making him loiter in the room. With her door closed, he knew Lena was taking off and putting on clothing and even that innocent knowledge titillated him. There was no denying what he hungered for at that moment.

Cordell had dared to separate sex and love and claimed to himself that he desired specifically one with her—which was true. Though with Lena, with the passion exploding through him for her, Cordell had learned that being in love and passionate could go hand in hand. Sure enough, long before that letter, he had loved Hope intensely. Even so, it was never like what was seizing his heart now. These sensations lived with him. They breathed with him. They were with him when he woke up, ate, glided down the street, did his work, sorted the laundry and went to the supermarket, and when he did anything. These emotions made him continually wonder: if she could sing with such passion, and now kiss with such passion, what would making love to her be like?

At the question, his body flooded with more excitement, and the essence of him became more aroused. Thoughts raced and progressed to fantasies. There were images old-fashioned people would have considered freaky. They were scenes that his sisters would have called nasty-to-the-bone. It all made Cordell recall a time when he was a puberty-aged boy. He recalled being so aroused all the time over this particular beautiful girl. It showed, too—showed where everyone could *see.* Unmercifully his sisters teased him about being nasty. So what would they say now? What would they think if they peeked into his mind and saw all the ways he wanted to please Lena?

Not only did he desire to be exotically physical with this woman, a woman who made him feel like he did as a boy, but at the same time a woman who made him feel like he never did before—but Cordell wanted to integrate everything inside him with her. He wanted to share all this emotion he had for her and unite it within her, and fill her with all phenomenal joy that filled him when they were together. He wanted to open his heart and soul and let his sisters see how he would easily die for this woman—and give to this woman everything that he owned—and share with her even his tears.

At times, he was certain he was living and breathing her. On occasions, it was as if she became inhuman and invisible and slipped inside him and became his soul. She was everywhere and anywhere, even when she was nowhere around.

Cordell walked down the stairs, wondering what she was doing in the other room. Once in the living room, he picked up a magazine, but his head shot up as she came down the steps. He was awestruck. In jeans, a tank top, sneakers, that smile and that face, he wanted her more than ever.

"You're one beautiful woman, Lena Durant."

"I'm glad you see me that way."

"Any man would see you that way."

There was horseback riding, but only a little. Lena was scared of getting thrown, and Cordell found the experience hilarious because of the faces she made, along with her repeatedly ending up backward on the horse. Succeeding that humorous event, there was a scrumptious meal at a seaside restaurant, but no rodeo. They were too late for it and debated going water-skiing, but the hovering sunset postponed that, too. So to round off an extraordinarily wonderful day, they planned to dance at a nightclub until dawn.

Entering the house, there was a race up the stairs to the closest bathroom, which Lena won. Smirking and folding her arms, she stood outside the door, also shaking her head. "You let me win, didn't you?"

"No, I didn't. I'm an old man. You have me by six years."

"So."

"So nothing."

"Well you—"

Swept suddenly into his arms, her breath and voice drowned away. Thunderously Lena's heart rang, but above its commotion, she heard him whisper: "Today was a day I'll never forget. It's been so long since I felt this good. Come to think of it, I probably never felt this good."

Clearly touched, Lena looked down, then back up again. The intensity in her eyes equaled his. "I feel the same way. Exactly the same."

"You do?"

"With all my heart and soul."

"Well, that makes me feel even better than I did already. And that's saying a lot." He smiled.

She joined him. "I want to make you feel good. But—but . . . well, I guess I'll shower and get ready to go dancing."

"Yes, I guess you better do that."

Quietly Lena closed the door. Cordell listened to the water running. He should have walked away and headed to the other bathroom. Instead he could only stand there. It was as if his hammering, racing, bursting heart wouldn't allow his limbs to move.

Eight

Lena heard romantic sounds sweetening the air as she came out of the bathroom and stood in the luxuriously decorated hall. Now how was she supposed to want to go dancing when he was playing a slow jam like this at home? The ballad, at least four years old, was an it-feels-so-disgustingly-good-to-make-love-to-you song. That's how anyone would have described "Whip Appeal" by Babyface. Listening to it, wholly enamored by its flowing of passion, Lena should have begun blow-drying her hair and curling it, but the seduction of the lyrics were irresistible.

Lena reminisced back to when that tune first hit the airwaves. Countlessly she played it every day. Robert and she were happy then. That being as it may, she wasn't anywhere near as blissful as she was now.

The mood of the melody growing more torrid, it lured Lena down the steps leading to the living room. As her feet glided, crushing into the golden carpeting, a hint of an erotic men's fragrance exuded. It staggered her with its sexiness, inviting her to ponder if that cologne sprinkled so evocatively on solely him, or did it invoke that mystique for everyone who wore it. But soon all the speculations were shoved aside upon Lena reaching the bottom of the stairwell—for there was a sight that took her breath away.

Lying sideways across the floor, Cordell was wearing a black silk bathrobe tied loosely. Rich brown facial skin shimmered in the candlelight glow of the room. The remainder of him that was exposed was alluringly hairy: a portion of his chest, a glimpse of his wrists, and the bottom of his legs. Beholding him like this, Lena wondered if there was any vision in the world more gorgeous; if there was something, she hadn't come across such splendor yet.

Slowly she sashayed toward him, appearing much calmer than she felt, giving no indication as to what his suggestive dress was doing to her. "Why aren't you getting ready, Mr. Richardson? That's no suit you're wearing there."

"I could ask the same of you." He propped himself up on an elbow, his eyes traveling from the dewiness of her face, to her white, gown-length kimono, to the lotioned feet he couldn't wait to kiss. "But on second thought, I'm not getting dressed because I'd rather be undressed around you."

"Well . . . I . . ." Lena stammered, feeling increasingly tongue-tied because of the heat in his eyes.

"Yes, let's hear it."

"Well—well I . . . I heard this great . . . this great sexy music. So what am I supposed to do?"

"Dance, that's what." At once Cordell hopped up, put the song on at the beginning, and scooped Lena into his arms.

They were so close, hearts were indistinguishable. Waists, hips, and torsos were stirring, twisting, arching with awesome harmony. Lena gazed up at him, finding his eyes burning down on her face. "I don't think we're going to make it to the club," she murmured.

"I don't think so, either."

There was the rhythm, the words, Babyface's voice vibrating, rippling, manipulating every note for all its provocativeness, beauty, worth. Amid this sea of ecstasy too, there were bodies meshing, hardness against softness, breathlessness and lips—lips that explored never deep and eager enough.

Cordell was the first to withdraw and in one inmost breath, he asked, "Do you feel me, Lena?"

"Oh, yes."

"Do you like what you feel?"

"Oh, yes."

"Ooh, baby, I know we've known each other only for about a month, but I feel so close to you. I need to be even closer. I want you, Lena. I want you so bad."

"Yes, Cordell. Oh, I want you, too. Please love me."

"I already do. I'm in love with you, Lena."

He sounded raspy and much lazier than the energy his limbs emanated. He pressed against her until she was down on the carpet, lying flat on her back. *Her,* their position, the moment, the ballad, the atmosphere, her clean scent, her sexiness, her gorgeous face, her voluptuous body, all entered him with a rush and balled into that explosive apex of his body. With a poignancy distorting the usual calmness of his facial features, Cordell rose up, somehow compelled to scrutinize her eyes, lips, the glow on her skin further.

Everything sensed and happening between them had assured Lena how he felt for her. Nevertheless, to hear it openly revealed made her plead with what sounded like her last breath, "Don't say anything you don't mean.

Please don't make a fool of me. My heart couldn't take it."

"I would never hurt you. I can't hurt what I love so much."

"I love the way you're looking at me now. It makes my body . . ." She closed her eyes and opened them slowly. "I feel like something so beautiful, I'm not even of this earth when you look at me like that."

"You're not. And I do mean what I said. Oh, baby . . . I . . ." He cupped her face in his hands and kissed her hard and long. Spasms of unquenchable desire, tantalizement, and an overpowering, insane need for total fulfillment, came in full force. When they stopped, Cordell rose up some more, his scintillating eyes devouring her. "Lena, you are so beautiful. Believe me. I mean what I say."

She took a deep breath, attempting to quell the excitement building in the base of her stomach, the excitement bellowing through her blood. Rapture was obviously and literally shaking her entire body. "I'm in love with you, Cordell. I know it's soon. I know it seems almost unreal and unbelievable. Too quick to be true. But it's there, and nothing and no one in this world can make it ever go away."

The scene had played in his mind so many times, Cordell debated if he was still dreaming about kissing away her kimono, her lacy bra, exposing her taut, round breasts, kissing them, being breathlessly roused by them, tasting them, handling them until he watched her become delirious and whimper with longing.

Lena became achingly alive as the feelings flowed over and inside of her. It was all too perfect to be reality. Only a fantasy was as beautiful as what was emitting between them, and only a fantasy was as beautiful as Cordell when his robe opened and dropped. His bare skin glistened. Rigid, firm, tight, dark, shiny, sweaty flesh, scented of lust and ready for her. Lena's hands roamed desperately. Her lips discovered each inch of him. It was too much. The euphoria of it all was too sweet to let go. This kind of moment, this once in a lifetime season of paradise, it had to be held on to, preserved, clutched direly for eternity. She would accept every drop and feel every measure of deliciousness, of delight, of excruciating elation until there was no more left.

Cordell kissed her all over, all over until every stitch of her clothes were off. Kissed hips, legs, nipples, buttocks, lips, toes, fingers, thighs and all in between, kissed until both were exceedingly enraptured by lips and fingers and could bear no more existing without totally becoming one.

Love had been a preciousness Lena assumed she knew, but it wasn't until he entered her heart that she finally knew love.

Love was more than his body pumping precisely for her satisfaction, grinding with a perfection that was wholeheartedly welcomed by her limbs, writhing to a melody only their souls could dance to. It was more than pleasure streaming in her that was exceptionally joyful, tearfully pleasing, unbearably thrilling. It was more than her granting all that was within her power to see, hear, and feel his unimaginable gladness. It was more than the act, an amorous exchange, via both common and unusual acts, which some considered raunchy, while both their souls understood it as a divine channel of astounding emotions, too overpowering to be contained in words, just feeling, just phenomenal feelings. It was more than

Lena could ever conceive, dream, imagine, something she never knew. It was more than words could describe. And when their resplendence was over—far, far too soon—Lena knew as undoubtedly as Cordell did that nothing would ever be the same. The world would never be seen in the same way. They could never look at each other and see what they saw before; now there was more.

"You're within me now, and I'm within you." Cordell proclaimed this when he eased from above Lena and lay by her side. "There's no way I can do anything now without thinking about you, without reliving what you made me feel, without remembering how it made me feel to see you so happy, to know I was making you that happy."

Lena gazed over at him. Perspired, exhausted, but tranquil, he was facing the ceiling. Lines creased between his brows.

Her eyes were cloudy, her body and skin drenched. Despite the wetness, she snuggled next to him and placed her head against his chest. With its bushy hairs, it felt like concrete against her cheeks, but was still somehow soft enough to be a cushion. She clung tighter, and as she did, she felt his fingers playing through the base of her damp hair. The gentle frolic over her scalp felt so good and relaxed her so much, her voice was so airy it sounded like it came from somewhere far. "I've never felt this before. I've never been made love to like this."

He planted a light kiss on her forehead and laced his large fingers in her hair some more. "I know. Oh, baby, do I know."

Sleep came easy. It came for both after a long awaited journey to an island of the soul now so awakened and so unknown.

* * *

The sunlight blasting through the chiffon gold curtains and creeping up the bed, nudging Lena to wake, was practically blinding as she sat up. When her eyes did focus, the first thing noticed was that Cordell wasn't cuddled next to her or in the bedroom. After that, there was the clock, displaying 11:13 A.M. in vivid green letters. Following that, she peered down at the barely there red teddy slipped over her. Smiling, she wiped the last remnants of sleep out of her sight and recalled how she wound up in Cordell's bedroom with lingerie on.

Bit by bit she remembered Cordell carrying her up the stairs to the master bedroom. Once inside, Lena treated him to a show of dressing and undressing, which brought a smile to his face that never left. Thereafter they celebrated their love with a bottle of champagne. Greatest of all, the evening was capped with more and more love-making.

Recollecting it all, she laughed to herself and stretched her arms high. The pungent taste of their nightcap was in her mouth, and brushed over her skin was the unforgettable scent of last night. But even with the door closed, Lena couldn't help abruptly inhaling another fragrance. Familiar, pleasant, hypnotic. Her first reaction was to open the door and dash downstairs to see what Cordell was up to. Yet as she passed the mirror and saw herself, Lena decided otherwise. She didn't need makeup to look pretty, but after their passionate night, all the perspiring and everything else, she looked greasy and raccoonish. Her mascara was smudged, granting her ring around the eyeballs. Her top lip had lipstick on, while the bottom one didn't. A tremendous fire-red hickey stood out on her neck. Plus her hair had that mussed I've-been-lying-in-the-bed look.

A wash of the face, an invigorating shower, and a hair brushing were fast on her agenda. Afterward she spotted an oversized "I Love New York" T-shirt flung over a chair. She slipped it over her head and headed downstairs. There was that fragrance again. The closer she came to it, she was sure it was roses, and Lena had to smile. When she reached the bottom step, the smile was a scream.

There were flowers everywhere. Red, pink, yellow, and white roses were scattered all over the place. They covered the sofa, the love seat, the chaise, the carpet, and everything else. There were myriads, and among them Cordell emerged from the porch with the newspaper in his hand. "Do you smell flowers anywhere?" he teased.

Her hands clung to the sides of her face. Eyes blinked and blinked. "I don't believe this." She kept turning toward each assortment of roses.

"Believe it." He stepped toward her. "I'm going to spoil you, Lena."

"You don't have to." And her expression darkened with her voice. "Baby, I'm spoiled enough."

His eyes locked fervently with hers. "I just wanted to do something special for you. You're my heart."

Lena ran over and jumped up on him. She hugged him so tightly her insides welled up with desire. They kissed lastingly, deep, ferociously until she reared back, her entire being heaving with the mad throbbings of their united hearts.

They gave each other a knowing look before Cordell clutched her the hand, pulling Lena down on the couch. "After last night," he said, "I had to do something special for you. You don't know what you did to me. What it all meant to me."

"I do know. I feel the same way."

"Lena, we can't just leave it the way it is."

"What are you saying? Really saying?" Her gaze carefully searched his face.

"I think you know. I'm saying . . . forever."

At that, her heartbeat quickened. "I would love forever with you." Though no sooner than the words were said, worry shadowed her face.

"What is it?" Cordell asked.

"I was thinking—what if Hope doesn't handle the idea of a divorce well? We're thinking that because she didn't love you that she'll leave easily. But what if . . . what if she just wants someone to take care of her? And what if she freaks out or something when you tell her because of that? Some people would rather have someone than no one at all."

He was silent for a second, biting his lip and thinking, before he said, "I will be talking to her doctors before she returns. I want to make sure that she can handle this after being institutionalized so long. And what you're saying is valid. As much as it hurts and saddens me, I've become a security blanket for her."

Lena nodded. "Just like I was for Robert. Sometimes I felt like I was some kind of super-weight glue holding him together. But am I giving myself too much credit?"

"Not at all. From what you told me, you were keeping him sane."

"So have you, with Hope. But if we are all that to these two people, can we unglue them, unravel their lives, and just go on with our own? Until recently Robert was good to me. Those years we were together and—"

But Lena was distracted by Cordell looking off. Instinct warned her what he was thinking. She touched his face. It was a sunset more than ever. Guiding it back to her, she spoke sincerely. "But never has he ever been as good to me as you. Never has he made me feel like you did not only last night, but all the time. Never have I loved him the way I love you. No man can ever replace you inside of me." Her hand delicately patted her heart. "Cordell, I love you so much I would die for you. You have made this time the summer of my life. Just you. Not even the music. Just you."

The following day, a lack of personal grooming aids forced them outside. They visited the local health and beauty supply store, but the sun ravished them so, it enticed them to remain outside. That day and days after, they enjoyed all sorts of entertaining things. They discovered more about each other, and all that they learned they loved. They shared. They laughed. They played. And throughout every venture, throughout every passionate look, throughout every phrase, throughout every discussion of her career, throughout every shopping spree he treated her to, throughout every breath, every touching of waists or chest or shoulders or holding of hands— emotions mounted. What existed now was more than they ever perceived was possible.

Even so, when two weeks had passed and Cordell had to return to his law firm, and Hope, he urged Lena to remain in the Cliffs.

"Without you?" she asked.

"You know I would love to see you every second of the day, but coming back from the city to here would be too much of a commute each day. I'd be worn out. No good for nothing. And I don't want to put off straightening out things with Hope. I don't enjoy seeing you behind her back, when she thinks everything is fine with us. It's not right. So I have to make it right."

"I admire and respect you for that."

"But I will call, baby. Call you so much you will get tired of me."

"I'll never get tired of hearing your voice." She swiped a lock of hair that tumbled over her eye and inched closer to him. "And I do understand."

"But in the meantime, I know you love it here. It's better than that hotel, too. You can get rested up before you start recording."

"When exactly is our meeting about the selecting the songs and the other things?"

"That's not until next week. Come to think of it, you can do this . . ." He thought for a moment. "After the meeting, you'll go to the hotel and get your things. Afterward you'll go to the apartment, get your mail and get the rest of your belongings, then you'll move in here."

"Move in here! I can't . . . not yet, Cordell."

He smiled. "Well, at least think about it. And I hope you thought about what I asked you."

He left early in the morning, sweet-talking her as he situated himself in the car. Dark suit, suave tie, clean shaved and that brilliant smile—and he captivated her. Lena would have walked on hot coals for him not to leave.

As soon as the last bit of the Jaguar's silver green was out of sight, Lena thought of something that would ease the pain of missing him: music.

She began rehearsing. She didn't yet know what songs

would be recorded. Lena was aware that her vocal chords were rusty. Not only that, her body didn't feel the same. Being in love, she realized, was draining. It took much out of her. She had to get accustomed to it—to this feeling—to all the love that Cordell was giving her. She had to get herself back in shape to do those vocal acrobatics.

It was the third day after Cordell left that Lena decided merely to relax. In the late afternoon, she sat out on the porch after watching some really interesting soap operas the entire day. That's when she glanced over, and who did she see but Darlene sitting on her porch, too.

Despite Darlene's constant dirty looks whenever Lena saw her, and regardless of Darlene whispering to her husband about Lena and snickering, too, whenever she saw her, Lena smiled and greeted the woman. "How are you today? How are those beautiful children? Haven't seen them lately."

Darlene just rolled her eyes.

And Lena just looked at her. Finally she reared her head back, then looked the other way. "Heaven help her," she mumbled.

Decked in a white, fitted jumpsuit, Tobia happened to be coming up her walkway. Like the first time Lena and she met, she was wearing several necklaces, rings, and multiple earrings, which would have looked shoddy on anyone else, but looked chic and sophisticated on her. When she spotted Lena, she detoured to Cordell's porch.

"Sit down, miss business lady," Lena greeted her with the familiarness of old friends. "How are you today?" For some reason Lena felt like she knew Tobia much longer, and much better, than she actually did.

Taking a huge breath, Tobia relaxed in a folding chair, spreading her legs wide.

"I'm tired, girl. Tired as I don't know who or what. But what you've been up to?" She leaned close to Lena and lowered her voice. "I've seen you and Cordell going in and out, and I've been hearing sounds coming from this house, too. Those sounds that I like!" Mischievously she raised one brow.

Lena grinned, glanced over at Darlene's porch sneakily, then made an effort to subdue her voice's pitch, too. "So you figured it out about us, huh?"

"Girl, anyone being around you could. When two people are in love, it's no secret. The whole world can see it. The whole world knows it. All they have to do is be around them for a while."

"We are that obvious?"

"You sure are."

"He's so wonderful."

"Yeah, that Cordell is a sweetheart all right."

Indisputably Lena had to agree. Yet at the same time, she was suddenly speculating—speculating if Tobia knew about Hope since Cordell and she were friends as well as associated through business.

Tobia, as if reading Lena's mind, nodded without hearing any question. "I know about her. She called his office often when he handled my case. I also sensed all was not right. And I must admit, certainly as a married woman, I don't like when women sleep with other women's husbands. But then again, as I've learned In this crazy world, you don't know what the real picture is until you dust beneath the surface. So I don't know the circumstances, and sometimes situations are not cut and dried."

"Thank you for not hating me for what I'm doing. A married woman would usually side with the wife."

"By now don't you know I'm not usual?"

"I'm beginning to see that," Lena said with a chuckle, but swiftly regained her seriousness. "And it's not like a typical married man fooling around syndrome. This is the first time both of us ever did something like this. You see, I just left my fiancé."

"For Cordell?"

"Not exactly. I was thinking about leaving him even before I came to know Cordell. You see, my fiancé, Robert, has been treating me like I'm his worst enemy lately, verbally abusing me, putting me down so bad, trying to hold me back from my dreams. He even threatened violence."

"Then you had to drop him." She stomped one foot. "Let that sucker go! For sure you know he's not right."

"I know. Strange thing is he used to treat me so well, but lately—" Dejectedly Lena looked down and when she gazed back up, understanding shone vivid in Tobia's face.

"I can see and feel your pain, girl."

"It has been pain. Too much to bear. But Cordell— beautiful Cordell, he makes me so happy. He makes me forget all that. And I know he loves me as much as I love him. He even had papers drawn up to put my name beside his on the title for this house."

"Girl, get out of here!"

"Yes, he did. Cordell even made sure to remind me about it before he left for the city the other day. Says he wants this to be my house and his—legally."

"Damn, he's serious as hell then! But what about his wife? Her name isn't on it?"

"She was not herself at the time that he was taking care of all the paperwork of purchasing it, and therefore wasn't able to sign. She was . . . well, she was recovering from a hysterectomy. Later she had a nervous breakdown."

"Oh, no."

Lena went on to tell Tobia about all the suffering Cordell had shared with Hope.

When she finished, Tobia mashed her lips together and shook her head. "My Lord! I had no idea he had to deal with so much. You would never know it. He is just as good a person as he can be. Cordell doesn't deserve that. No good-hearted man like him does."

"No, he doesn't."

"I'm so sorry to hear all this."

"Me, too. She never put her name on the house's title because she's been in and out of sanitariums, just trying to get her bearings. She doesn't like to leave their place in New York, either. And when she became better, he practically dragged her up here, but she was never interested in this house, and he never made an issue of her signing her name on any legal documents."

"So are you going to do it?"

"Well, I am flattered. And even though she's done Cordell so wrong, I don't believe I can do it. After all, even if she didn't love him as a wife, she did carry his children—so *she's* earned the right to have her name beside his, not *me.*"

"You're all right, Lena."

So comfortable Lena felt with Tobia, she was about to share more details of her love life, when unexpectedly Darlene startled them by yelling over toward the porch.

"Tobia, are you going to Mary's party?"

Tobia looked like she didn't want to answer, but after a moment, she remarked, "If I'm not too tired from all this working."

Darlene flashed her gap. "You better go have some fun and drag Reuben along. I told Edgar I have to have me some fun before these kids come back from my parents to go to school next week. I'm going." She sniggered. It was a bizarre-sounding laugh, like it came from a horse. However, Tobia didn't join in her amusement.

Instead Tobia gazed at Lena and suppressed her voice, even more than before. "That's a piece of work there."

"I know," Lena responded lowly. "But at least she spoke to you. Since the day Cordell brought me here, this lady has been so miserable. She won't even say good morning to me. And I see her speaking to all the other people on the block, all the other women, the men, the mailman, too. And when Cordell and I go out and come in she's always staring at me and rolling her eyes. Sometimes she even points, and I guess that's because I love wearing sexy clothes for myself and for Cordell. She points and snickers about me with her husband. But he's always nice. He'll just look when she points. He's always talking to me about the weather, his kids, the garden. He's such a nice man to have such a yucky wife."

Tobia stretched her eyes. "He is? Girl, we have to go in the house and talk."

"What?"

"Let's go inside, so we can get loud. Come on, let's go. Because Edgar—that Edgar over there—" She stood up and gawked at his porch. "He's nice all right, especially when it comes to coonie pie."

Lena laughed. "Tobia, I haven't heard it called that since I was a child. My great aunt used to say that."

"Well, you heard it from me today. Edgar is not just being nice to you, girl. That's one horny old dog when it comes to a pretty woman. He would screw a tree if it had nice leaves and could screw back."

All titters, Lena and Tobia went into the house. Once they were cozy with soda, salty chips, some music, shoes off, lying sloppily over the floor, the conversation resumed.

"So what's Darlene's story?" Lena asked. "Why does she roll her eyes at me so much?"

Tobia crunched a potato chip. "Jealous," came out muffled, and after a swallow, "She knows her husband. She knows how he acts around a real pretty woman. Somebody told me she used to be pretty. But you see her now, don't you?"

"She's jealous of me?" But Lena wasn't that surprised. She had seen that familiar envious glint in the eyes of pathetic, hopelessly insecure women all her life. Every so often, a member of the tiny, dinky club would always pop up.

"Jealousy can be such a sick thing," Tobia elaborated. "It settles all in your face, making you look miserable and mean and ugly. Sometimes I believe some people get so wrapped up in it, it kills them and they don't even know it. You know what I mean?"

"One hundred percent. But she's jealous because she thinks her husband has a roving eye, and she thinks I'm the type to catch a rover's attention? So she dislikes me for how I look, even though she doesn't even know me? Well, all I have to say is heaven help her."

Tobia nodded. "Exactly. And she hates you dressing all sexy, showing up your face and body. Instead of admiring you, and feeling good that a sister is looking so good, and trying to get some tips—in her sick mind she's probably mad because she could never look like that. But there's even more to it than that, girl. Any pretty woman with a nice shape Edgar sees, he walks up to her, acting all nice, but he's really on the make. He's been a real headache for Darlene. Everybody knows how he is. So watch out! And sure as hell Darlene knows he's on the make for you. That witch knows her husband. She knows what he likes."

"I take it you don't care for her?"

"I sure don't." She took a sip of soda, then set down the cup beside her leg. "There's just some people you feel a bond with; others you don't."

"Tobia, I know what you mean. I really do."

"Like you, for instance. My instincts tell me you're what you appear to be. And you have to rely on your instincts about people sometimes."

"That's precisely how I feel." Lena reached into a Bonton bag and grabbed a handful of chips. Munching them, she revealed, "I was telling Cordell that just yesterday about you." She grinned.

"But my instincts tell me that Darlene stinks. She's always talking about any woman who's prettier than her and with a nice shape, saying the woman isn't all that. That's childish mess. She's always bragging, too."

"She is?"

"Ooh, girl, what are you talking about—she can brag! She hates it when people have what she has, or more. Her husband, that Edgar, the droopy-behind fool is rich, you know? Some big-time banker. That's another thing, too: she don't want no pretty woman to come snatching her pockets. You know what I mean?"

"So she's like that, too?" Lena stood up and went to the CD player to change the disc. Relaxing back on the floor, she shook her head. "She's something."

"Oh, yeah. And more. And you know that party she was asking me about?"

"Yes, the one that one of the neighbors is giving?"

That's when Tobia suddenly looked strange. She couldn't even eat any more of her chips and soda.

"What is it? Go on, say what you were about to say."

Tobia was reluctant. Finally, she expressed, "Lena, now I talk a lot, and I might talk a little crazy, too, but I'm not the type to instigate a mess and start confusion. But I like you. Feels like I knew you a while, you know?"

"I know. The same here."

"Now if I tell you something she said, give me your word, you won't hang her by her ashy heels."

On the edge of her seat, Lena would have promised anything at that moment. "I promise. She said something about me, didn't she? About me and Cordell, right?"

"Now you won't do nothing? Right? You promised."

"I'm cool. I won't say a word."

"Okay." She paused, then, "I overheard Darlene talking with Mary, the woman having the party, in my shop, the other day. Mary saw you and Cordell and thought you were his wife. She said that she wanted to invite you to the party, but after what Darlene told her, the woman agreed that she wouldn't ask you to come. But don't even worry about it."

"I'm not. I have a wonderful, exciting life to live. One that Darlene could only dream about."

"You sure do. And the best way to get back at a jealous person is to make them more jealous of whatever it is they're jealous of. So that's *you!* She's jealous of your looks, and wait until she finds out you have an exciting singing career. Just let her eat her heart out. The best way to do that is to make yourself the best. Keep on being the best in every way. Keep being classy, and successful, and warmhearted, and beautiful as you are—that's all. And as far as your relationship with Cordell—that is yours. It's not her business. That fool has no business of her own. Why else would she be in yours? Isn't she pitiful?"

Tobia had to be the craziest but most level-headed person Lena ever came across. Lena loved talking to her and simply spending time with her. In the days that came after, if Lena wasn't rehearsing and Tobia wasn't busy at her lingerie shop, they were shopping, or attending novel readings, or listening to good music, or eating at the best restaurants. When Lena left for the meeting in New York the following week, her new love and her new friend made her feel like she had been on a faraway and unforgettable adventure. Now she had to face the music—literally. Best of all, she would be reunited with Cordell. She was afraid. She was excited. She couldn't wait.

Nine

Those eyes—slanted upward at the outer corners so uniquely—they granted her the look of a character in a dream who was too beautiful to actually be real. Above all Lena's physical features, they captivated Cordell the most. Those eyes are what lured him, beckoning his own to explore farther down and elsewhere each time he saw her, as he saw her in the conference room.

At times, he truly had to make an effort to concentrate on her interests. Face to face with Lena again, after their paradise in the Cliffs, made those memories that were always with him—that she carved into his heart and soul—come closer in his mind's panorama. He wanted to hurry up with this meeting, but at the same time, he was intent on her receiving all that she deserved.

Two hours later, they were high-stepping into Centerfields, ready to celebrate. As soon as Patty and Manuel caught sight of her, they scrambled over. Lena hugged them both and shared great news about her steadily rising career. Placing glasses of water on the table, Manuel couldn't dim his enormous grin or stop shaking his head. "Wow, Lena, you're really going to make it. I just know it. Don't forget about me when you're on top."

"She's too sweet to be that way," Cordell injected, his eyes sparkling, his lips tilted in a gentle smile.

"I could never forget someone as kindhearted as you," she told Manuel, but swiftly shifted her gaze to Cordell.

Patty carefully observed the lawyer and client exchange, while Manuel winked at Lena. "So you won't forget my free records and concert tickets. And don't forget your old friend needs a new car after you get your first mil. My car is raggedly as hell."

Everyone chuckled. "Now you're asking a lot," Lena said humorously. "But what I can commit to for now is the records and tickets and also a party."

"They're giving you a party?" Patty asked. "So quick, even before a record is out?"

"It's not her party," Cordell answered him.

"No, it's not," Lena confirmed. "But we can invite people, and I want you both to come. The label is having a party to celebrate the release of two of their other artists' albums, and during the party they're going to introduce me as a new singer signed to the label. Some of the press will be there. It's a publicity thing."

"Yes," Cordell added, "and we would be glad to have you both there."

"Sure," Manuel agreed eagerly, staring at Lena, then Cordell. A moment later, he was attending to other patrons.

Patty, on the other hand, made himself comfortable at the table. "Lena, you know I missed you. I love you, you know?"

"I missed you, too, Patty. Love you just as much."

Cordell was sipping some water. When he put down the glass, he was smiling. "Anyone would miss this beautiful lady, and love her even more."

A funny half smile creased Patty's lips. Equally as fast

as it appeared, it vanished. "So, Lena, did you get your contract and other matters squared away really good?"

"More than good. My wonderful attorney here"—she gazed fondly at Cordell—"my wonderful attorney managed to get me a very hefty advance and other great terms, too. I'll be getting together with the producers, songwriters, publicists as early as next week to get started. Plus I have a speedy release date. That's real important, I've learned through all this negotiation stuff." Her hand was stroking Cordell's. "I couldn't have received all that without this man."

"That so?" With a vague expression, Patty looked from Cordell to Lena. Abruptly he stood up. "I have to tend to things. I'll talk to you before you go."

The instant Patty left their table, Cordell and Lena began making plans. There were exhilarating plans for her career. There were also plans to be together every weekend and often as life permitted, and particularly for him to ask Hope for a divorce and start proceedings. He still hadn't done so, because she had extended her stay with her folks out West. Yet this early evening when he arrived home, he expected her to be there. Then he could ask her. Cordell had spoken to her doctors. They felt she could handle it.

So with Cordell's single status soon approaching, Lena had decided to remove her things from the hotel, go by the apartment and move her belongings in Cordell's house in the Cliffs. Residing there, Lena could be near him even when he was nowhere around. Cordell would help her move her possessions into the house. More wonderful, he would stay there with Lena until after the weekend. Since that was the case, he would notify his office that he would be working from his Jersey residence again.

They were preparing to leave when Manuel approached the table. "Patty wants to talk to you, Lena."

"Why doesn't he come right over?"

"He's in his office. He wants to talk to you there." He eyed Cordell warily. "Alone."

Cordell sipped his drink. "Go ahead, beautiful." He took another swig. "I'll try not to get too lonely."

Laughing, Lena went to a backstage office, where the stench of old cigars floated around Patty. Perched before his mirror, he appeared unlike himself.

"What's up? If it's about the party, I'll make sure you get your invite."

"It's not about the party, Lena."

"What then?"

"You. You and *him*."

"Him? You mean Cordell, my lawyer?"

"Is that all he is?"

"My manager, too. Why?"

He became silent, facing the mirror, before, "Robert's been here looking for you."

"He has?"

"So you left him, did you? Not going to marry the creep? Good for you. He was a bum. Not good enough for you. You need a hardworking man."

Lena didn't know why it still bothered her when Patty bad-mouthed Robert, but it did. Even so, her spirit was too high to be dampened. Ignoring the remarks, she asked, "He's really been in here looking for me?"

"Yes. He knows he's not allowed here after what he did that first night, but the creep burst in here anyway. I had to have him thrown out again and again. He bad-

gered Shell and Michael, too, when they came in one
night. And Manuel, he had it in for him when he didn't
know where you were."

"Oh, I'm so sorry. I have to apologize to Manuel. I
hope he didn't hurt him. He thinks Manuel is trying to
get next to me. He caught us dancing at my apartment
one day. I'll straighten him out, though. I'm getting ready
to go to my apartment to— I'll—I'll be seeing him
soon."

"Boy, does he need to be straightened out. He gets so
foulmouthed. I'd like my fist to go some rounds with his
head. Usually a big mouth like that has nothing to back
it up."

"Is that why you look so troubled?" She didn't think
it was, but she inquired anyway. *There was something
else.* "You were worried about what was happening with
me, huh—with me and Robert?"

"That's part of it," he said. "But I'm also concerned
about you, *period.*"

"Why? Everything is going great. Thanks to you."

"No, it was you, Lena. Your talent. But about that
guy—" He looked frustrated.

"What guy? Cordell. You've seen him in the club. As
I said, he's my attorney and my manager."

He scratched his bald spot. "That's all?"

Grappling with how to answer, Lena inhaled and exhaled softly. Sooner or later her friends had to be told
the truth. Most importantly, she could trust Patty. This
would go no farther than the room. Hope wouldn't learn
about it before Cordell told her. After all, this was Patty
she was talking to. The man who helped her accomplish
a heartfelt dream. He merely desired the best for her.

"Cordell is a very wonderful man."

Patty flashed that same half smile that appeared at the table. "I see. It's clear you think so."

"He's also the man I love."

That made Patty quiet and drew an odd expression across his face. "He's a lucky man."

She further explained his situation. Patty agreed to keep the secret, but when she left the room, Lena could tell he wasn't happy for her. Something dispirited reeked in the air. Perhaps he thinks I'm moving too fast with Cordell, she reasoned. Then again, a person would have to be inside each of their skins to know what they shared. The only way Lena could possibly describe it was to say she had been touched in a place in her heart and soul that she never knew existed.

Practicing how he could tell her in a way that wouldn't be devastating, Cordell froze before entering his front door. With his stomach knotting, he rehearsed telling Hope about why they needed to be divorced. What's more, he would tell her about going to the Cliffs for the rest of the week and the weekend. He wouldn't mention Lena, though, unless Hope asked if there was someone else. Even if Hope didn't love him, but just solely depended upon him, and had become accustomed to him, it could be rather unsettling to learn someone was taking her place. People became comfortable with each other. They felt a security in consistency, especially unstable people. He didn't want to hurt Hope. On the other hand, he refused to continue hurting himself. However, when Cordell stepped inside the house and saw Hope on the couch watching television, what Cordell didn't count on was seeing, feeling, and sensing it again: there was this something about her lately. It stirred within him that old, familiar, overpowering urge to smoke.

It was obvious Hope still wasn't the woman she had been. Undoubtedly her illness prevailed. Yet something about her was different. *Off.* The eyes—when she glanced at him—remained lifeless, pained, but at the same time filled with something he couldn't fully discern. Different also was the way her body moved. Gliding through the house from room to room, her motions were altered. And when Hope spoke to him, sedately, as she always did, as she did at that moment, in some way the sound was an unfamiliar voice.

"You had a nice trip?" he asked.

"It was pretty good."

"Did you get out and do anything?"

"I watched television. I didn't want to go out."

"But you have to start getting out. You have to start really living again, being a part of the world."

"Like you, Cordell? Your eyes are so alive right now. It's like you're glowing inside and it's coming right out at me. Is your work so interesting and making you feel so good that you look like that?"

There was silence.

The oppressiveness of guilt, joined with the knowledge that he had done acts so unlike himself, made Cordell hesitate in responding. He shouldn't have felt this way. After all, she didn't love him. God knows she didn't. The letter proved she never had. In spite of it, Cordell persisted in feeling the need to honor this sick woman as his wife. And with his conscious clinging to that fact, there was great awkwardness in asking the life-altering question. It required so much energy. On the other hand, with Lena absorbed within the depths of him, it was impossible for Cordell to begin backtracking now.

Love was keeping him going as fast as the words rolled out. "I have something to tell you. Hope. A great deal of thought has gone into it. It's right for us both." He paused. She was hanging on every word. "I ah . . . I'm going on a trip to the Cliffs. Soon. In a few hours. And before I left, I needed to tell you something." He took a deep breath and stared at her hard. "We should get a divorce."

"Should we?" She sounded so plain it was startling.

"Yes, we should. I know you don't love me, Hope. I read that suicide note."

"You read that note? Was it the one I wrote to Mama?"

"Yes. It killed me."

She looked down, her gaze suddenly wild and searching the floor. "Just about everything has killed me. Losing those children killed me . . . and—"

"Hope," he almost yelled, snapping her head up to him. "I want a divorce and you should want one, too. I'll provide for you very generously. I'll always show I care. I'll always respect you in every way. You already know I will. But we're not making each other happy. We both deserve more. We can end this graciously."

Cordell expected Hope to finally agree. He had explained the benefits to her. She had to see it. By no stretch of the imagination did he anticipate what he heard.

"I don't want it. And don't go on the trip."

"What? You don't want it?" Something seemed to lift him by the top of his head, carrying him aloft the earth. "Can't go?"

"No, I don't want a divorce, and I want you here with me."

Above his shock, Cordell heard a commercial. Hope turned the dial to another channel. When the theme song to her favorite show played, she peered up at him. "I've been thinking about the babies a lot lately, the hysterectomy, too. I need you with me, Cordell." She revealed this as emotionless as her demeanor. "I know you like working from home up in the Cliffs. I know that's why you're going. But I'm not ready to go up there yet, and I would like you to stay with me. So could you stay home with me instead? This afternoon, the rest of the week, and the weekend?"

Reluctantly Cordell nodded. What else could he do? Abandon her when she was obviously still ill? For all this to sink into her head was going to require more time. "Let me call the office. I had told them I would be working at home in the Cliffs. Let me tell them my plans have changed. I'll make the call in the bedroom. I don't want to interrupt you watching your program."

"Okay."

Indeed Cordell did phone the office. But not before he rang Lena's hotel room. There was no answer. She probably was getting her belongings from the apartment. He would try again.

Riding to the apartment, Lena wondered how she would behave if she saw Robert. Heaven knows she prayed he was out somewhere. Somehow she believed he would see *it* instantly when he looked at her. In the past, he teased her about having affairs. It was all merely a joke then, all the razzing about smelling another man's

cologne on her skin. Funny, she thought, how jests could
so easily become reality. Once, to Robert and herself,
the notion of her being with someone else was as ludi-
crous as money growing on trees.

Considering how Robert had treated her lately, many
women would have deemed Lena justified in loving
someone else. That being as it may, even with a magnificent man like Cordell to share her heart, it was
strange for her—so strange Lena occasionally viewed her
life as some other woman's. It was like a friend of Lena's
had lain in bed with a man who wasn't her fiancé and
let him do everything imaginable to her, and that friend
yearned for him do it to her every chance that he could.
It was like a co-worker had disclosed this to her in confidence, but the only one Lena would share the secret
with was Robert. After telling it to him, they would be
grateful this circumstance had never crept into their life,
and Lena would assure him it never would.

Except there was no friend. It was Lena's own predicament. Her own nightmare that accompanied her
around lately, always lying at the bottom of her joy no
matter what she did, or how pleasant everything was. It
was there with her now, larger than life, to unravel her
peace of mind when she confronted Robert.

As she came closer to her destination, the place where
she had made a home with a man for two years, Lena's
actions hit her hard In the heart. Physically she felt nau-
seous and achy, and by the time her hand opened the
door, guilt had her trembling. Prayers wouldn't even
make it stop. It was solely when she put forth what she
really gained did Lena recover some composure. It was
when she envisioned a life with Cordell. Despite being
conscience-stricken, there was no way to regret a mo-

ment with him. He was as much a part of her as her
own breathing.

Wandering through the house, Lena was surprised at
the neatness. By no means was Robert sloppy, but not a
perfect housekeeper, either. It was unusual not to see a
dish on the dining-room table, nor a piece of paper that
fell out of his busy pockets onto the floor. Although when
Lena entered the bedroom, she saw books scattered
across it. On closer inspection, there were test papers,
too. Robert had been teaching again.

The flushing of the commode, the fall of sink water,
and the bathroom door opening snatched Lena's attention. She sauntered into the hallway, and there was
Robert.

He wore the silliest smile on his face, and his eyes
were red and watery. Seeing him this way, instantly Lena
recalled the urgent messages he had left. "I was real
busy with the record company," she said, hoping to re-
lieve his distress. "Really, really busy. That's why you
haven't heard from me."

"That's good," he said flatly. Nevertheless he still
didn't look right to her. His voice didn't sound right. He
headed into the bedroom with Lena on his trail.

"Robert, what's wrong? Tell me."

He flopped onto the bed and pulled a hanky from his
pocket. Dabbing at his eyes, he spoke between strange
laughter. "These damn allergies are going to kill me. But
forget me, how are you?"

Hastily she sat next to him, her scrutiny and worry
obvious. It made him look everywhere to avoid her eyes.

"Robert, what's wrong? Why are you so upset?" She
grabbed the handkerchief from his hands, but it didn't
make him look at her. Nonchalantly he started picking

up some of the papers surrounding them until Lena grabbed his hands, forcing him to meet her gaze.

"What is it? What has happened while I've been gone?"

He rubbed the back of his neck, and out of nowhere a tear began to fall. "I'm losing my mind, Lena."

At the conviction in his tone, a wave of alarm blew over her. "Why do you say that?" Lena sat up straighter, her heart racing, her body braced for the worst.

"I was in the hospital."

"What happened?" Her heart was speeding. "Oh, my God, what happened? Oh, I'm so sorry I wasn't here for you. I'm sorry I didn't return your messages."

"I took some pills."

"Please don't tell me that." Lena's hand flew up and covered her mouth. "No, Lord." Water bundled in her eyes.

"But I wasn't trying to do anything to myself, though. Oh, no." He chuckled oddly. "It was a mistake. I just had this headache, and I wasn't thinking clearly. I haven't been thinking clearly lately. I go somewhere, and I don't remember traveling there. I put things in places and I forget." He sniffled, then wiped some tears. "I start to say something, and a second later I forget it. So I took the pills. Then I took some more too soon after, and I took more and more. For some reason, I wasn't aware of time. I just wasn't aware, period. But I'm okay. I'm okay now."

"Yes, you are okay." Frowning, Lena kneaded her fingers across Robert's back. "Don't ever forget that."

"Oh, Lena, I don't know what to think sometimes." He shook his head. "I don't know. I had a great-uncle who had mental problems and killed himself. He slit his wrists. Maybe it's in our genes. I sure feel like I could lose it sometimes lately. Feel like getting off this rocky road often, but I never do. It's just a stupid thought when things aren't going my way. But now with this, who knows what could happen."

Lena refused to picture that image. Closing her eyes and opening them, she knew she couldn't bear it.

"Things like this make you think about what matters," he went on. "This even made me start teaching again. I didn't have to teach. I could have just studied for the bar, but I wanted to do something significant to help get myself together. Besides that, I felt like helping somebody do something meaningful.

"Otherwise I could go mad, Lena. That's how it is when a man loves a woman so much he can't think of anything else except her. He can't live without her. And when she's gone, his life is over. He feels like he might as well die. For what else is there if the woman he loves just stops loving him? What's worse? The rest of his world, too, starts crumbling and falling down."

Because Robert's hands had gestured wildly as he uttered those last words, a textbook fell off the bed. Two test papers tumbled off, too. He didn't pick them up. Because he couldn't. His eyes were too busy burning inside Lena's. Soon nothing moved.

Ten

How it wrenched his heart postponing their plans, but Cordell explained his dilemma to Lena by phone. Fortunately for him, she was very understanding about Hope. Often she expressed her sorrow at how sick his wife was. Yet now he knew she was not only considerate of Hope but patient with her, too. Besides, she expressed that Cordell was worth waiting for forever. Thereafter other arrangements were made. Regrettably they couldn't be together until after the weekend, after his workday on Monday. For their rendezvous, they chose Centerfields. Between now and then, he wanted to hear her voice as often as possible.

All their changed plans aside, Cordell still wanted Lena in the house. "I'll send the movers to the hotel and the apartment for your things like we planned."

"I can't do it now. Not yet."

"Not yet? Not yet?" Shock registered loud in his voice. "What do you mean?"

"I'll stay at the hotel awhile."

"Why?" He could sense something amiss. "What changed? What happened when you saw Robert? Is this his doing?"

"I'm staying—I'm mo— I think Robert attempted suicide."

"He did?" With his surprise, there was a hush. "When did this happen?"

"It was happening when I ignored Robert's messages," she lamented. "He took some pills. His body is recovered, but he's not all together."

He took a deep, walloping breath. "That's rough. I'm very sorry to hear that, Lena. But It's not your fault."

"I just can't go right now with him like that, and Robert so upset."

Silence.

"Cordell?"

"Yes, I'm here. I was just letting all this sink in. I hate this happening. But I don't want to be insensitive to your feelings. You were going to marry the man. It's only natural that you feel concerned. But really, it's not your fault."

"I don't think it is."

"I *know* it isn't."

"But I think he needs me. I felt so sorry for him. I just want to do something to make this all right."

Cordell heard all the emotion in her voice and was silent once more. When he did utter something again, it came out raspy and low. "You still love me, don't you? Seeing him again didn't change that, did it?"

"No! Baby, I love you. I love you more than you'll ever know. What I felt for Robert is no longer there. It's gone. I love you. I'm *in love* with you."

Cordell took a deep breath and another deep breath. "Thank God. You had me worried there for a minute. Whooh!"

"Don't worry. Just love me back."

When the conversation ended, Lena assured him her only interest and intention with Robert was moral support because of the sad events that were happening to him. The hotel would be her residence until she relocated to the house in the Cliffs. She mentioned this to Cordell more than once.

At two in the morning, in the darkness, in the bed, in the guest room of his home, Cordell continued being immersed in the recent developments with Lena. There was no doubt she was in love with him. Everything they shared and did and felt when they were together and apart guaranteed him of this. In spite of this, though, it caused him grave discomfort to know she was so accessible to Robert. From what Cordell knew about him, he was certain Robert was going to use this predicament to his advantage. Persuading Lena to move back into the apartment was his objective. Cordell knew this like he knew there wasn't a sound in the room.

Faint moaning and movement against his back caused Cordell to sit up and brought his concerns into the bedroom with his wife. He had originally gone to bed in the guest room, but Hope had been having nightmares. He ran into the room, and there she begged him to just rest beside her. She was afraid. She was also very restless. More than once while he lay down, she had brushed against him and let out a soft sigh that sounded almost sexual. It made him wonder how he would handle it if she wanted a physical relationship after years of not having one. For an eternity, it seemed that in bed they were merely body parts sailing by one another, occasionally bumping as each traveled to their destination of a restful sleep. They were bodies accustomed to each other, comfortable being near one another, because time and their life's order demanded it so. Of course after each day, it was Cordell's tiredness that dragged his eyes shut, but it was also that serenity, which came with the sameness of each day being no different from the last.

Now abruptly change had snaked in to disrupt the tranquility and was stealing his rest. It was a metamorphosis that was bittersweet. On one hand, he was a man feeling a joy unlike any he had ever experienced. On the other, he was a man like those men he loathed. Men who were tormented, insecure, and had no idea of who they were, so they cheated on their wives, because another woman, disconnected to his problems made him shove them aside. Another woman offered something new. She extended a pleasant distraction from the realities he was too cowardly to face, battle, and conquer. And when this mistress became a nuisance, demanding a little more, some substance instead of an affair, insisting on being the next wife, he dropped her and sought a new diversion. A fresh model to assist in his escape from reality.

Except Cordell couldn't identify with them. By some standards, he had no problems. He was highly successful, enjoyed his profession, loved himself immensely, and knew completely who he was. In fact, most would have believed nothing was wrong in his world if they didn't know of the miscarriages and Hope's state. But he had learned to live with his wife's condition, just as he had accepted that his children had died. The powerlessness of the loss had gripped him so vehemently his tears refused to burst from behind his eyes anymore. They merely dwelled in that place where he stored his most critical sufferings during life. There wasn't even any time to revisit them. If he went near there, or stayed there a moment too long, he wouldn't have been any good for Hope. She had always needed him more than he needed to grieve.

She brushed against him again and turned in the opposite direction. Cordell was glad he couldn't see her somber face. Lately she was hard to look at. Each time he did, something balled in his chest, dug up through his throat, and somehow strangled his voice. Was it wrong that he asked her for a divorce when she was straight out of the mental hospital? Yes, it was true she didn't love him. Yet even with that realization, how had he summoned up the nerve to be unfaithful? Sometimes the amazement of it all made him feel like he was out of his body. It was as if he was watching this guy being with his wife, while in his head he was replaying conversations with the woman he loved, and feeling hot over and over again, reminiscing about the lovemaking with that woman. This man he watched deserved a lashing. Hope had loved as much as she was capable—as much as her difficult life had allowed her to.

Certainly he felt used and betrayed by her. She had wanted him for baby-making. But did she deserve what was happening? Getting a baby from your husband's sperm—even if that was all she wanted—wasn't an atrocity. A married couple producing a child didn't make the fool he was making of Hope. This debate was so prevalent, it made him smoke again, at least a pack a day. Smoking at the office. At home with Hope he smoked, too. Never around Lena, though. Lust and love pushed the pressure out of sight. Hence, the urge, too, disappeared.

Observing Hope's small frame rising and falling with her breathing, Cordell wondered when he could ask her again about the divorce. When would it be the right time to possibly destroy a woman who was destroyed enough? He couldn't answer. There was only the rumbling from within, facing him from the time he woke until he was deep in sleep. He could no more stop feeling Lena inside his bones, his blood, his veins, his heart, his soul, every tendril of him, than he could refuse the oxygen God bestowed on him to breathe.

Cordell eased back down under the covers, fighting the need to smoke right then. Though when he felt a piece of paper on his arm, he cut on the lamplight and pulled down the covers. He expected a bill or one of the notes he'd scribbled, which fell out of an entertainment law book he read earlier. It was neither. He peered down, and lying in the middle of the bed was a sonogram picture. It froze him. A shiver rolled across his shoulders, too.

Centerfields was lively with hordes of people and rocking music when Lena entered and spotted Cordell at a corner table. He didn't see her, so she took the opportunity to pat her hair some more and dab on a little more russet lipstick. Not so noticeably she glanced down at her pink, fitted mini, taupe pumps, and taupe bag, then gazed back up hoping she would look gorgeous to him.

When she approached the table, he stood up. His eyes told her all she desired to hear, even before he confessed it.

"You look so beautiful."

"You look succulent."

"Yummy. Go ahead and bite me then."

They sat, and the fire was there. Lena had never experienced merely a gaze making her feel naked and stroked all over as she did then. She hoped her scrutiny did the same to him.

Manuel popped up and gave her his customary peck on the cheek greeting. "Hey, lady, you come to see me again? Can't stay away from my sexy body, can you?"

"I'm obsessed. Stalking you, too."

"She sure is," Cordell joined in. "She told me about the hot and heavy affair you two have going on."

Manuel smiled but swiftly turned it off. "What are you two having?"

Cordell looked at Lena. "Lady first."

"I'll have a sparkling cider. Real, real cold, too."

"No problem. And you?" He didn't look at Cordell.

"Give me anything. I'll try anything. That's how good I feel tonight."

Manuel sped off, and Lena had spoken only three words when Cordell's beeper went off.

"Where's the phone, baby?"

She pointed to a distant hallway. "Over there. Don't make me wait now."

He brandished a big smile. "Be right back."

Lena studied him walking away. His movements were of a man who knew his importance. The air around him was his. The floor barely held the weight of his presence. Lena was proud and stimulated. Narrow, hard hips dipped flawlessly in navy pants, and a paper-white cotton shirt wrapping shoulders molded so far apart, and arms as hard as this table her elbow rested on—stirred fantasies that rivaled the unforgettableness they experienced in the Cliffs.

A hard-rocking band had Lena's attention when Cordell was out of her line of vision. It was at that moment she also noticed Patty mingling through the club. She anticipated him coming over, greeting her, and chatting like he normally did. Lena looked forward to it when she first sat at the table. She wanted to remind him again about the record company's party. From a distance, he had been watching her and Cordell. Lena waved to him, but she guessed some customer or one of his employees had dug up his bad side, because Patty didn't wave back.

The mood hadn't changed. While sitting there alone, she waved to him again. Incensed, he was leering in her direction, then turned his head away. It was funny. Almost instantly, she saw him smile at a patron.

Manuel setting the drinks on the table grabbed her attention. "The party still on?" he asked.

"Yes, and it's at the Potomac. And did I tell you it's for the release of these two other artists' albums, the girl group who did 'Keep The Love Coming' and the guy who sings 'Always In My Heart'?"

"You told me it was for some other acts, but I didn't know it was *them*. Those are two hot ones! But you're better, Lena."

She blushed. "I don't know about better, but this girl is sure grateful! I'm so excited that they're going to introduce me as a new and upcoming singer. I can't believe I'm about to record an album. What a blessing! Thank God."

"I already do. For you." He winked. "Where's he?"

She didn't like the way he pronounced *he*. "Who? Cordell?"

"Yeah."

"Why did you say it like that?" Her tone was playful.

"Just asking. He left?"

"No, he had a phone call."

Manuel folded his arms. "That's your new man?"

Lena just looked at him, her mouth propped sourly to one side.

He started sniggering. Words were breaking through. "Hey, I had to ask. You a super-fine lady. If you're free, then I'm in the running, too." He stretched out his lean arms.

Lena was so tickled by this she was turning another shade. All she could do was urge him, "Get out of here! Go on. Do your job. Get on out of here. Get!"

They both were trading looks and laughter when he faded into the crowd. Shortly after, Cordell returned looking distraught. While sitting back down, he revealed, "It was Hope. She told me she wants me to come home early tonight. Said she just wants me there."

"Just wants you there? But nothing is wrong with her?"

"No more than the usual. You know . . . the depression and all."

"To just sit, or lie down, or watch television with her again? All that time. Baby-sit her?" Lena heard the ugly way she was sounding, and wanted to calm herself, but couldn't. "But what about us? Tonight? That's all that has kept me going these last days, knowing we would be together in every way tonight."

"I know."

He reached across the table and clutched her hand. She savored the way it felt when he touched her, something this easy. Even so, she was too agonized to appreciate it the way she usually did. She was too busy wondering what would Cordell do. More than that, Lena longed for him to tell her without her having to ask. With all her effort, she prayed that answer would be the one she yearned to hear. Amid this, Lena also knew that perhaps this was a good time to share her most recent news, too. They could put everything on the table at once.

"I have to tell you something."

Cordell released her hand as an invisible flurry of tension waved over him. *No, it wasn't that.* "Did he convince you to move back into the apartment?"

With her mouth moving and no sound coming out, Lena searched his face.

"No, Lena. No!"

In desperation, she leaned toward him. "He is really bad off. And he's on the couch at night. I told him I can't sleep with him. I didn't tell him about you yet, because that would hurt him too much. But Robert knows that I don't feel any grand passion for him anymore. He doesn't try anything, either."

Cordell bit his lips and looked everywhere but at Lena. "I don't believe this. This can't be happening. I don't believe this."

"But this way I can help him." Lena leaned closer. "I can convince him to get up and go teach every day and study for his bar, and also get professional psychiatric help. And working and studying will make him stronger. It'll build up his self-esteem, and eventually I can tell him about us. I'm there just for strengthening him. He begged and begged me. He even got on his knees and cried like a baby. He said he just needed me there.

"And I know he said the pills weren't intentional, but if they weren't, taking so many was definitely caused by him having a breakdown. If I told him I was in love with another man, it would throw him over that cliff. And he's been nice to me, too. Not so dependent and demanding. Cordell? Cordell, look at me? Look at me and say something. I'm putting up with Hope. I'm putting up with her when I'm getting really tired of her!"

His eyes shot to her. The expression on his face, she had never seen it before. "I guess he's like Hope . . . somewhat at least. But it doesn't make me feel better knowing that. Somehow I think he is playing you, Lena. Playing you well."

"I know what I'm doing."

"It's only a matter of time before he's trying to ease you back in his bed!"

Lena reared back. She could feel her nostrils burning, signaling that she was about to cry. She wanted to stop the water from downpouring, but when she heard the sobs easing between her words, it was too late. "Do you really believe I could so easily sleep with him after I told you I love you? Do you think I can just go from man to man, from one bed to another? Do you really think I can sleep with a man so easily, just because I slept with you so fast? Well, I happen to believe that what we had went beyond time and sensibleness, and even most of the ugliness of this earth. But maybe I was wrong!" She lunged up from the chair and hurried to the entrance.

"I'm sorry," met her face when she was swung around. "I love you so much. I trust you. And I will handle it. I will. If that's what I have to endure to keep you in my life, I will." The promise was followed by a smothering embrace, a winding parting of lips, a lazy tasting of tongues.

From the suite's terrace, there was a view of a shipping dock. Every so often, the boisterous bantering of the men below, loading and unloading merchandise, hurled up to the third floor where dusk peeked in, casting another glow onto two stripped, quivering bodies. They were already shimmering with the oil of desire. The scent of it, too, made them hunger each other more. No pain, no tears, no worries—just souls listening to their rhythms singing a song of never enough.

Eleven

The celebrating at the Potomac was as energizing as New Year's Eve. Moving in every direction among the three landings of the dance hall were myriads of invited guests—from celebrities to those ecstatic partyers clad in their fanciest, most expensive, sexiest garb. Raging drumbeats slammed. Lights rotated from purple to red to midnight blue and lastly black. The disc jockey hyped up everyone with hip congratulations to the honorees, and when he mentioned Lena during the introduction to one of the club tunes, a thunder of applause and *Yea's* slipped through the music. Robert, who was conversing with Shell and Michael, stared over at the woman he hoped to marry and broadly smiled.

Lena tried to be modest about her happiness. What's more, it was easy not to feel it completely when she considered how things had turned out tonight. Beside her joy, there was a sadness. The kind that solely a friend can detect, even when you're in the midst of a crowd hanging on your every word, even when you're talking, smiling, laughing, and outwardly confident.

Lena had no inkling that Tobia had arrived and was observing her. From appearances, one would have assumed she flagrantly basked in the outpouring of attention, praise, and well wishes for the future. Except the one who knew better snaked from behind her and with lanky fingernails covered Lena's eyes.

"Who's this?" she asked.

A long kiss sound. Another longer kiss.

"Humph, that's no man. That's for sure. Must be a woman sucking a sour lemon or a—"

Tobia uncovered Lena's eyes and hit her on the arm. "Now you're getting crazy as me."

They both laughed, hugged, and pecked each other's cheeks. Lena reared back, inspecting Tobia's colorful African outfit and her usual plentiful, but gorgeous, display of jewelry. "That outfit is too gorgeous," she complimented her.

"Isn't it? Girl, I'm too sharp." Tobia twirled around and around, provocatively jiggling her wide hips.

"Whooh!" Lena shouted. "Please don't hurt somebody!"

"I intend to—and look at you."

Lena was wearing a black, sequined, strapless ankle-length dress with a sweetheart neckline and a thigh-high split. She started to entertain Tobia by prancing around, mocking her buddy's modeling moves. Deep down, though, her heart wasn't in it. Instead she asked, "Where's Reuben?"

"Home sleeping. I'm so mad at him. He promised to come with me. But nooooo—I'm getting ready and the fool is sleeping! Then he wakes up and tries to get ready, but he starts falling asleep again."

Lena tried to look amused. However, it wasn't working. Studying her, Tobia stated what she had been speculating.

"So Cordell stayed home because Robert insisted on coming, and he didn't want to make you uncomfortable.

And also because Ms. Wifey probably wanted him to stay with her."

Lena peered down for a moment. Staring back up at Tobia, she couldn't disguise the hurt. "Right on both accounts. Tobia, what good is a night like this, a night when I am finally recognized as being a recording artist, my lifelong dream, when I can't even share it with the one I love?"

Tobia patted her on the back. "I can feel your heavy heart, girl. But after all the stuff you told me about how you was dogged, all I can say is tell the other one. Tell him! Where is he, anyway?"

Lena pointed with her head. As if he knew the two were discussing him, Robert excused himself from Shell and Michael and walked right over.

Lena put on her most contented face. "Tobia, this is Robert. Robert, this is my best girl, Tobia."

They exchanged greetings. All were chatting and swaying to the music when Manuel danced over. He was shaking his slim hips in front of Lena. "Want to dance, good-looking?" he challenged her.

With amusement curling her lips, Lena looked him up and down. "Dance with you? Dance with you? Mister, I'll burn you up on that floor. I do cut a rug when I want to."

She glanced at Robert, who was extending Manuel his evil eye. "I'll be right back," she told him. They headed to the packed dance area.

A hit club tune was playing. They both were flaunting their style and litheness, like they did in her apartment that day. Manuel was loving this dance with Lena. His wide smile took up all of his thin face. On the negative side, however, he couldn't let the cocktail tray pass him by. With a drink eternally in his hand, he was showing Lena some new captivating steps. She was strutting some fresh steps of her own. Mindful of Manuel's every move, Robert was talking to Tobia.

Exhaustion was cramping Lena's knees by the third song. Sluggishness clutched her feet. Her forehead and armpits were drenched. The top back part of her dress felt clammy, too. She needed to go to the ladies' room and freshen up. Nevertheless, Manuel had drunk too much. That's why he pulled her arm too hard when she attempted to go.

"No, I'm tired. These dogs of mine can't go much more. One of these other girls around here will be glad to dance with you."

Discreetly she slipped her arm out of his grip, but had paced only a few steps when he clenched it again. "Please, Lena," he begged. "Baby, please—dance with me?" He did some outrageous contortions with his buttocks and hips, which made him look so ridiculous many snickered.

Lena didn't want an even bigger scene. She followed Manuel to another spot among the partyers. A breath later, he took another swig of a drink and handed the empty glass back to the waitress with the cocktail tray.

Despite his growing drunkenness, for a while they were dancing civilized. Though as the music progressed and the drinks kept flowing, it seemed to affect Manuel in ways Lena never dreamed of. He was winding his butt and hips, putting his legs and arms into it, lifting them, throwing them, getting downright sensual in his every motion, and soon after downright funky and nasty. And why did Lena ever turn her back to him while he behaved this way? The next thing she knew he was on her backside. She struggled to escape. But with the strength of a thousand men, he held her to him. *Tight.* Like he was . . . like he was . . . All who saw, their mouths flopped open. Tobia, Shell, Michael, the guests, and even Patty surfaced and gawked from the sidelines. However, Lena didn't have to tussle for freedom for long. In a blink, Robert was there. He had Manuel by the collar.

"I knew you wanted my woman!"

Manuel's eyes stretched tall as they could, making him look extremely surprised and unable to blink.

Robert swung. The fist caught Manuel's left jaw. He was stunned, and he staggered just in time for a knee kick to send him soaring to the floor. People gasped, gaped, the music stopped, and Manuel scuffled to get back up. It was a rocking, wobbling, dizzying effort. So much so that Patty and others rushed to his aid. Yet when he shooed them away, curiosity forced them to watch. Again he strove to stand and strove again. He had almost managed it, too, if he hadn't stumbled and did a full split. In shock, Lena grasped the sides of her head. Everyone else, except Robert, gawked. His eyes had narrowed to slits while many attempted to help Manuel. Nonetheless, he was stubborn and chose to sit, still not blinking, still looking so surprised.

Tobia stepped forward and squinted down at him. "What in the hell's wrong with his eyes?"

There were simpers, but Patty answered with a straight face. "They always look like that when he's drunk."

Manuel belched. "Who's dwunk?"

"You, damn it!" Robert blasted. "But still it's no excuse for what you did! The disrespect! When people are drunk, they do what they always wanted to do when they were sober, but they didn't have the nerve then!"

Lena threw her hand forward. "Stop! Somebody help the man up. Robert?"

Robert pretended he didn't hear. His heed remained on the object of his wrath. Instead, security guards surrounded and began pulling up Manuel. Once on his feet, the surprised ogle fixed on Robert. "You—you tupid fool!"

Panicking, Lena was eyeing the guards, motioning for them to drag Manuel out if they had to. However, so entertained they were by everything, they were taking their time.

"Please take him out!" she yelled.

Manuel yelled louder. "I'll go! Yeah, I go cause"—he burped—"cause I don't want to embarwiss my fwen." Then the surprise focused harsher on Robert. "But I hate you! And—and it's good for you, too!"

Robert waved him off. "Go home, stupid. You don't even know what you're talking about."

"No! No, not me," Manuel insisted. "You—you're the fool. I know a sequet that—"

"Take him, somebody!" Lena cut him off. She began pleading with one of the security guards, but Manuel was dogged.

"I know a secret that—that would make you the biggest jackass at the party. The—the biggest jackass that ever lived." Manuel peered at Robert a minute, then burst out with hysterical giggles. While he was being escorted to the exit, his hilarity reverberated throughout the club. In Lena's ears, it sounded like the wicked witch in the *Wizard of Oz.*

An announcement on stage from Shell and Michael about the celebration just getting started whipped the crowd into a festiveness and eased some attention from what had just occurred. Michael even joked about being scared of Robert. "With a fist coming at me like that, I would have looked like I just saw Casper the *unfriendly* ghost, too, and also like the tipsy gentleman did, I would have done the funky chicken and a perfect split, too."

Everyone laughed, including Robert. The music started again. The partyers headed to the dance floor.

Shaking her head, Lena strolled over to Robert. "Robert, you just could have pushed him off. He had no right to get fresh with me, but you didn't have the right to beat him up like that."

"What the hell did you expect? He was out of hand. What kind of man would I be if I let him do that to my woman, and I just stood there and did nothing?"

But I'm not your woman, echoed inside Lena's head. Yet outside she just looked at him, didn't answer, and soon a few people called her over. Edgar, Cordell's neighbor in the Cliffs, even popped up, shocking her, offering a sloppy kiss on the cheek and gushing that Reuben told him about the event. Oh, God, another problem, Lena thought—although she fastly decided she had to keep Edgar and Robert apart. She couldn't have Edgar asking something in front of Robert that would reveal the true nature of her relationship with her attorney.

Shell and Michael introduced her to a music magazine editor. There were others to meet—celebrities, bubbling regular folks, and somehow through all the mingling and business, Lena wandered into an empty arcade room. Needing just a little quiet to absorb the wonder and dramatics of the night, she closed the door, and it was then that she saw him. Perched in the corner, in front of a game that was obscured by the open door, was Patty. Odd as it appeared, he wasn't playing. He was simply standing there.

"What are you doing in here by your lonesome?" Lena asked.

"I could ask the same of you."

He didn't look at her. His gaze aimed straight ahead.

"Did I do something wrong?"

"Now what would make you think that?"

"This cold act you've been giving me lately. I don't understand. Has the world gone crazy, or is it just people I know?"

He still wasn't making eye contact. "Oh, you know a crazy one all right."

"Wasn't Manuel something?"

"The other one was a lot worse. What are you doing with him anyway? You're supposed to be so nuts over that lawyer."

She gazed down, then back up at him. "Robert took some pills. He says it wasn't suicidal, but I don't know. But he did admit to having what could be a minor breakdown, and I've been trying to help him, by sticking with him for a while and trying to convince him to get some professional help."

"Somebody ought to tell Robert what's going on so it could put him down a peg. Then you would be free of the jerk." Patty tossed his hand at her. "Fooey! Let him go crazy if he wants to. He thinks he can bully everybody! Well, he would certainly get off that high horse if he knew he wasn't the only one you're sleep—"

Suddenly there was a hush. The sole sound was Lena curving around him, so she could see directly in Patty's face.

Tensely his blue eyes locked on hers, and there what she saw, she wasn't sure of. "What exactly are you saying, Patty? Just say it straight out. You don't mince words. It's not your style."

"Come on, Lena." He drudged up a dry smile, which soon collapsed with the rigidness of his voice. "You're juggling Cordell and Robert at the same time."

There was something in his tone.

"No, I'm not. I'm just staying at my old place, and that's all. I'm Robert's companion, not lover. Don't worry. I'm a big girl and can take care of myself. This is really bothering you, isn't it?"

"Let's just say I'm interested. Maybe I will tell old high and mighty man. He needs knocking down. So what if he goes off the deep end. I'll make sure you're out of the way. He's always disturbing my place in those tirades when he can't find you, and humiliating Manuel like that. He's rotten."

In his tone, there lingered something. It cautioned Lena this wasn't at all about Robert. And her secret being dangled by someone she believed was a friend made her head throb. "You would tell Robert, even though you obviously know that he doesn't know about us? You would do that, knowing you could cause so much commotion in my life by making Robert fall apart? Just because you're mad at him? I thought you were . . . I trusted you. I had this deep intuitive feeling about you, that you were a real good man."

His face changed. He looked scared, helpless. "But I am what you thought, Lena." He clutched her by the shoulders, and the old gentleness was soaking his voice. "I am a good man. Can't you see that? I've been hoping you would see that, but all you see is *him*. And how long do you think you can keep it from that rat? It's no secret. Who do you think you're fooling! It's no secret when two people are in love! It's only a secret when one person loves someone—and that someone doesn't even know!" With that, he frowned and backed away from her. "I love you, Lena." A flash later, he dashed out the door.

Lena was flabbergasted. She had no idea. If Patty had thought of her in such a way, what else in this world appeared one way when it was another? Was this floor she stood on really a floor? Confusion circled her.

When Lena reached the first landing, Tobia took one look at her and gasped, "Girl, what happened to you?"

"I thought I knew someone." She wiped a wayward swath of hair from her eye. "I guess I didn't know him at all."

"A *he*? Did you say *he*? Don't tell me there's another one?"

Lena looked down and smiled sadly to herself. She gazed up at Tobia. "The man I used to work for, he likes me. That one—Patty."

Tobia sucked her tooth. "Is that all?"

"It's a big deal to me. I had no idea he thought of me that way."

"Girl, I wish all these men were after me. Of course, I wouldn't give in to them, but I sure would tell Reuben about it. Maybe he would get worried about somebody stealing me. Then he would stop working so much—and, Lord, that sleeping all the time. And did you check out that droopy Edgar? Nobody invited him. I'm going to get Reuben for his big mouth. He woke up long enough to tell that horny jack about this party."

The next morning Lena was awakened early by the aroma of something fried and greasy. After washing her face, showering, and throwing on a kimono, she found herself lured to the dining room. Home fries, fried chicken, and a plate of salad sat attractively on the table.

"For you, Lena," Robert announced and pulled out her chair. Along with a mile-wide grin, he wore a red and white apron.

Starving and showing her appreciation, she settled before the food. "I really thank you for this. I really do. I'm so hungry. Last night took a lot out of me." She reached for the basket of home fries and raked a huge portion onto her plate. Robert then shoved a hefty thigh next to them.

"Thanks," she said, reaching for the ketchup, then pouring tiny drops over each fry. Picking one up, she raved, "Looks good, too."

Robert untied the apron and relaxed opposite her. "I decided to give you a southern breakfast. One of the things I know you—" He halted in midsentence, seemingly amazed at her chewing and relishing the food. "Oh, the way you do that makes me think of things . . . we could . . ."

The suggestion was ignored. She simply continued nibbling the chicken and fries, all the time cooing, "Ooh, this is good." She licked her fingers constantly.

"I remember how you told me about those visits to your great-aunt down South"—he picked up a chicken leg and was biting into it as he talked—"and how she always made you fried chicken and home fries in the morning."

Lena chewed and nodded. "That's right. My sweet Tee Tee, rest her soul. You remembered that?"

"I remember a lot, Lena," he said with all the intensity that abruptly shimmered in his large, dark eyes. The look made Lena so discomfited, she looked away for refuge and luckily saw the paper nearby. A page was open, and her heart galloped at what she saw. Her mouth even dropped. For there was a picture of herself displayed right before her.

"Yes, that's you," Robert said with a chuckle. "When I saw it, I had the same reaction. That's why I laid it there. I wanted to surprise you and see your face do just what it's doing now, light up."

"Yes, that's me!" she shouted. "Me and Edgar on the celebrity page. My God, I don't believe this! I'm no celebrity."

"Who's Edgar? I saw him at the party. Is he a music exec?"

She had to think of something.

"Oh he's—he's a neighbor of Tobia's."

He nodded. "And how did you meet her? She's a trip."

"Oh . . ." She thought. "Through friends."

He nodded again. "You look great in the picture."

"Thank you." She concentrated back on the photograph, reading the details beneath it.

"So where was your lawyer and manager? When am I going to meet this guy?"

Lena stiffened. She peered over at him. "Why?" came out automatically. "I—I mean, why worry? You'll meet him soon enough. He was ah . . . he was home with his wife."

"Oh," he remarked and was swept into silence, feasting on the last drop of chicken.

Lena appeared to shift her interest back to the paper. Inwardly, though, the words blurred. She was too busy wondering what Robert would ask next. Most disturbing, how would she answer?

"But I have to say this one thing that's been on my mind," he said suddenly.

Panic abounded, but it was camouflaged as she gazed up. "What's that?"

"That fool, Manuel. There was something weird. Even though I didn't show it, it made me feel funny when he was saying that stupid stuff. What did he mean by a secret? Shell and Michael even looked at each other."

Lena shrugged her shoulders, masking the fear that was now banging inside her. "Who knows?" she answered coolly. "Manuel's crazy sometimes."

"And who cares about him?" he said tersely, but with a smile. "We have better things to talk about. Right? Your career is moving full steam ahead."

"That's right. It's really happening."

"If I didn't have class all day, and studying for the bar after, I would go with you to see you work."

His begging eyes pleaded with Lena. What they requested disheartened her: Robert was seeking an invitation to drop everything—drop his life and join her bandwagon.

"I would like you there, Robert. But maybe it's better if you get into your thing."

"Sure," he said flatly, but she could see his unhappiness with her decision. When she searched close enough, Lena could see that restlessness, too, the kind that led to the frustration that always unleashed against her.

Why couldn't he just give one dream his all, and work like hell, and pray for the best? Why was he always jumping from one thing to the next? Lena questioned all this because she had grown tired of not merely Robert's verbal abuse, but his everlasting instability. Wasn't it time for Robert to be a man, or just a person, and have a purpose, a mission, or some passion in life? What's more, as much as Lena didn't want to do it, she kept comparing his weakness and insecurity to Cordell's strength and confidence.

"Your dreams haven't changed, have they?" she asked him. "I know you're really into your teaching right now, but you still want a legal career very badly, don't you?"

"Yes," he mouthed blankly. "I'm working on it. Like I said, after teaching every day, I'm home studying for the bar."

"Good. Because when I'm not here, you'll be busy, too."

"What do you mean when you're not here?"

"I mean I'll be out a lot," she explained, thinking of her conversation on the phone with Cordell the previous night.

"You have to come home and rest sometimes."

"Of course, I do. But often I'll be so busy we might hardly ever see each other. I'll be in the studio much of the day and probably the night, too. And on many weekends, I'll be staying next—I—I mean with Tobia."

"Tobia?" His upset was apparent but controlled. "What are you going to be with her for?"

"Because I love it where she lives. There's an ocean roaring behind her house, and it provides a real calming effect on your senses. There's peace there that I need. It's the perfect atmosphere for me to get into my music and rehearse. I have to really stay focused if I'm going to do my best."

"But what about me?" Subtly his voice was rising.

"What about you?"

"I want to be with you. Don't you want to be with

me anymore? What does that look like for you to be spending your weekends with her when I'm here alone?"

"It looks like a woman trying to pursue her dreams. Robert, I need my space."

"From me? Am I that horrible?"

"No, you're not horrible. You're a sweet man when you want to be, but I can't forget when you weren't and when you're not. More importantly, I moved back in here with you only if you wouldn't put pressure on me for a real reconciliation. You said you needed me near because I could help you cope with your problems and help you feel stronger, and I would stand by you as you went through therapy, which you still didn't do yet! Robert, I can't make you a promise that I will again agree to marry you, when I know that I won't. But I do want to stand beside you for a while to help you build your life. And I want to do that by helping any way I can."

"You're going to change your mind?"

"Change my mind about what?"

"About staying until I'm together, then moving on."

"Robert, you're not really hearing what I'm saying to you."

"Yes, I am. But you're going to be too much in love with me to go. I will make that happen." Smiling, he stood up from the table and began gathering their dirty plates.

As Lena watched him placing them in the dishwasher, she inhaled deeply. *This won't work,* she thought to herself.

"So everything is going well in the studio?" Cordell asked Lena during a stroll through Central Park. It was late morning, with the humidity already smothering, but neither cared. Holding hands, they had sunshine glistening over their moistened skins. They had the wondrous sight of a toddler frolicking on the grass and bigger children playing baseball scattering about them. They had a horse and carriage showing a tourist couple a side of New York outsiders rarely see. They had the ducks from the pond they passed by. But even with all this natural splendor, they existed in a world that embodied only each other. Cordell didn't even care anymore if the wrong people saw them with each other.

"Everything is going extremely well," Lena gushed. "I love every minute of it, too. The whole process of picking the songs, trying them on my voice, working with the musicians, doing the rough cuts, then re-singing them with the full arrangement. Oh, Cordell, it's so exciting! It's like everything about this is so perfect for me. I fit right in it. For the first time in my life, I feel I'm doing what I supposed to do. It's the summer of my life, just like you said!" Lena was so spirited about this, she raised their bound hands in the air. "I feel purposeful, and I know something great is going to result from all my effort. I can feel it!" She looked up at him, dropping their locked fingers.

His gaze sparkled, matching his smile. "I love to hear you talk like this. You are so into it. And I'm going to make sure I do right by you with all aspects of the management. I only want the best for you, Lena." He squeezed her hand tighter.

"I only want the best for you. And speaking of the best . . ." She paused, taking in his sexy profile against the backdrop of trees and sky. "Well, speaking of the best, you've made this the best time in my life. I feel so happy, and it's not because of my dream coming true. Only a person can make you feel what I'm feeling. Only a person you're in love with."

No amusement on his face, Cordell ceased moving and delighted in her lovely face. No words could have made him happier than the ones spoken by her. He bent his head and watched her tremoring mouth steadily closing in on him. But just when he was about to feel paradise, a volleyball bounced from nowhere, hitting him hard on the leg.

"Sorry, mister," a puberty-aged boy giggled out, retrieving the ball, and looking back at his friends who sniggered, too. The youngsters hurried off, but in the distance Cordell could see them watching him and Lena.

Both chuckled but were also now aware of others observing them. Some young, some old, they all smiled with lips and eyes.

"Are we that interesting?" he asked.

"We must be," she said, humored by this. "Guess folks don't see lovers kissing in parks anymore."

"Yes, I guess so," Cordell said, the gaiety vanishing from his face. "There's been so many terrible things happening in the parks lately. The kids don't even have a safe place to play like we did. That's a damn shame. We have to change that."

"Now this is something," Lena said, shaking her head. "You and I feel the same way about this, too. When I was working at the insurance company, I wanted to get involved in something to help kids in my spare time. Yet every time I began to try, Robert always stopped me. He claimed it would take time from him. So I let it pass. But he's not going to stop me anymore. When my schedule slows, I'm going to get involved to help these children, even if it's only for a few hours once a week."

"I'm so glad you feel that way." He raised her hand and kissed her knuckles. "But somehow I already knew you did.

"But similar to your situation, I couldn't get involved because of my spouse. But it wasn't that Hope didn't want me to get involved in such activities. It was just that I visited her anytime I didn't use working. But one of these days . . ." He peeked over at Lena, then looked to the direction where they were headed. "One of these days when we're together, I mean really together, we'll do these things. We'll do what's always been in our hearts. Everything."

They walked on farther, passing a couple spread out on a blanket, immensely enjoying each other.

"I sure wish we had time to do that today," he said.

"Me, too. If only Robert wouldn't have taken up so much of my time this morning."

"Was he making a big deal about the picture with Edgar? Did he ask who he was?"

"He asked. I said he was a neighbor of Tobia's, and that I met her through friends. He accepted it."

Cordell nodded. "And how has he been acting?"

"He's been nice as can be."

"Has he—"

In reply to the unfinished question, Lena gazed up at him tenderly. "No, he hasn't pressured me to make love to him."

Looking ahead, Cordell sighed. "I don't know, Lena. I don't trust him. With the way he is, how could he live with such a beautiful woman and not try something?

With all his frustration, who knows what's going on his mind. Plus, he's not stable."

"Let's forget Robert for now. Just trust me and what we feel for each other."

"I do trust you. And I want you even more." Erotically he shifted his gaze over her body. "I'm glad you spent this time with me, no matter how short it is. I just had to see you. I even had my secretary reschedule my second-favorite client for later in the afternoon. You know who the first favorite is."

Her lips curled up. "You did that for me?"

"Don't you know by now that I would do anything for you?"

"Thank you."

He stopped walking, his actions causing her to do the same. Lost in her unbelievable eyes, Cordell cupped her face so softly it was if he was scared it would evaporate. Tilting her head, Lena rubbed his hand against her cheek and watched him move closer to her. She inhaled his exotic scent as he breathed, "Lena . . ."

"Yes?"

"Lena," he murmured again, letting his eyes divide between her eyes and lips, "you don't have to thank me for spending time with you. That's my pleasure."

Determined fingers crept across her cheeks and traced the outline of her lips, their movement languishing in the center. There his thumb stroked into the crease, sensuously tugging open her mouth so his tongue could thoroughly seek its prey.

Twelve

Wanting a dream, believing in a dream, visioning a dream, are simple matters. As soon as the seed of her purpose was sown, Lena fathomed this. However, the experiencing of your greatest desire is an awakening to reality; it's a discovery that a dream is not only an investment of hopes, but time, energy, and all that your will shall muster. Because of all the lengthy rehearsing sessions and the endless hours at the recording studio, Lena treasured a peaceful, precious moment of leisure on Cordell's porch. With Tobia pattering and sprawled out in a patio chair beside her, Lena luxuriated in the peculiar warmness of early November. Out on the pavement of the driveway, Cordell stirred about his car, repairing various items in the interior and exterior.

Automobile grease smeared stains on his Indian-brown complexion, bringing to mind the soiled mechanics who worked on Lena's Maxima from time to time. Searching, screwing, pushing, delving, coiling, Cordell had worked up such a sweat he had taken off his flannel shirt and had soaked the tank top that had been underneath. Tobia was chattering nonstop, but nothing was intriguing enough to budge Lena from her obsession. Regardless of what engrossing information her confidante was relating, Lena's attention remained steadfast.

"That's one good-looking man," Tobia asserted, observing a soft profile, embellished with long, dark curls. "But of course you see that. But that Robert isn't too shabby looking, either."

Twisting her mouth sourly, Lena glanced at her friend. "Please, Tobia, don't mention him." She looked back at Cordell.

"Robert's acting up again?"

"No. Actually, in many ways, he's been nice." Outstretching her arms, she leaned back in her folding chair. "He's even been understanding."

"Maybe he's strong enough for you to tell him about Cordell? And you can leave, too."

"Not yet. If I left or told him about Cordell, there's no telling what he would do. My conscience can't handle that. He still has signs like he's having a breakdown. There are these *off* things that he does. So I have to help him, so he can handle it. I'm always trying to get him to go see a psychiatrist, too. But he refuses to go, and he just keeps doing those *off* things. Robert even cries a lot. Late at night, I can hear him in the bathroom. It's so, so sad—a grown, macho man who looks so strong."

"I think he knows you're listening. Maybe he wants even more of your sympathy than he already has. By now he knows that's all that's keeping you close by. I don't trust him."

"I don't think he's faking it. He's really hurting. Nothing is going right: his relationship with me, or the teaching, or studying for the bar. I can tell he doesn't want to do either. He's still jumping around from one thing to another. No, he's not doing it yet, but he's talking about it. He'll meet a preacher, and he'll have the nerve to say he's going to do that. Or he'll hear a tape of one the songs we're recording in the studio, and he'll say he's going to study music theory and learn to play an instrument. He's so confused."

"I knew a man like that once." Tobia nodded. Her eyes trailed into the horizon. "Knew him well. He was the jack of all trades, but the master of none."

"Exactly! That's Robert. But I think he could master something if he just gave it time, and himself some discipline."

Looking dazed, Tobia started rocking. "Maybe he could do that, but this man I knew didn't." Her concentration held to that horizon. Eyes grew foggy. "He kept on turning this way and that way, and soon he didn't know which way was which. He kept comparing himself to others, too. Measuring his failures against their successes. He went from job to job. Never had money. But I told him what to do. But our preacher said it to him better. He said, 'Flowers, some may bloom in the same season, but if you really watched them, really did, they don't bloom precisely at the same time. They have to sit—sit and listen to God first. Then they'll bloom. Each after it has listened. Each in its own time and way.' "

"That's true," Lena said but was sidetracked by Cordell suddenly revving up his engine.

"The trueness of it can burn into your soul."

"But who was this person?" she asked, listening, but still concerned with Cordell. "Did he get it together after that?"

For the answer, their gazes locked. But shockingly Tobia's eyes were covered with water. "It was my brother," she mouthed flatly. "He jumped out the window. He doesn't have to worry about what he's going to do anymore."

Lena made a motion to hug her. Except Tobia stood too fast.

"I have to be getting back to the shop." Her thick fingers whisked across wet cheeks. "Those girls talk to each other too much when I'm not around and ignore my customers. So I'll see you later, girl." She stepped onto the pathway. "Dinner at my place at seven?"

"At seven we'll be there."

The back of a head swathed with short hair, and the rear of a stout physique, adorned with vibrant garb, faded into the distance, leaving Lena feeling silly. For even though she wasn't weeping visually, she was certain she was crying, too. It tugged her heart that Tobia lost someone obviously so beloved by her. Worrisome also was the question this story triggered: was what happened to Tobia's brother, Robert's future? Especially if she left him?

The ocean's roar was startling against the stillness of midnight. Clad in a pink bikini, Lena stretched flat on her back, mesmerized by the stars, the moon, and the gorgeous man at her side. Bare chested, adorning baggy swimming trunks, Cordell propped on an elbow, surveying the face and body he couldn't get enough of.

"What are you thinking?" he asked.

"About today." The sky still transfixed her.

"It was a beautiful day, wasn't it?"

"Tobia's barbecued chicken and corn fritters and okra and that peach cobbler made it even better. My God, that woman can cook!"

He lifted a brow. "But you can cook another way."

Lena curved her lips slyly. "You're fresh."

"But you like it."

Within a heartbeat, passionate lips were slow dragging over Lena's face, rousing pleasurable tingles within her satiny depths. Purring faintly, she brought her arms around his back, urging his seductiveness to pleasure her further.

Her whimpering, him moaning, their erotic writhes invited more reckless touching and all the magnificence that each knew awaited. Eagerly Lena welcomed his wealth of affection with kisses and caresses. What she didn't count on, however, was the faint brush on her arm. It was succeeded by another brush, and another, and yet another, until creeping was on her shoulder. Lena sprang up, clumsily bumping Cordell aside.

"What's wrong, baby?"

Yet she was already paralyzed by what was plodding higher on the silken flesh of her shoulder. "Get it off," she spoke lowly, gaping at a ladybug. "Get it off, baby. Please. Please. Pleassseee."

Laughing, Cordell briskly plucked the creature from her skin. Lena gawked at her arm, her shoulder, then started twitching.

Shaking his head, Cordell was uproariously amused.

"What's so funny?" She lightly punched his arm. "That sticky thing could have—could have—"

"Killed you!" His hilarity thrived. With it, he yanked her down on the sand, easily positioning her back against his chest and open legs. Getting cozier, his arms wrapped around her chest, and there invoked feather-soft kisses along the sides of her face. Such tenderness charmed him into sharing his greatest wish. "When I'm free, I'm going to marry you."

Hearing that jerked Lena's heart. She couldn't even speak, just listen on.

"And when we have our daughter, I'm going to teach her not to be afraid."

"When we have a daughter," Lena echoed. The thought made her misty.

He took a deep breath. "Sounds nice, doesn't it?"

"It sure does."

The ocean bellowed and permeated the hush that followed. Children—the image of their innocent souls made them think.

"You would make a good father," she professed. "I just know it."

"Think so?"

"Just as easy as I know my own father."

"And speaking of your father, you don't talk about him. I haven't heard anything about him since that night we went for a walk after one of your performances. I've told you everything about mine and my mother, but you hardly ever tell me anything about my future father-in-law."

"Father-in-law?" She felt warm at the possibility.

"And why wasn't he at that party? I know you said he didn't want you to give up the security of your other job for it, but by now he must know this is going to lead to something big."

"No, he doesn't know."

"He doesn't?"

"I didn't tell him about my career move. He's still traveling abroad. He sends me postcards everywhere he travels, but I can't bring myself to get in contact with him and tell him about my new life."

"Why, Lena?"

"Because—until he sees me doing something really

outstanding with it, he's going to knock it. There is no million dollar royalty check yet to show him. There is nothing yet but my great hopes. My father isn't a gambler, especially since his sister killed herself when she couldn't make it in music. That's why he can't conceive of music taking me anywhere but down. And who knows, even when I'm a success he might not be there for me. He had a vision for my life, and right now I'm not living up to his expectations. I could never contact him and tell him I quit my job to record an album. I just want to remain happy as I am at this moment. And I am happy. With you." She was adoring the sky. "You and I are what matters now. You're all I need. If my father doesn't believe in me, I know you always will."

"As sure as I live and breathe. I know you believe in me, too. You've practically put your life and future in my hands."

"They are good hands." She maneuvered her body so she could face him.

He paused, intoxicating himself, his gaze cruising slowly over every inch of her. "You know I feel like a kid lately," he whispered, "but then again I feel like a man I've never been before. A very happy one."

Sultrily Lena shifted over his muscular form. She felt his strong hands, pulling her hips tighter to him by her buttocks. Straightaway his growing arousal ignited a mountain of desire within her, making her femininity creamy and so anxious for him.

"Lena," he moaned, "you don't know how good you make me feel. And I could never describe in mere words what a precious gift you are to me, but I"—his eyes lowered to her lips—"but I can show you."

Ravenously his lips claimed hers, calling forth a rush

of ecstasy to flood his being. The explosion of his arousal hit him hard in his masculinity. It spurred movement of his limbs and fingers so beguilingly, they summoned every pleasure center connected to her heart.

Kneading her moistened hands across the muscles of his back, she was treated to the sinful lusciousness of his tongue. The erotic wandering of it between the honey walls of her mouth, combined with the earthshaking allure of his sexiness, were tormenting her with longing. Succumbing to the surge of need streaming through her, Lena pressed her body against him, and whimpered so softly, "More."

Overjoyed to grant Lena's wish, Cordell leaned back, his sight never leaving her. Spellbound by her love-drugged eyes and overall seductiveness, he let it all bewitch him before he eagerly untied her bikini top and shoved the bottom past her thighs. As her bare, voluptuous form glistened underneath the moonlight, his breath grew heavy, his eyes grew wide.

"You never stop taking my breath away," he whispered. "You're so beautiful, Lena. So unbelievably gorgeous."

"So are you," she responded, sliding closer to him, lightly clutching the elastic of his shorts and freeing his prominent treasure that she loved.

Breaths grew heavier. Every stroke was bolder. Moans of agonizing happiness escaped each time Cordell teased the tautness of her breasts with expertly loving fingers. Later he worshipped them like the most delectable fruit with his mouth.

The titillation that her roaming hands caused across his throat, shoulders, hairy chest, quivering stomach, thighs, and where she thrilled in between ignited a flame too sweltering to bear. Sensitively at first, his fingers entered and stimulated the pith of her desire. Before long he replaced them with the sweet penetration of his love. Soft, satisfied cries fluttered through the air.

With his face smothered in her breasts, then sliding to her neck and reclaiming her lips, the incredible bliss of their melting bodies spread through him like wildfire. He moaned gently at first, but then like a man about to fall from the edge of the earth.

Swept higher into their raging fire, Lena provocatively glided her hips to the rhapsody of their soaring emotions. Feeling his hands all over her, through her, and finally gripping her buttocks to thrust himself deeper in her silken treasure, she had known nothing in life more rapturous. Not even their last time was like this. She screamed her pleasure but wasn't heard. Untamed kisses suppressed the sounds.

With his head shot back, and her body throbbing, pulling him farther and farther within, welcoming him so deep, where he was bewitched by joys only dreamed of, the inconceivable bliss overcame him. It overcame her. Stroke by stroke, their nerves rumbled with pleasing, potent, crazy sensations, with them holding on and on and on to that last strain of sweetness until it couldn't be withstood anymore.

Afterward they lay naked, entwined with each other and wrapped within a huge beach towel. Moments later, they headed inside the house, holding hands, nibbling fingers, smiling and kissing. Sleep was extremely restful.

The sunshine reaching through the curtains was vivid when Lena woke during midmorning the next day. She awakened remembering that she wasn't sleeping too deeply. Earlier she had hazily heard Cordell mention he was going to the supermarket. Breakfast groceries he had to get.

She washed up and dressed in a T-shirt and jeans. When she opened the front door, air hit her that was warmer than that of the night and yesterday. "It's a strange November," she thought aloud. "But I'm not complaining."

Sitting barefoot on the porch, she decided to wait for him. Nothing was worth waiting for like one of Cordell's southern breakfasts. His fried chicken, with severely seasoned skin, was mouthwatering. Grits added another scrumptious dimension. Added to it, the sautéed tomatoes on the side spiced everything up more. No, she thought, as her throat moistened and stomach panged with hunger, she didn't mind waiting for that. Besides, looking at him across the dining room table was more appetizing than the meal. And then there were the memories of last night.

Nevertheless, among the scintillating thoughts, Lena didn't count on being abruptly distracted by Darlene sitting on her porch, too. Unlike Lena, she didn't appear to be anticipating the treats of a lover. From her expression, she was expecting to rid herself of rage. Lena didn't bother to say good morning. The greetings always went unanswered anyway. The soundlessness was interrupted, however, when Edgar came out of the house and the screen door slammed. He was smiling at Lena and Darlene was obviously bothered by his simpering, and the combination of the two opposing sentiments encouraged Lena to speak first.

"How are you doing today, Edgar?"

"Fine, and you?"

"Wonderful. Just wonderful. Very glad to be alive on such a beautiful morning." She wanted Darlene to know how happy she was.

"That's good. And how's your music coming along?"

At that, Darlene was silently snarling.

"Great," Lena responded. She loved his wife's expression. "The music is going better than expected. I'll be sure to give you a complimentary copy when the album is complete."

Darlene rolled her eyes.

"I'll be waiting. And let me know about any more parties. That one was something."

Lena crooked her mouth to one side in amusement. "Don't I know it."

"You made me a celebrity." He tittered. Darlene rolled her eyes much harder. "Everyone was coming up to me, telling me they saw it."

"It? Oh, the picture? They did?"

"Yes. I came out pretty good considering I was so tocked up."

Lena's lips broke into a full grin. Tittering some more, Edgar went back into the house, leaving his wife outside.

Lena heard another neighbor's lawn mower cutting grass. Trailing it was an ice-cream truck sailing by. There was also a resounding of an ocean tide that was so mighty it floated from the back of the house to the front yard. That's why Lena truly believed it to be another outside sound filtering her hearing, when Darlene's voice cut through, coming out low and from somewhere far.

"I saw the picture, too," she said.

Lena looked around and across at the other porch. Outrage had polished a shiny circle in the center of Darlene's

forehead. Fury had narrowed one of her eyes into resem-
bling a claw. The woman grasped her hands on her puny
hips, while a stomach had the nerve to protrude a considerable distance above them. Far worse, nostrils were
spreading and waving to Lena.

"You're talking to me?" Lena asked.

Promptly Darlene flashed her an eerie smile. "Who
else could I be talking to, neighbor? You're certainly
mighty friendly with my husband."

Lena dragged up a crooked smile, too. "Because I'm
a friendly person. I try to be everyone's friend, even
yours."

Darlene chuckled. "Well, being friendly can get your
feelings hurt sometimes, especially when you're doing it
to sell something. Sometimes people don't want to buy
what you're selling, no matter how much you wiggle it
around in front of them. Sometimes it's just too cheap
and easy."

With that, Darlene marched inside her house. When
the door slammed, a hanging plant unhooked from the
awning and the pot broke against the concrete. Lena was
so mad she wished that pot was Darlene's head.

Days later

He was in a field. The Georgia fields he loved to tram-
ple through as a child. Strangely enough, there were cotton, apples, peaches, and grapes all sprouting up from
beneath the ground. Cordell thought this was bizarre that
they would all grow like this. Inquisitiveness and taste
made him reach down to gather some. Nonetheless, when
he did, day turned to night. It was the bluest of blackness.

He was petrified—not merely of the dark or the sudden change, but of a larger than life figure. It was enormous, like a building approaching, or a giant, or a monster. He couldn't tell who or what it was, though Cordell knew he had to fight. There was something in the hand of the creature. Something huge and sharp. It pointed. He knocked at it and punched at the creature. Though the more he battled, the more awake he became. Gratefully he was no longer dreaming. Instead he was watching Hope. She had come into the guest room where he slept. In the dark she was so frightened of, she was creeping toward him.

His heart was racing. Sweat poured down his face. Blood pummeled his ears, but immediately he grasped her by the shoulders when she sat on the side of the bed.

"Are you okay, Hope? Are you all right? Why are you up now in the dark like this?"

"I was sleeping," she said. "Sleeping lightly and I heard you in here having a nightmare. So I woke up."

"I'm sorry."

"It's not your fault." She put her legs up in the bed and eased into it.

Uncomfortably Cordell slid over.

"It could happen to anybody," she went on. "You sure were upset about something. When I was a kid, I used to have dreams that made me upset when I did something wrong. My folks would tell me it was my conscience coming after me."

Cordell observed her a second before responding. "It was weird. But I want to forget it. I just want to make sure you're okay."

"I'm okay. Just tired."

She turned her back to him and soon he heard breathing. He tried to go back to sleep, but his heart was beating too fast.

Thirteen

Lena placed the headphones over her ears and went through the rituals of sound-checking with the engineers and the executive producer. It was one of her stranger moments. Somehow she felt very spiritual, almost illusory, like she was looking down upon this spectacular scene in a young woman's life, rather than standing before the microphone, being that young woman, priming herself to perform the last single on the album. If all went smoothly today, this would be the concluding recording session. It would be the closing of one extraordinary chapter and hopefully the beginning of a far more wonderful one. So for a brief moment, Lena had to wonder was this all real.

She knew the heavenly sensation had to do with the *summer of life* Cordell often spoke of. Happy as she was feeling, undeniably it had blown its breath in her life. Proof was not solely the fruition of her musical aspirations—but mostly because of the man she loved.

Thanksgiving, Christmas, and even Valentine's Day were endured without the warmth of his shoulders since his wife needed them for strength; her condition was declining; the doctors stressed that Cordell not push her with the divorce. They just had to be patient. Lena had survived the loneliness because her dream was being attained, and the man she'd always dreamed of was sharing it with her. Cordell was her inspiration when she stroked those notes so magically in the microphone each day. It was the liberation of the harvest of her love-filled spirit. It was the outpouring of passion that overflowed from herself and into him, burying itself within the depths of his soul, so that it scintillated outside of him, reflecting throughout all of him—especially his eyes when he walked in the room.

Seeing that Lena was busy, Cordell didn't nuzzle her like he was tempted to, but blew a kiss. Shortly after, he entered the engineer's booth, and from behind the glass he blew another kiss. Viewing the various faces in front of her, Lena was determined to do her best.

Forty minutes later, the recording area was more popu- lated and all were cheering. There were the musicians, the engineers, the producer, and loudest of all, Cordell. From across the room, Lena was sashaying toward him. An embrace was seconds away. It was only the unex- pected sight that emerged, which halted Lena from reach- ing her destination.

"How's my beautiful lady doing?" Robert greeted her ostentatiously. "Did you finish it up today, sweet thing? I could tell by the way you look that you did." But before she could reply, a scandalous tongue catapulted in her mouth.

"Robert, don't!" Promptly Lena pulled away. She caught Cordell from the corner of her eye. Seething, he was trying to look everywhere but in their direction.

All during the laying down of the tracks, Lena had convinced Robert to stay away. It was her space that she needed, she informed him; he had to find his own. There- fore Lena was more than startled and discomforted to

see him, particularly since Cordell and she had become
careless with their affections.

So mouths had reason to become speechless. Added
to that, the funny looks Robert received made him scan
around warily. Even so, when everyone purposefully
switched their attention elsewhere, he again focused on
Lena.

"Can we go home and do some real celebrating?" he
asked loudly enough for all to hear.

"No," Lena answered, mindful that lips were parting
all over the room.

"But I can make you very, very happy," he said ani-
matedly, almost like he had been drinking. But Lena
smelled nothing on his breath.

Stern-faced, Cordell stepped forward. "Is there a problem? Has something happened? Did someone send you
over here?"

Smirking, Robert eyed Cordell up and down. *Lena's
stomach knotted.* "No, no one sent me over here." *All of
her blood jumped up in her head.* "I'm here because of
my lady—Lena." *Her heart couldn't even beat.* "And
who are you?"

"Lena's attorney and manager, Cordell Richardson."

"Oh, yes, you do look familiar," Robert raved on,
"from the pictures in the paper and magazines with my
lady. It's about time I met you. The photos made you
look younger, though."

Lena inhaled.

"Is that right?"

"But hey, who cares about that. You're doing a good
job."

"I think so. Plus I have a great client." Consciously
Cordell didn't look at Lena.

"And that was a nice advance you pulled off for my lady, too. We've been living good off of it, too. I was even able to resign from teaching last week. I hated it, man. But I'm taking the bar soon."

Lena put her head down.

"Oh, really?" Tension lined Cordell's forehead. "The bar isn't easy."

"It will be for me. Then I'll take your job and represent my lady. Put you out of business." He snickered and nudged Cordell on the arm. "Just kidding, man."

But Cordell knew he wasn't. He looked at Robert real hard, but Robert switched his focus to Lena. "So are you going to celebrate with me?"

"Robert, I want to hang around here and do some things."

"But the album is finished."

"But the marketing isn't."

"Sure I couldn't interest you?"

She inched away to a secluded area of the studio, making him trail her. "Robert, we have an agreement," she spoke lowly. She shot him a knowing look.

"Well, I anticipated that. That's why I picked another way I could spend time with you if the first one didn't work." He looked around, then lowered his voice as he looked at her. "Well, I talked to a therapist over the phone today. Will you come with me for a consultation? Today? Right now? For the consults you can just walk in."

She didn't need to speculate. Therapy is what he needed so desperately. Once into it, he wouldn't need her as a crutch anymore. In low tones he attempted to convince her further to accompany him, while helping gather sheet music. Moments later, they were heading toward the exit corridor. Wearing an arrogant expression, Robert was gaping at all the guys, including Cordell, before boasting, "Me and my fine baby here are taking off, fellows. I'm going to try and take her out on the town tonight. We're going to do it up right in every way. I'm a lucky man, guys. A real lucky man to have this woman. Any man would want to be in my shoes. And you don't know the half of it!"

Lena was furious about what he told them but didn't want a scene. She simply headed toward the exit and before she was out of Cordell's sight, she gazed back at him. Still as death, he was watching and watching. Soon the woman he loved and her ex-lover were out of view.

"It doesn't matter if the sun isn't out," Lena told Tobia as they relaxed on a bench in Central Park. "To me, it's still a nice day to be alive." Exuberantly she threw her head back, facing the perilous clouds that hovered above, then looked back down. From her viewpoint, nothing detracted from the burgeoning beauty of spring surrounding them. "And I'm so glad you invited me to that fashion show. It was really fun."

"It was fun, wasn't it? That long drive up this morning didn't even bother me. And I knew you would love seeing all that sexy lingerie."

"Yes, I did!" Lena piped, rolling her shoulders, mocking the moves of the models that strutted on the runway. "But really, I thought that new designer's stuff was the sharpest."

"Ooh, who you telling, girl!" Tobia enthused, her hands gesturing so wildly a finger brushed her lipstick and that finger brushed her blouse's collar. Quickly wetting a tissue, she began wiping and crooning on, "The new kid on the block is sharp! He was well worth my driving to New York this morning." She rubbed harder. "Matter of fact, I'm taking a big order with him for the shop."

"Good. As soon as they arrive, I'm coming to spend some big-time money."

The stain was gone. She looked up at Lena. "Not necessary. As a matter of fact, girlfriend, I'm giving you all of the designs free. That's my present to you for completing your album."

Wide-eyed, Lena reared back. "You're kidding me?"

"Has Reuben stopped sleeping?"

Bursting into laughter, Lena leaped over and hugged her.

"Oh, thank you. Thanks so much. Cordell is going to be thanking you, too. He loves those hot nighties. Loves to take them off, and I love him to take them off."

There were sniggers, but when they separated, Tobia's eyes glittered more than her smile. "Girl, Cordell knows he has your nose holes open! You sure love that man. You're always talking about him and thinking about him. *Always!*"

"I can't help it. It's like I dreamed him and he appeared. I feel love like I never thought was possible."

"So now you have to do what's right and make everything even better."

"You're talking about telling Robert?"

"What else is wrong with your life besides him?"

She frowned. "I don't know about telling him right now, Tobia. His therapy isn't going too well. The doctor said that his head is not in a good place. Sure he can act to people and show off, but really he's so insecure and troubled."

"That's his problem."

"He's been saying lately that he feels even closer to me than before, and that if I left him, he would take his life. He says he loves me so much, he would kill himself."

"Hogwash! He should have thought of that before he was mistreating you. And talking about killing, I know what he killed! He killed your love—not you! And what's the point of him quitting that job? That doesn't make no kind of sense. What is he supposed to do with his time, watch you use yours?"

"I told him he shouldn't have quit."

"What did he say?"

"He says he needed more time to study for the bar."

Shaking her head, Tobia mashed up her lips. "You're the most patient, understanding woman I ever knew. I would have left that wandering hog on his tail a long time ago!"

"I can't kick someone when he's down. And he's been real sweet to me."

"How sweet?" Tobia raised a brow.

"Not that sweet."

"Good."

"Besides, he supported me in every way before."

"That was then, girl. Today is today! I don't care, Lena. You have to tell him. I know Cordell wants you to, too."

"I want him to tell Hope about me, but he hasn't. Her doctors keep telling him not to pressure her anymore about it. Why does he have to keep putting his life on hold because she's so fragile? Where does it end?"

"But she's really, really sick upstairs from what you told me."

"Robert is, too. Everyone can't see him like I can. He hides it, but if you knew him like I do, you'd see his fragileness."

"Whatever you say. But I wouldn't keep a wonderful man like Cordell waiting and waiting. Anything can happen, and you will wish you had never waited. Your freedom can be gone in a snap. Your mind can be gone in a snap. Even your life can be gone." Tobia stomped one foot. "You know the florist shop down the block from my lingerie shop was robbed the other day, and they shot at the owner, but missed him." She started fanning and stopped. "Girl, that was too close to home. So that there proves that at any time, anything can rob you of precious things you can't get back.

"So don't let it rob you before you've received the joy to the fullest. Tell Robert and walk off into the sunset with Cordell. Enjoy him as long as you can. He loves you. And that night when he was so proud of you, I saw it more than ever. He was just beaming that night."

"Which night? You and I have been going out a lot lately."

"You know, when your record company threw that party for you for the release of your album."

"Oh, yes."

"Girl, I looked at his face when you were giving that speech, and he was so happy and so proud. God, that man loves you."

"The feeling is so mutual."

"And I been meaning to ask you, how did you keep Robert away that night?"

"His doctor gave him some medication to relax him. It made him very drowsy."

"I see. That was some party. I danced all night."

"I was so surprised Reuben came with you. He does sleep a lot—I saw when he fell asleep while you two were slow dancing."

They both cackled.

Sobering some, Lena shook her head. "Uh-uh-uh. And Tobia, wasn't Edgar a cut-up on the dance floor? I danced with him so many times. Who told him about it, Reuben again?"

"Yes, and I wish he hadn't." Suddenly Tobia was scowling. "He should have stayed home with his wretched wife."

Lena studied her face. "Okay, let's have it. What did *she* say about me now? Cordell and I have been getting a lot of press lately, and she's no doubt been keeping tabs on us. What is it? She wants to know all of my and Cordell's secrets?"

No answer. Tobia tightened her thin lips, making them look hard as pencils.

"But we do take very professional-looking pictures," Lena explained, "simply like an attorney and client posing together. God knows, we don't want his wife finding out about us like that, through the press."

"You don't have to explain that to me," Tobia voiced defensively. "I'm your friend, remember?"

"Of course, I remember." Suddenly looking frazzled, Lena shoved an escaping curl from her eye. "I guess I'm just upset all of a sudden because I can tell by the look on your face that Darlene has said or done something horrible. So what is it? I know she knows Cordell was married to Hope. Hope was at the house before, years ago. Or does she think I'm married, too? Tobia, I can handle it."

"Okay." Tobia nodded. "Somehow she knows you were engaged to someone. That's old news. She told this old lady on the block, who told Reuben. Besides that, Edgar saw Robert's little show at that first party the company had for you. But it's not that. It's not even Darlene. It's him—Edgar. You know all those pictures he asked you to pose for with him?"

"Yes. And I did it because he's nice. Despite what you said, he's always been nice to me."

"He's nice, all right."

The tone indicated a storm coming. But from Edgar? "What did he do?"

"He's been showing those pictures around."

"So?"

"So nothing. He's been talking, too. Telling everybody he's been with you."

"Been with me?" Her heart somersaulted in her chest.

"Girl, I mean *been with you.* Like you and he are getting together. And whatever you do, don't tell Cordell when you talk to him. He'll beat all the sag off of Edgar's drooping tail. Besides, he has a surprise for you on Saturday that will make you forget all this mess. He told me all about it. You're going to love it."

Yet Lena didn't hear about surprises. She had already heard about Edgar.

Lena knocked on house number 331 like she was pounding Edgar's face. Common sense had warned her not to confront him. Nevertheless, outrage got the better of Lena, convincing her otherwise. She was fuming mad at that jowled skunk, as Tobia so adequately named him. Nothing but lies Edgar had prattled about her after she had been so kind to him.

The door cracked slightly. A voice Lena loathed was yelling back through the house. "Get back. Go somewhere and play while I answer the door." As well, when it opened fully, there was the creature she loathed to match with the voice.

The children crowding around Darlene's dress tail were forgotten. Seething, the woman's eyes shrank to slits as she glared straight ahead.

"What in the hell are you doing knocking at my front door?" She looked Lena up and down. "There is nothing in this house for you!"

"I would like to speak to your husband, please. If he's home, tell him Lena Durant would like to see him. It's important."

Darlene swung back, throwing her hands on her tiny hips. "You have a lot of damn nerve! But no way are you going to take my man without a fight."

Lena snickered. "I don't want Edgar. Please. And the reason I'm here is because he's been telling lies about me and—"

"The reason you're here is to flaunt your trashiness. You want to make me look like a damn fool! I've seen all those pictures you've taken with my Edgar at your so-called bashes. You're always inviting him to those parties. And I've heard those stupid rumors."

"They are lies your husband has been putting out. I have nothing to do with Edgar."

Darlene's lips balled in a puny circle. "They are put out by you! I see the way you look at my husband and prance around him. You're nothing but a prostitute. You're

Cordell's prostitute and trying to put my husband on your list."

"I'm not a prostitute! But you're one dumb chick if you think I'm after him." Lena reared back, looking her up and down. "Do I look desperate?"

Darlene didn't answer. Fuming, she slammed the door.

The ambience of the posh, candlelit restaurant highlighted the spell that beguiled Lena and Cordell. Everything was perfect—from the silver trays piled high with lobster, to the raspberry-scented candles invigorating their love-drugged senses, to their sizzling love talk, to the mellow jazz playing in the background. However, when suddenly the music took an unforeseen turn, Lena's surprise tilted her head. No longer was there smooth jazz floating from a compact disc, blowing softly from the overhead speakers, weaving mellifluously through varied conversations. Abruptly replacing it was an extremely loud radio. Naturally it didn't blend with the atmosphere. Hence, most were wondering what was going on. Except watching Cordell's oddly amused expression, Lena started to become suspicious.

That was right before the disc jockey announced, "And here's a new ballad called 'Irresistible.' It's from a young lady you're going to be hearing a lot from. Just listen to this unbelievable voice. Here's Lena Durant and the first release from her new album entitled, *Lena*."

The delirium of hearing herself flowing from the radio surpassed Lena's wildest fantasies. Staring at Cordell, her eyes welled up with water.

"I hope you like your surprise? I know it wasn't sup-

posed to hit the airwaves until another six weeks, but I
fought with big boys and pulled some strings."

"Oh, baby, thank you. I can't tell you what—"

A waiter with a microphone interrupted by lifting
Lena's hand. Squeezing her slippery palm, he revealed
to his patrons, "This is the young lady you're listening
to right now. That is her lovely voice. Let's all go out
and buy this one. It's a fabulous song. It will be a classic."

Applause and applause and more applause were nearly
deafening.

"You did this for me?" Lena managed above the clapping and yells. She was lost in the dark pools of ecstasy
facing her.

"I would do anything for you, Lena. If you don't believe it, just feel my heart. It never lies."

His gaze never leaving hers, Cordell brought her hand
against his heaving chest.

But many hours later, all that existed of Lena was the
fragrance of bottled blossoms emanating from Cordell's
skin, his shirt, his pants, and the suit jacket slung over
his shoulder. Outside the door of his condominium, it
continued wildly arresting his senses, inviting him to stop
so that once again he could inhale and appreciate her
sensualness. Oh, how he remembered the way it mingled
with her natural scent, sprinkling so seductively over her
neck, and behind her ears, and along the jawline of her
softly sculptured cheeks—and then there was the chasm
of her bosom.

Momentarily Cordell felt compelled to close his eyes.
Her body—he was frozen reliving their lovemaking. She
had looked so beautiful and happy tonight. The kind of
beauty and happiness a man will reminisce about when

he's old and taking out magnificent scenes of his life, which made the days worth living.

Opening his eyes, Cordell faced the grim door to reality. Confronting it, he again felt strongly what he had been feeling lately. He was living two lives. One of passion, excitement, and unconditional love. The other, the one he was about to enter, of anguish, stress, and burdens. It all made him crave a smoke.

Hope had phoned him in midmorning at the office, needing nothing more than his presence by her side later that night. Otherwise he wouldn't have left the hotel room so early, with Lena blowing him kisses, while wearing a see-through black nighty in the doorway. Nevertheless, it was more than the sweet promises of her beautiful body that linked his heart with Lena's. Much more than that—with all of his being, Cordell knew they were kindred spirits. Instinctively Lena knew him and she loved all that he was. With her, he wasn't wanted because he was successful, or because he was financially secure, or because he was a son or a brother, or because he could make babies. With her, he was loved simply because he was Cordell Richardson, and Lena thoroughly understood who that individual was. She treasured sharing everything with him. She supported his dreams, believed in them, created new ones for him. She enriched his life with every positivity that came to her. Over and over, she had expressed that he was the most important person in her life. More than that, she had showed it. In short, she valued him—valued him in ways no other woman ever had.

With images of their permanent future firmly in mind, Cordell pondered now if he would have the courage tonight—the courage to ignore what the doctors warned him against. Not only would he ask Hope for a divorce again, but he would tell her why. He would tell her there was someone else. Surely she wouldn't want to be with him if that was the case. Even though sick, Hope had pride. It would hurt, but he was hurt every day that he played along with what the doctors advised. Cordell was tired. He wanted what was making him tired to stop! After all, in his own opinion, Hope had improved considerably lately. She was more talkative and, overall, far more alive. Occasionally she cracked a joke, and several times she asked Cordell to accompany her to various places.

However, when the door opened Cordell was jolted. Assailed by the horror of the unexpected. At what he saw, his heart dared to plunge through the skin on his chest. His head pounded. Drums played in his ears. Without even being aware of it, stark shock was pulling him farther inside. More and more astonishment hailed him. His house was wrecked. A burglary?

He called for Hope. Heaven help the ones who harmed her, he thought, sweeping through the house, shouting her name and searching. No answer. No answer. Not an utterance anywhere until he reached the basement. With her hair mussed, her clothes disheveled, her eyes wide with frenzy, Hope saw Cordell and screamed. When he attempted to get near her, she screamed again and shriller.

"Get away! Get away! Get away from me! Get *awaaayy!*"

An envelope was held tight in her hands. Business-sized and lavender, it resembled the variety type purchased in specialty stationery shops. But what was most striking was what Cordell spotted when her grip loos-

ened. Writing was boldly captioned where her fingers
had covered. It read *PICTURES OF LENA AND COR-
DELL.*

Cordell reached for them and gawked in shock when
they met his hands. Someone miserable and evil had
come into play, photographing erotic shots of Lena and
himself. Sneaking around, lurking, someone had devoted
much time to this eerie project. When Cordell looked
back up at Hope, there were daggers and tears in her
eyes. Panic overtaking him, he quickly grabbed the phone
and dialed the ambulance.

Fourteen

Shuffling around the bedroom, preparing for a publicity shoot, Lena glanced at the clock repeatedly, and each time she cursed—9:35 glowed in vivid green numbers against the black backdrop. Realizing time was quickly slipping away, she put the finishing touches on the upswept style she was wearing and rushed to the closet. Why had she overslept, she asked, yanking out two outfits. Because she was dreaming of Cordell, she cheerfully answered and laid out two pantsuits on the bedspread. Either the pastel pink or the chartreuse, she was deciding, when the telephone rang.

"Lena?" the dejected voice on the other end greeted her.

"Cordell?" His tone froze her. "Cordell, what's wrong?"

"I'm at the Waybrook Mental Institute. It's Hope."

"What about her?" Unconsciously she held her breath.

"I discovered her last night having a breakdown."

"Oh, Cordell, I'm so sorry."

"So I am. For many reasons. You see, she had pictures in her hand when I found her after I came home. They caused it. Pictures of you and me."

"Of us? What . . . publicity photos from the magazines or papers?"

"No. Pictures that made her extremely upset. She's seen the press pictures. These were something else."

"What were they?"

"Someone took intimate pictures of us."

"What? How?"

"I don't know. Whoever it is, is a nut. They sent them anonymously by mail, too."

"What?" Lena was shaking. She couldn't believe this.

"They were in a fancy envelope, too. And they were labeled: 'pictures of Lena and Cordell.' "

Astonishment, bewilderment, and outrage evoked a long awkward silence from Lena. A thousand worries crammed her brain by the time she uttered, "I can't get over this. Who could be so cruel?"

"The devil could be that cruel," Cordell answered angrily.

"Oh, God, Cordell. I didn't want her to find out like this."

"I know. We both feel that way." Then Cordell became quiet. Lena could almost hear him thinking. "Could Robert have done this? Maybe he knows and is trying to get back at me."

"Impossible," Lena assured him. "If he knew, believe me, both of us would, too."

"Where is he anyway?"

"His therapist suggested he go to this facility upstate. I was with him last night and this morning, and he clearly didn't know about us."

"If you say he didn't do it, he didn't. Anyway I have to go."

She anticipated him saying when they would be together again. Lena knew it was selfish, but she wanted something to hang her hopes on after this stressful conversation was over. Cordell didn't sound like himself. It was frightening. He didn't sound affectionate or attentive at all.

"So you're going to hang up now?" she asked, hoping for some words, some affection, some feeling, some love, some reassurance that their relationship remained unchanged.

"Yes, I have to go. Goodbye."

When the phone clicked, without a parting "I'll call you later," or "I love you," or "I'll see when I can see you again," alarm swept through Lena. Was this a real goodbye? Did it take this tragedy to make Cordell see that he was making a grave mistake? Self-centered as it sounded, she needed him, too.

Lena struggled not to let insecurity overtake her. She planned to proceed with the publicity shoot but soon found herself canceling. After hearing such disheartening news, she could no more grin and pose for pictures than she could function at anything. Thoughts plundered her energy, luring her to the solace of the living room couch, where she mindlessly thumbed through magazines. Page after page after page, she didn't see any of the publications' artistry, but herself, Hope, and Cordell.

She tossed them all onto the floor. Yet as the hours increased and she gained a clearer head, there was rage brewing. Who was the perpetrator of this tragedy? That's where her energy should have been aimed. Who had done this?

Her mind rummaged through all the people who knew of her relationship with Cordell. Of them all, she could come up with only two who had threatened to tell Robert. Perhaps they had decided to tell Cordell's wife, too.

Straightaway Lena ran to the dining room and sorted

through the unopened mail. It had really stacked up. Interviews, taping videos, and photo shoots had kept her busy, while Robert had been consumed with therapy. Nothing had been opened in about three days.

She rushed through the envelopes until she found an interesting note. It was a postal note for Robert, specifically. He was instructed to pick up something.

It took her minutes to reach the post office with the note in hand. The clerk gave her a hard time at first. Solely Robert was supposed to sign for this mystery item. Nonetheless, when the woman recognized her from a music magazine photo and article, she was so smitten she bypassed the rules.

Lena didn't open the envelope until she stepped back in the apartment door. In light of Hope's reaction, she was afraid to. However, when courage did abound, Lena's mouth gaped open and hands flew to her mouth. She dropped the pictures. She picked them up and studied them again. She dropped them again. They were— They were—

They were close-up pictures of her and Cordell making love. In neither photograph could she specify where they were taken or whether at night or day. The lens had focused so close to them that their surroundings couldn't be seen, merely them, their faces and largely naked bodies.

Lena's head was swirling. The earth was moving. The air was overheated. She couldn't think straight. That's why she responded to her first suspicion. Dazedly she headed to Centerfields and confronted Patty and Manuel. Luckily the brunch pack hadn't come in yet.

After Lena spouted an earful, they both gaped like she asked them to come ride in her spaceship.

"Lena, you have to be kidding," Patty responded, his distress so obvious.

"Lena, I would never do that," Manuel added, looking like he could cry.

"But you two threatened to tell him!" Lena sniped. "The last time I saw you two at that party, where Manuel made a fool of himself, both of you threatened it in one way or the other!"

"I was drunk, Lena," Manuel defended himself. "Though I truly wanted to hurt the guy, I wouldn't have the nerve. Most importantly, I couldn't hurt you like that. I care about you, despite what you think. Why haven't you dropped by? Are you still mad at me for dancing so freaky? I'm sorry. I was terribly attracted to you, and it came out weird when I was drinking. I'm sorry. I won't bother you again."

"That goes double for me," Patty threw in. "I was just yammering the night of that party. I would never do such a thing. That sounds like a real wicked one to me, to go and take those kinds of pictures. What a spy! And those things I said to you, and that anger I had about you and Cordell, it was only because I, too, was attracted to you. I was jealous.

"I'm a man, Lena. I'm big, fat, bald, and maybe ugly, but I'm a man just the same. With feelings. Where is it a crime to fall for a beautiful, sweet, dynamic woman? I meant you no harm. I'll stay out of your life."

Both went on, attending to their duties as if Lena weren't there. Observing them, she couldn't walk away with things the way they were. These were her friends— her friends that she watched with a sadness to their gaits and motions that made her feel guilty.

"Patty?" she called. "Manuel?"

Manuel peered up first. Wearing a scowl, Patty gazed up, too. He began lighting a cigar.

"I'm sorry, guys," Lena apologized. "I'm so sorry. I'm under pressure now. I meant you no harm, either. I care about you both. Manuel, you're a flirt, but a harmless one and a sweetheart. And I love you, you know, Patty?" Lena began to say more, but as she did, sobs broke in her words. Both men approached her. Soon Lena was swallowed within their combined embrace.

"Who could have done this?" Tobia asked as she sifted through the pictures a week later.

"Cordell said the devil," Lena replied and wiggled her back in the cushions of his sofa.

She had just arrived at the house in the Cliffs, hoping Cordell would be there or at least call there. He had her beeper number, the record company knew her whereabouts at all times, and since everything had happened, he hadn't phoned Lena or returned her calls.

In the morning, Robert had set out on another trip to the health facility upstate. He would be out of town for almost two weeks. Hence, it presented no problem for Lena to unwind in the Cliffs for a while. Staying at Cordell's home made Lena feel close to him. Not only that, but every second she prayed he would come through the door or ring the phone.

Tobia put the pictures back in the envelope and laid them on the coffee table. "It's not those gossip magazines. They would just print them if they couldn't be sued. This sounds like a devil close to home to me."

"But who?" Lena leaned forward. "I can't think of who would take such time and go to such effort. The energy to contrive such evilness. It's so sick. It required research, too. Damn!"

Tobia nodded and squinted her eyes like she was recalling something. "Let me see those pictures again."

Lena handed them to her and studied her scrutinizing them. "What?"

"There." Tobia pointed to a spot on one of the extremely, extremely compromising photos. "That's it right there."

"What?" All Lena saw was Cordell's knee by her finger.

Scanning above the knee, she would have been embarrassed if she weren't so mad.

"I don't get what you're pointing at, Tobia."

"Well, I know that it's very close up, so close you can't see the background, or time of day, but detective that I am, I see a speck of sand by Cordell's knee."

"Sand?" Lena gasped and took another look. On closer inspection, it was a speckle of sand.

"Were you two together by an ocean or beach?"

"Only here in the Cliffs. Several times, but late at night. We wouldn't flaunt what we were doing."

"Well, you had an audience." She tossed the pictures on the table again. "An audience of one frustrated busy devil. Someone who had the time to do it."

"And the money to purchase expensive equipment that could shoot long range and in the dark."

"And someone who also had knowledge of how to find out where someone lived. And you know, come to think of it, last week these two women—friends of Darlene's—came into my shop. They were just talking—didn't know that I knew the woman they were talking about."

"They were talking about Darlene? You didn't tell me this."

"Girl, I've been so busy I forgot. Anyway, they were gabbing about how Darlene tracked down some woman Edgar was cheating with last year. They said she went to the library and got all kinds of computerized records and telephone books and such to find out all kinds of information about this chick. So there." Tobia gave Lena a knowing look.

Lena gritted her teeth. "I could break her goddamn neck!"

Tobia stretched her eyes. "Damn, I didn't know you could cuss."

"I can kill, too! Right now!" Lena hopped up and began pacing.

"Calm down, girl."

"No! Why should I?" She began stepping harder, faster. "Because of her, Cordell's wife is in the hospital. And I know it sounds cold, but he's by her side, instead of by mine. And not only that, I might have lost him."

"Don't think that way, girl."

"It's true, Tobia. Why doesn't he call? He could just let me know if he's alive or still thinking of me or something. Do I still matter to him?" She wanted to cry, but she shook her head to halt it. "Oh, God—if he doesn't love me anymore, I'll go crazy, too."

"I don't know why he doesn't call. But I know love like his for you can't just vanish into thin air. He loves you, Lena. Maybe he had to learn how to deal with what's happened—quietly."

"I don't know, Tobia. I just don't know anything anymore."

"Yes, you do. You know who did this to you two."

"That I do."

"So what are you going to do?"

"I can't stoop to their level. All I want is Cordell."

"Well, I can stoop," Tobia said and hurled herself to her feet.

As she straightened her clothes, Lena asked, "Where are you going?"

"Next door," she answered, strutting to the front door with Lena trailing behind. "I saw them sleeping on the porch when I came over here. Maybe they still are."

"Tobia, what are you up to?" Lena said frowning as they stepped outside and saw Darlene and Edgar snoozing on the porch. Sprawled out in her folding chair, Darlene's head was laid back. Her mouth was wide open. Across from her, Edgar was sleep with his paper on his lap. He looked so innocent in a tiny hat, legs crossed in khakis, and wearing a short-sleeve plaid shirt.

Lena marched behind Tobia as she quietly came upon their step, up to the porch, took off her shoe and hit both of them on the head with it. *Whack! Whack!* Instantly they awakened, their eyes swirling, rubbing their heads and gaping at Tobia.

"Bees were on both your heads," she lied to the bewildered waking faces.

"They were?" Darlene asked and straightened her wandering sight on Lena's leer.

Rage was breathing at her and Edgar. "Edgar, you're a lying scum, telling people we have a thing going on. Please! It will only happen in your dreams."

"You have the nerve!" Darlene defended Edgar. Scowling, he was quiet, watching and massaging the lump growing on his head.

"Shut up!" Lena demanded. "I know what you did. I

can even prove it," she lied. "And I could get you into some serious legal trouble for doing it." She didn't know if this was true, but the least she could do was scare her. "You took photos of us without our permission, and you can be prosecuted. Cordell is a lawyer, remember?"

Darlene looked worried. She swallowed.

"That's right," Lena went on. "But that's not even what matters to me really. The point is you hurt me, and I never did anything to you but tried to be friendly. You hurt Cordell, his wife, and tried to hurt someone in my life, when you should have been just getting rid of a man who's no damn good!"

Unable to withstand any more torture, Darlene covered her ears and dashed into the house. Seeing her enemy so defeated, Lena should have felt triumphant. Instead, for some reason, she felt like running somewhere, too. Satisfying as telling off Darlene was, it didn't erase one most horrifying fact: she hadn't seen Cordell and he hadn't called in a week.

Fifteen

As Cordell approached Hope's hospital room, he could think only of Lena. He hadn't called her since he informed her what happened to Hope. It wasn't because his feelings had changed, either. Quite the contrary, they were more intense. She had been too patient with his situation with Hope. The next time he spoke to her, Cordell wanted to tell her that his wife and he were divorcing. But first he had to let Hope know this. The doctors claimed she wasn't ready the days before. Now they said she was. Cordell didn't feel he could utter a word to Lena until he straightened out this part of his life. She deserved that courtesy.

"You look terrific," Hope gushed, overjoyed to see her husband entering the muted yellow room, embellished with many comforts of home.

Shocked by her expression, but more so her cordialness, Cordell sat slowly in a chair beside the bed. "You look great, too."

"I'm so sorry, Cordell. So sorry I couldn't handle it."

"You don't have to be sorry. You don't have to apologize, Hope. You shouldn't have been subjected to those pictures."

At once, she looked away, seemingly focusing on a lone portrait of three bears hanging on the wall.

"Hope?"

Upright and sideways her heed remained.

"Hope?"

Nervously she brought her interest back to him. "I guess I have to talk about it now. Well, at least I thought I was ready to. But now that you're here—"

"What?"

"I don't know where to start, Cordell."

"You don't have to start anywhere."

"Yes, I do. You see, I don't care about you and that singer."

His mouth gaped. His chest raised. "You don't?"

Closing her eyes and opening them, she shook her head. "I wasn't a wife to you, and that's why she took my place."

"Hope, let's not lay blame. Let's just rectify this situation so that we can make it best for both of us."

"That's what I'm doing. I'm trying to tell you what I want, what I need. I need you, Cordell."

Not believing what he was hearing, he stood and obliviously faced out the window. "You want to stay with me?"

"Yes. I reacted so strongly to those pictures because you mean everything to me. Why else do you think I wanted you near me so much? Why do you think those pictures hurt me so bad? Only love can cause such a reaction, Cordell. I didn't go ballistic because I was accustomed to having you around or because I was used to you taking care of me. And if it was just a matter of you disrespecting me, I could have even handled that very easily. But it wasn't those things. *It was you giving my love to someone else that hurt.* I love you. I love you so much."

"How can you say that?" Frowning with amazement, he spun around. "What about that letter you wrote when you attempted suicide?"

"Things change." Desperation glazed her eyes. "And you must feel something, too. You never deserted me."

Shaking his head, he turned back to the window, seeing nothing, but hearing everything.

"And you never . . . you never treated me like you knew. You never did anything until . . ." She looked off, then quickly found her way back to him. "Cordell, I'm sorry. I really am. And it pains me to say that I felt that way once. But believe me, things have changed. After the babies died and I couldn't have any more, I thought there was nothing to live for. But you stuck with me. You made me see that there was a reason to live. You cared about me so much. You loved me so unconditionally no matter what I did. And lately it really began to hit me."

"What hit you?"

"*You!* How wonderful you are. Like never before, I started to really see you and what I saw I loved. Couldn't you tell? Haven't you noticed things about me lately? I tried to make myself look more attractive for you. And didn't you notice how I wanted to do things with you? Things that I never wanted to do before. And I even tried to get you in bed at night. I tried so many times to seduce you by going into the guest room, brushing up against your body, hoping you would grab me and make passionate love to me like you used to. But this time, I would love you just as passionately back. This time, I wouldn't be with you just to make a baby. This time it would be because I loved you more than anything in the world."

Overburdened by this news, he took a breath. "This

is . . . I . . ." He rubbed his forehead. "I wasn't expecting this, Hope. I thought you wouldn't want to be with
me after this."

"You thought wrong."

She stood from the bed and came behind him. Burying
her breasts into his back, she nestled the side of her narrow face underneath his shoulders, and her arms slid
around his waist, resting together on his flattened stomach.

"Cordell, don't leave me now. I'm being released today, too, and I want to go home with you, as man and
wife. Don't give up on us. Let her go, and let us live.
You love me still. I know it. She just satisfied your needs.
We have real love. We've been through so much, and
we're still together. Don't kill me by rejecting me. I
wouldn't want to live. Now that I've found life, don't
take it back from me. You're my world now. Don't take
it from me. If you did, I would surely die. I wouldn't
botch it up next time. One way or the other, I would be
gone from this world."

Lena was counting days. To fill them, she did anything. Several times she considered cutting her hair. She
pinned it up to envision how striking it might look, then
let it tumble to her shoulders when she recalled how
much Cordell loved lacing his large fingers in the long,
satiny ringlets. Her nails and toenails, too, needed attending. She painted on Rub Kisses one day, Magnolia Petals
the other, and lastly she cleaned off the peeling leftover
polish of Mad Magenta. After all, who was she trying
to look good for?

Lena cleaned, too. Not that Cordell's home was dirty.

On the contrary, it was spotless. However, her mind was busy with unpleasant things, so Lena had to indulge in something to grant some equilibrium. She dusted in the attic repeatedly, scrubbed the kitchen, washed sheets in the linen closet that were absolutely immaculate already. She even rearranged the living room furniture each day, until once while she was doing it the telephone rang. It was the wrong number. She exploded into tears.

Cordell's lack of contact stressed her so. Endless times she picked up the receiver with his office and beeper number on the tip of her fingers. However, a nagging deterrent always halted her: if Cordell longed to hear her voice, he would have contacted her. A person could reach another person if they *really* wanted to. It was that simple.

A thousand days and nights had seemed to pass within merely eight. Lena was so tired of the waiting, the not knowing, she was constantly meditating, praying, but equally slumbering, dreaming, drifting off anywhere, everywhere, especially in the living room where memories of lovemaking haunted her most. But the reality of his absence dawning on her more and more, she faced what had to be done.

It was time to return to the city and handle the numerous affairs of her life. Plenty of promotional work had been scheduled when she last saw Cordell. Most importantly, there was a black-tie awards banquet and party tomorrow evening, given by the record company. Via fax, Shell had sent an invitation, stressing her attendance at the ceremony and a memo stating to prepare a succinct speech for the acceptance of an award. Additionally, he forwarded clippings of her outstanding reviews in various papers.

Of all the label's new artists to be honored, Lena was

supposedly the most successful thus far. Since its brief release, "Irresistible" had shot to the number-three spot on the R&B charts and number two on *Billboard's* Pop 100.

Such spectacular news should have elated Lena. If only she could have shared her victory with the one she loved, it would have meant everything. Yet such splendor wasn't to be. Sadly Lena smiled, coming to terms with the truth.

Standing, tidying her clothes, she prepared to abandon this fantasy world she had lived in. Seconds passing, she headed up the stairs to pack. Yes, it was time—time to return to reality, but mostly time to accept a heartbreaking fact: it was over; it was over; it was over. Cordell didn't love her anymore. Perhaps he never had.

Sixteen

"Why won't you ever touch me?"

Glistening, Hope's naked form heaved with frustration, her knees digging into the mattress, her voice impassioned as her body's heat. Rejection thrust her leer at Cordell's back. Clad in blue silk pajamas, he was sitting on the side of the bed, his face buried in his hands. No longer able to endure this emotional blackmail Hope was plaguing him with, he finally curved his head around to look at her. Truth blazed in his eyes, and she despised it.

"You're still thinking about her, aren't you?"

Racking his brain for the least harmful words to convey his thoughts, Cordell turned back the other way. "Hope, I really hate hurting you."

"But you do still want her, don't you?"

She maneuvered around the bed to better view his face. Avoiding her, his posture permitted beholding solely his gorgeous profile: an oval, unobtrusive forehead, the mildly sloped nose, the mouth just full enough to look luscious, and a calmly masculine chin. It was all wrapped in the smoothest, sexiest brown skin. God knows she hungered to kiss it and him, everywhere. Yet to her disheartenment, his interest aimed straight ahead.

"Why can't you make love to me?" she persisted, praying he would merely glance at her. "Aren't I beautiful anymore?"

Lips parted, but they were wordless. Aggravated, Hope could only let her slender hands gingerly hold his cheekbones, steering his concentration to her.

His brows netting together, Cordell nodded. "Yes, Hope. You are still beautiful."

"Then why?"

He looked off, frowning and harshly rubbing his face. Studying him, she lifted his hand and kissed It. "Well, I guess it's going to take time to get her out of your system. We've been home only a few days. After all, she was satisfying your needs after they were unfulfilled for years."

A glower met her pleading eyes. "Don't talk about Lena like that. Don't cheapen her."

"Why?" Subtly and provocatively she shifted her thigh against his. "Because she's so priceless between the sheets?"

"That's low," he said, feeling pity where long ago desire would have been. "Before, you would never have talked like that about someone."

"Because I was always a little, weak fool."

"You're not a fool. You're a very classy lady."

"Is that why you won't touch me? I'm not some little, pathetic, fragile creature who can't be tampered with or she might break. I need some love, Cordell. I can give love, too. Just give me a chance."

Determined to possess what she fervently desired, Hope brought her quivering lips against his temple. Instantly he stiffened. Taut breasts flattened into his rib cage, inflaming more and more of Cordell's flourishing sorrow for her. It all inspired him to stop avoiding the inevitable and spring to his feet. The charade was over.

"I'm sorry, Hope. I really am. But just because I'm here with you right now, it doesn't mean that I have intentions of making this marriage work. I don't. It's over."

She was shaking her head. "No. No." Suddenly looking embarrassed, she snatched up a housecoat that was rumpled amid the covers. Wrapping it tightly around herself, she was adamant. "No! No! Don't say this! You don't mean it!"

"I can't keep you alive," he explained softly, earnestly. "You say that I'm your world, but I can't be. You say that you would take your life if I wasn't in it, but by saying that, what are you saying about yourself? You are a very special human being without me or anyone else. But you have to find something within yourself to keep you alive. Even if I did love—even if things were different, you would need more than me to keep you alive."

"You don't mean what you're saying."

"I do. Please don't make this harder than it already is. But every person needs a purpose, something that makes them feel fulfilled, and it's not another person, not a lover or a baby. It's just something that helps him love himself, something he can contribute to this world in his own special way. It's part of many other things that helps us build self-esteem. Self-esteem makes us cherish ourselves. It makes us love ourselves. Without that kind of love, without self-love, it's hard to love someone else fully or healthily.

"When someone comes into your life, they are a gift from God, the greatest blessing there is. They are blessed in our lives to enhance it and offer their love. And I . . ." His eyes trailed into the horizon. He hated hurting her.

This was the woman he vowed before God to honor and love. This was the woman he shared so many years of his precious life with. This was the woman he believed he would share forever with. Most remarkable, she had carried his children. This was the woman—

"And you can't give me your love anymore, right?"

He stared at marbles of water crowding her eyes. "No, I can't."

"Was that so hard to say?" Making the belt of the housecoat tighter, she wandered aimlessly around the room. "So when did you stop?" She gave no visual contact, just roaming and finger-grazing chairs, walls, dressers, and such. "When did your feeling for me go? The first time you went to bed with her?"

Anger was stealing into her voice. Cordell yearned to assuage it, but he had to be honest if this torment was to be finally finished. "It had nothing to do with Lena and I making love." At that, she slapped against her stomach and a sickened expression distorted her features. "It had everything to do with how you treated me and mostly that letter."

"You shouldn't have read that damn letter!" She slammed her fist on the chest. "It wasn't for you anyway! Can't you forget it? I told you I don't feel that way anymore. I love you."

"I know you do."

Desperately her eyes lunged at him. "Then why can't you forgive me? Why can't we go on and not look back?"

"Because I can't, Hope. I just can't." He paused, looking into a place it seemed only he could see. It was that place of darkness, of anguish that was engraved within him when discovering he wasn't loved. So many years it had lain in his soul, clenching its thorns of loneliness, always snaking out from the corners of any happiness, reminding him he wasn't connected with any other creature on this earth in spite of him giving all that he had, and all that was within his power.

So now he stared at the one who didn't love him and stared at her until he heard himself whisper, "I've learned that when you break someone's heart as tremendously as you did mine, no matter how much the person tries to make up for it, the damage is done . . . and mysteriously all you felt for them changes. I don't know why, but it just does. It just does."

Silence held her a moment, her tearful glare darting around the room before it found him again. "It's so funny—after being given away at birth, and losing all those children, and my womb, I should have known the next thing to lose was my won't-do-nothing-wrong-to-me husband." She chuckled dryly.

"God, Cordell, if there was anything that was dependable in this world, that was solid and unchanging, I thought it was you. You!" She lowered her head, mindlessly peering down. "I loved you the best way I could. As much as I could. You know that."

"I know, Hope. I understand. I really do. You wanted children. You wanted that kind of love because you wanted to give them what your natural parents didn't give you. Your doctor told me that years ago, but I figured it out, too."

"You know, I never could figure out why my birth parents didn't want me." A hoarseness was coating her words. "Why they didn't look for me to learn about who I was. How could you leave a piece of yourself out in this crazy world helpless?"

"I don't know. But I'm very sorry you suffered because of it."

"I always said if I had children, I would give them so much love they would burst from it."

"I know you would have."

"But we both know that's impossible, right?" Then her eyes looked stern in his. "She can have children, can't she?"

After a moment of reluctance, "I believe so."

"Beautiful. Just beautiful. And you love her, don't you? I mean love her the way you used to love me?"

"I don't think you can love two people the same way."

"I think you're right. Because I see something in your eyes right now. You're thinking of her. You love her so passionately you can't even breathe without thinking of her. I see it. I saw it before, too. You love her more than you did me, don't you?"

"Hope, don't do this."

"Don't you! Answer me, damn it!"

"I didn't want this to happen like this."

She threw her hands up in the air. "I don't want to hear it. I don't even want to think about you and her anymore. Because before those pictures came, I already knew. You think I didn't know why you wanted a divorce so suddenly? I'm not stupid. The signs were there. The late nights. The trips. The perfume on your clothes. And that look in your eyes. You were always somewhere else."

The ballroom of the President Chateau breathed excitement, enlivened by a fabulous band performing instrumental versions of unforgettable R&B classics, along with hundreds of debonair gentlemen in tuxedos and ladies with chic coiffed hair, who were adorned by elegant evening gowns. With Shell and Michael constantly at her side, shuffling about, introducing her to myriads of executives, celebrities, industry personnel, and other attendees, Lena appeared to be the happiest belle at the ball.

Dressed in a black velvet, off-the-shoulder gown trimmed with white satin, she was a stunner. Lush, caramel-hued skin dazzled within the lambent glow of the room, accentuating mink-brown eyes and alluring, red-glossed lips. Such attractiveness framed what appeared like millions of silken, dangling curls. It all drew admiration to her face and body again and again and again. Most appealing, her smile, wit, and interesting conversation struck a high chord with everyone. To all meeting her, Lena was down to earth and a pleasure to be around.

Shell was navigating through the traffic to get some cocktails when Lena found herself alone with Michael. He was peering down at his watch, and Lena was feeling the overwhelming need to get away. All this pretense of being happy was wearing thin.

"I think I'll take a powder in the ladies' room."

Michael tugged up his glasses by the middle. "Do you really have to go now? We don't have long before they start giving out the awards."

"I'll just be a few minutes."

"All right. But hurry back. And I hope you have that little speech ready?"

"I do. And I'm going to thank all the wonderful people who helped me so much, including you and Shell."

He smiled bashfully. "And what about Cordell?"

"Him—him, too," she stuttered.

"Where is that guy anyway? I thought he would be here."

Lena maintained her composure despite her sinking heart.

"I don't know. I guess he had business with his firm."

"Probably so. Shell and I haven't seen him lately, and we have a lot to discuss about your career. Besides that, I was just wondering where our buddy is. Cordell is cool people."

"Yes . . . he's . . . cool."

"The last time I saw him, me, him, and Shell were talking about taking a little trip and going fishing. We're all country boys, you know. Just lost the accents though." He was tickled.

Lena feigned a grin.

"Well, I'll be by the bar with Shell. Don't be too long now."

"I won't."

Bypassing the ladies' room, Lena headed straight up the stairs to the terrace. Once reaching its towering landing, she scoured it quickly, then exhaled with relief. The terrace was exactly how she hoped it would be—completely empty. Finally she was free to look as miserable as she felt.

Overlooking the picturesque skyline, Lena clamped her hands around her forearms and strove to adore the view. New York was startlingly beautiful from this elevated landscape. Office building windows were illuminated like decorative torches against the obsidian sky. As well bridges were radiant, their lights arranged along the cables, forming intricate, captivating designs, which all bounced onto the water, making it shimmer and appear entangled with a billion tiny moons.

So lovely, Lena thought, but it was observed for only a second. For the more she tried to appreciate the scenery, the more she couldn't see it. Fading it into the background, and even robbing her joy from tonight's honor, was Lena's sustaining heartache: Cordell hadn't called her, hadn't seen her, had forgotten her so easily, and therefore didn't love her anymore. Or had he ever?

That burning in her nostrils, that warning signal that cries were imminent, had just begun creeping—creeping so steadily it was only the presence felt behind that stopped them and startled Lena into whirling around. Then there, with a sexuality emitting from him that ignited her own, was a sight of sights—the one who affected her like no other—and the love of her life—who she was now so unsure of.

Repressing the sobs that would vent her pain, Lena looked astonished to see Cordell standing there. Fiercely her heart pounded at his nearness. Swiftly her blood warmed.

A black tuxedo molded breathtakingly to the broadest shoulders and mountain-thick arms. Daring further, her quest roved up to penetrating, shimmering eyes. Beaming from them, Lena believed she saw all the desire, passion and love that once embraced her heart. Except surely that couldn't be. His actions had indicated otherwise.

"How are you, beautiful?" he voiced serenely, attempting to allay the sea of ecstasy he felt mounting within him. "I missed you so much. But I was determined not to miss this night. Though I've been away from you, I've been keeping track of everything." He lowered his head, his stare burning in hers, then seeking her lips. However, as he was about to taste what he hungered for, for so long, Lena backed away. In a flash, she faced the skyline.

Undaunted, he came behind her. "Baby, if this is about my not calling, I can explain."

"Can you?" She didn't look at him. "It's not necessary."

"But it is." Gently, he clutched her arms and curved her around to meet his gaze. He could hardly think, could barely talk for looking at her. His body screamed to kiss her. He ached to love her so erotically. God knows he had missed her so.

"Lena, I know I haven't spoken to you in a while. But I've had good reason. I wanted to end my relationship with Hope before speaking to you. After what happened, I didn't want to come to you again with nothing that was certain. I had given you too much of that already. I wanted to hand you something real. I vowed to myself that I wouldn't waste your time until I could do that. Now I can. I am free. And I want to be with you . . . forever. I want you to be my wife. Lena, I love you so much."

"You sure have a funny way of showing it. Cordell, I was at your house waiting for you. And then when I didn't see you, I at least expected a call. There is such a thing as a phone. Remember that invention! Now why did it take nine days for me to finally see you? Were you with Hope? Holding her and rocking her fragile mind together and then maybe saying 'maybe I can rock something else back together, too.' "

"Lena, you know better than that."

"I know she's home. I called Waybrook. They could give me that information, if nothing else."

"Baby, I was trying to get things right. I've done so much wrong with you. All this sneaking and hiding to try and spare Hope's feelings. You're too beautiful and precious for that, Lena. You didn't deserve that. I should have done the right thing from the beginning and told

Hope about you, but I didn't. That was so wrong to you. Lena, I wanted to give you something solid. But I thought you were so secure with us. I had no idea my not calling had turned you into a wreck."

"Well, it did! By the way, Darlene was our culprit."

He frowned. "Darlene? Why?"

"Because she's a big dummy, that's why. Anyway I don't care about her. And I don't care about you, either. So go."

Brusquely she swung around again. Fury was choking her, but at the same time Lena was waging war with irrepressible desire. Why was she feeling so much when he had done so wrong? Or was it only wrong in her mind because she had been afraid? Afraid deep down where there burned memories of Robert? Did she think Cordell had suddenly turned on her, too?

"Lena, I know you don't want me to go. I saw it in your eyes. You want to believe me." He eased closer. "You want to show me how much you love me." Subtly his head arched above her shoulder. Hot, pleasing breath tingled against her neck. "I know you do."

Slowly Cordell began grazing the sides of her arms, the sweetness of his fingertips invoking her to momentarily close her eyes. Oh, God, how Lena wanted him but didn't want to be a fool. She had been Robert's fool too long.

"I thought—"

"What?"

"I thought—"

He swerved her back around. "You thought I didn't love you anymore?"

"What was I supposed to think? And I still might be thinking it?"

At heart, though, she was sensing his sincerity. It weakened Lena, surrendering her to the eagerness sweeping her in his arms. Her body was succumbing, but her mind was trying to fight it. "So you were with Hope every second of the day?"

"Not every second. And always wherever I was, my mind was always with you. Surprisingly she told me that lately . . . lately she had fallen in love with me."

"In love with you?" She blinked.

"It blew me away, too. Then she implied that she would kill herself if I left her. So I went home with her. I wanted to break it to her gently about how I felt for you, so we could finally get everything out in the open and I could come back to you and tell you that I was free."

"How did she eventually take everything?"

"Not well. She was furious because I would never touch her and because it was clear I didn't love her anymore. So the divorce is in the works."

This was all too shocking, Lena thought. "Is she going to be all right? What if she—"

"She'll be all right. She's different now. She has it much more together in spite of what happened. We talked. Actually she's very talkative. But forget all that. I'd rather hear something from you." He paused, softly tracing her entrancing eyes. "Tell me you still love me. Just tell me that. I had no idea what my not calling was doing to you. I thought you knew my love for you would never change."

Lena searched her favorite sunset, wondering how she survived those days without it. "I guess I was subconsciously comparing you with Robert. I was caught up with worry over what happened, and then you didn't call.

I thought if he had changed on me, you would, too. I was really upset and wasn't thinking clearly. I'm sorry." She hesitated, taking her pursuit to his lips. Want moved her closer. "I do still love you."

Three hours later, a limousine glided along Fifth Avenue en route to the Hyatt Hotel. Laughing, talking, and sipping champagne within its plush comfort, Lena and Cordell thoroughly enjoyed the travel accommodations to their luxury suite.

"Did you tell Tobia about it?" Lena asked, her appreciation of him sliding sinfully over his body.

"I wanted everyone to be there who you loved and who loved you." Studying her every move, he took a swig of his drink.

"You're so good to me, Cordell Richardson." A kiss blew at him. "And you invited Patty and Manuel to come, too? I was surprised to see them there."

"All for you, pretty lady."

"I'm very grateful." Eyes still devouring him, her finger torpidly circled the rim of her glass. "I wish I had a chance to talk to them, instead of just seeing them in the audience when I gave my speech. But you rushed me out of there so fast."

"That I did." Nodding, he slid over to her, bringing himself so close their thighs rested against each other. Afterward he set his drink in a holder, then took hers and did the same. "I had to have you to myself. Couldn't wait any longer. It's been too long. It's time to put everyone else aside for a while."

"Yes," Lena agreed joyfully, contradicting the sadness that washed over, lowering her head.

Watching her lids slip over the eyes that increasingly disarmed him, Cordell sensed something amiss and lifted her chin.

"What's wrong, baby?"

"I was just thinking about something. Don't pay me any attention."

"I love paying you attention. But I think I know what's wrong. It's your father, isn't it?"

She looked amazed. "How did you know?"

"Because I know you, Lena. I feel what you feel. Sometimes I sense things you're thinking even when you're not even around."

"I know what you mean. I feel the same for you. It's weird, isn't it?"

"No, it's not weird—it's love. But you love someone else, too: your father. And you were wishing he was there tonight."

"If only I could talk to him about what I'm doing with my life. But to be honest, I thought he would have called me by now. My records are on the radio. My face is in the press."

"You haven't heard anything from him?"

"He wrote me from Budapest at Christmas. He was having a beautiful time. He told me that he and his companion decided on extending their stay and traveling to many other places. But since then, nothing. I'm surprised."

"Maybe Robert's been hiding the mail from you to spite your father. You said they dislike each other."

Now that worried Lena, but she cringed at entertaining a thought so awful. Instead she stared up at Cordell. "Enough about all this. I want to get into you." She circled her arms around his neck.

Explosively his body crushed to her, and the arousal that was building and building ever since he saw her was now unbearable. He couldn't wait until they reached the hotel. Promptly he tapped the panel separating them from the driver.

"What are you doing?" Lena purred, peering at him hazily.

In response he smiled, then dragged his head away when the panel opened.

"Yes, sir?" the driver said sprightly.

"My good man, would you do us a favor?" Cordell reached into his pocket, grabbed his wallet, and removed five one hundred dollar bills. Handing them to the chauffeur, he inquired, "Could you drive us somewhere really quiet and leave us alone for a while?"

"Oh—yes, sir," the driver agreed with a huge grin. He briskly tucked the bills in his jacket pocket. "Yes, sir."

"We're alone, finally," Cordell slurred, watching the chauffeur head down the street. He closed the limousine curtains and looked back at Lena. "You're so beautiful and I want you so, so bad." His voice was husky with contained excitement.

His lips parted hungrily. As they did, Cordell took in every inch of Lena before his scorching gaze settled on her mouth. Breathless for her taste, he gathered the woman he loved in his arms. Closer they came, with features blurring, until he claimed her kiss with savage intensity. Turned on by her responsiveness, he pulled her body tighter to him, his tongue thrashing sensually throughout the velvet warmth of her mouth. A flood-tide of pleasure spiraled through his body, out of control. Lust and love tightened the already roused treasure he so desperately ached to give.

A roaring sea flooded in her cache of love. It overflowed with each soul-drenching wind of his tongue around hers. It compounded with the vigor of his hard body embracing hers with his surging strength, it all filling her with such ecstasy the emotion was almost intolerable.

Lacing her hands through his hair, then coasting along his neck, shoulders and broad back, she longed for more and more of what he was endowing her. Never could she get enough of his teasing and thrilling her lips, tongue, and mouth—ferrying her to a wispy cloud of rapture beyond compare.

Neither could Cordell receive enough. The forceful domination of his lips descended to her neck and all over the prickling heat of her shoulders. Letting her head flow back, Lena succumbed to the sweet sensation, then came forward to worship him with the same.

"Oh, yes, baby," he moaned, beholding her through passion-glazed eyes. "I can't get enough of you."

"I can't get enough, either. Give me more, Cordell. More, baby—please."

Fingers mingled through cascading, satiny ringlets—and when the furor of the moment would turn her head aside, he buried his face in its lushness, drugging himself with its chaste scent. Succeeding such exhilaration, his fingertips began to lay another claim. Carefully his hands unzipped Lena's gown, and soon she felt it slinking down her inflamed flesh, bundling around her tiny waist. A red lacy bra tempted him to discovering all the succulence that was underneath. Quickly he unclasped it. It hung loose. He slid it by the straps down the length of her arm.

Breath caught in his throat seeing her exposed, glistening temptations. "You're so beautiful," he drawled, switching his preoccupation from her breasts to her face, and her face to her breasts. "God have mercy."

"And you make me feel so beautiful looking at me that way."

"Oh, baby I—" he rasped, his words cut off by her leaning forward, offering her sultry nectar.

"Oh, yes," she purred, gripping his lowered head as he suckled an erect nub deep in the hot cave of his mouth. Gasping with delight, Lena propelled her limbs into him further.

With an expertness possessed solely by him, his mouth grew more ravenous with its crusade, titillating her sensitive nipples with tender and fiercer handling before granting the same to her entire breast. Her sweeping lashes shadowing her cheekbones, she watched the pleasure her body was giving him and felt more of her own.

His hands caressed the fullness of her bosom lengthily, treating her to all the bliss her ravenous appetite could contain. At the same time, his mouth returned to hers in fiery demand. A waterfall of joy streamed from her core.

Seeing his thriving passion and highly experiencing her own, provocative handling tugged off his jacket, shirt, and all underneath, leaving his muscular arms and bare, broad chest for her delight. Kisses rained over the path of one shoulder to the other and down the smoldering skin on his arms. She was especially soothing and affectionate to the areas where he was most sensitive. A breath after, soft hairs that scattered about his chest were seductively brushed by the sides of her cheeks.

Her hands were like little flames, groping muscles on one arm and carefully caressing the other, all of which triggered her attraction to him to erupt in a blazing frenzy. Delirium seized them both.

Knowing she couldn't withstand much more exquisite torture, Lena freed him from all the apparel that hindered their becoming one. Instantly her arousal was unendurable at his full beauty, as was his when he proceeded to finish what he started.

"Do you like the way I touch you?" he asked, his hands suddenly reaching underneath her dress, pulling it up to her thighs.

"More than anything," she breathed.

"I'll do anything you want, anything that pleases you."

At that, feathery kisses enraptured her hips, thighs and legs, stirring delicious sensations up and down her spine, while Cordell gruffly yanked the gown past her hips. When it reached her ankles, it was tossed aside. He stroked and planted kisses up her leg. The only thing stopping him was the red lacy panties and sheer, coffee hosiery that were next for shedding. In the dire plight of freeing her, kisses again christened her flesh in that endeavor. In turn, Lena's mouth and hands feverishly pleasured him at whatever erotic zone she found herself.

When finally she was totally unclothed, his breaths were erratic, his eyes were misty with desire.

"I have to have you," he moaned as the urgency of his needs made him position above her, his weight bringing her down onto the billowing black cushions. At once, she felt his manly hardness wedging deep in her stomach and at various points of her writhing form. Swept away by its invitation, she explored every inch of his flaming limbs.

Infused with the eagerness of passion, his hands moved everywhere—her breasts, stomach, ribs, and soon ferreted out the wet mound of deliciousness between her thighs. She wriggled with elation as his magical fingers pleased her, making her so euphoric she was about to explode. Greatly yearning to give as good as she received, Lena stroked his cherished prominence until it seemed he couldn't breathe.

"Oh, yes. Oh, baby, only you could turn me on like this."

Panting, Cordell shifted his body over hers, using his knees to spread her legs apart. Both knew no more could be withstood. Staring in her beautiful face as she gazed up at him so desperately, he was determined to grant them their ultimate joy.

A hot, lingering, deep-throated kiss stirred her unquenchable fire, while her system was finally shocked by his love melting into her moistened depths. Frozen by the luscious feel of each other, both were still for a moment, savoring being completely connected until their hearts craved for more.

Excruciating excitement rippled through their veins. He moved erotically, slowly, then savagely, then altogether varied, immersing her in his sweltering masculinity, while her impassioned hip fluxes worshipped him with her evocative rhythm. He cupped her by the buttocks, thrusting himself deeper into her splendor. At the same time, she enraptured him with a puissance that rendered him helpless to a glorious, wild fever.

Their lips entwined ceaselessly, fulfilling wickedly lustful promises. Their hands caressed, searing feverishly through every portion of slippery, naked flesh. All the while, they were experimenting, discovering, experiencing all the magnificence of each other. The jubilant rush bursting through their blood grew stronger with every kiss, every stroke, every breath, every push and pull, every swagger, every whimper of ecstasy.

Swaying with the magnificent stride he lastly set, they longed to be part of each other forever. Yet that wasn't to be, they learned, as their loins gushed with liquid fire. It rocked them, enthralled, and spellbound, transporting their souls to that highest plateau of love.

"My Lord, Lena," Cordell mouthed breathlessly, flinging himself aside her, then pulling his shirt across them. "You drove me out of my mind." Lightly his lips brushed hers. "Baby, I'm so in love with you." His captivation roamed down her body. "Ooh, you were so sweet."

Loving to hear that and feeling overwhelmingly satisfied and peaceful, Lena smiled. "You made me feel things I never imagined. I never thought it could be this way."

"But it is." He leaned over, plundering his tongue inside her mouth until they both lacked breath.

"What are you trying to do—kill me, Cordell?"

He was grinning. "Oh, no, I think that's what you were trying to do to me."

She searched his amused expression. Clearly very gratified, he also looked exhausted and drenched with perspiration. In spite of it, he was the sexiest man alive to her. "I'm so happy we made up."

"Me, too." He bit into his bottom lip. "As a matter of fact, I want to show you that we have really, really made up."

"Huh?" She was puzzled.

Answering her curiosity, he rose up and reached over

at his jacket. A small navy box was lifted from the pocket.

Stunned, Lena sat up gawking. Scrutinizing her reaction, Cordell didn't keep her in suspense, either. He simply opened the box, and there stood a tremendous glittering diamond ring.

Tears welled in Lena's eyes. "Oh, Cordell."

"It's beautiful, isn't it? Just like you." Softly he drank in her loveliness. She was breathtaking, even soaked in the sweat of their lovemaking. "Lena, you are the most beautiful, wonderful woman I have ever met. And I'm so thankful God brought you into my life. You are a precious, blessed gift. I want to treasure your sweet love every day. I want to make you so very, very happy every day. So it would be the greatest honor of my life if you be with me forever. Will you marry me, Lena?"

"Marry?" escaped in a whisper. She looked down, ignoring the water pouring down her cheeks.

Delicately he wiped some of it, then exquisitely kissed the lingering wetness away. It all evoked her to caress his hands as their eyes met again. She shook her head. "Oh, Cordell . . ."

His brows raised. "Oh, Cordell. Oh, Cordell," he teased. "But what about a yes?"

"Yes! Yes! Yes!"

Sealing their merger of the hearts, his warm mouth clung to her lips and his tongue sought hers in tantalizing ravishment. Desire escalated again, but realizing the chauffeur might soon return, they struggled to calm themselves. With their fascination leaving them lost at the sight of each other, Cordell somehow tugged his interest away long enough to remove the diamond from the box and slip it on her finger. Holding it out, marveling at it, Lena shook her head again. Hair flapped by her eye, but she didn't care about shaking it away. She was in love and just proposed to by the man of her dreams. Nothing else mattered.

"So when are you going to do it?" he asked abruptly.

"Do what?" She was cheerfully examining the ring.

"You know, tell Robert."

Lena stiffened. Her smile dimmed. "Oh, that."

"Yes, that. He has to be told, baby, so we can get on with our lives. Now you told me that last time I saw you that he was going to some mental health facility upstate. Did he go?"

"Yes."

"When will he be back?"

"He should be returning soon, unless he's home already."

"Good. We'll see if he's there tomorrow. If he is, I'll come with you."

With a strange curve to her lips, Lena managed to nod.

Seventeen

Never had he seen a woman so gorgeous. His jaw propped against his hand, his elbow denting into the bed, Cordell was motionless observing Lena sleeping. Her full, dewy lips closed softly, bowing up faintly at the corners in mellow contentment. Several times he kissed her lightly. Doing so, his fingers threaded lithely through her hair. Untamed, it spilled carefree over the pillow, surrounding her face in an awesome halo.

Her skin was glowing. The hue of caramel dusted with chocolate, it looked luscious in the early afternoon sunlight that sprinkled through the room. Nevertheless it was those eyes that mesmerized him most. Even closed, their beguiling slant captivated him, making Lena appear like a doll.

Approximately ten minutes into his enchantment, lashes fluttered and languidly her lids opened. Squinting up at him were warm brown pools, with depths reminding him of fur.

"Good afternoon, Mrs. Richardson."

"It's that late?" Stretching and straining to see better, Lena grinned mischievously. "I'm not Mrs. Richardson yet."

"Will be soon. And how's my beautiful baby today?"

"Wonderful, just wonderful." She smiled. "How is my baby?"

"Drained, but very, very, *very* happy."

She giggled. "And what part of last night is the most memorable for you?" She outstretched her arms farther.

"Oh, the banquet was very nice, but the limousine was truly unforgettable, just as it was when we came back here. Ooh, can we have another replay?" He lifted her hands and grazed her knuckles with his lips. "And after our replay, we can go get things settled with Robert."

Lena's expression changed.

"What's that?"

"What?" She turned her back to him.

He eased her back over. "What's that look for?"

"I don't know. I'm so happy, and I just hate hurting Robert."

Cordell sat up. "Lena, please let's not go through this. Robert has to be told about us. Hope knows and he should know, too, so we can move forward. I don't want you staying with him anymore. That would be crazy. It was hard enough before, but I put up with it. But now I've had enough of it."

"You don't understand, Cordell. He's just coming back from this mental hospital. And he's coming from there because he's still an emotional wreck, and then I'm going to spring this on him."

"He's a man. He can take it. You've been tiptoeing around his feelings for too long. What am I supposed to do now that I'm free? Let my woman live with another man so he won't kill himself?"

"Baby, it's just so hard to hurt him when he's on the verge of losing it. Yes, I've told you that he's calmer and nicer and hasn't verbally abused me in a long time, but still he's not right; he's unstable. When I'm at the apartment, many nights while I'm lying in the bedroom, I can hear him in the other room crying. Crying like a baby.

"We have everything, and he has nothing. And my just deserting him at such a hard time could really send him over the edge. I can't bear that on my conscience, could you?"

"Yes."

"Cordell!"

"Well, I could! Because he treated you wrong and he killed your love. But now it's time for him to be a man and deal with the consequences of what he did. He had a beautiful, beautiful woman who loved him. All he had to do was love her back—that's all! But no, he had to treat you like his worst enemy. So he shouldn't be that surprised that someone else would die for what he so greatly took for granted. The hell with him, Lena!"

Aggravation had lined his face, but Lena heard it more in his voice. "Cordell, don't get upset. Just try to understand my side. We will tell him . . . just not now."

More exasperated, he took a deep breath. "When, Lena? When is it a good time to tell him? Ten years from now?" He threw back the covers and brought his legs over the side of the bed. Reaching for his pants, he was shaking his head.

"What are you doing?" He didn't answer. He merely stood, slipped one leg in his slacks, followed by the other. Watching him zip them up, she asked again, "Cordell, what are you doing?"

"I'm getting dressed," he said tersely. "I need to go for a walk."

"Cordell, don't be mad at me." Yet her words bounced

off his back. Quicker than a blink, he was in the bathroom with the door shut.

Water was running. Listening to it pouring with high
pressure, Lena was pacing the floor. After what seemed
like an eternity, the door opened and he walked out.

"I want you to see my side," she insisted. He was
easing about the room, gathering his socks and other
items.

"What is there to see, Lena? You want to baby this
grown man. Or maybe—"

"Maybe what?"

"Maybe something is still there."

"How could you say that?"

The phone ringing intercepted his answer. Cordell
snatched it up, listened intently, and piece by piece his
face began to shatter. When he hung up he gazed dazedly
at Lena. "That was Reuben."

"What's the matter?" Her body was shaking from his
expression. "Why do you look like that?"

"It's Tobia. She was shot in her shop. A robbery."

The ride to the hospital was a blur. Time had no measure, no distance, no depth. People didn't even exist. There
was solely Lena with Cordell racing beside her. In a
heartbeat, they were entering an intensive-care room.

Grim, devastated, Reuben sat in the corner with his
head bowed in his lap. Cordell went straight over to him,
and thereafter they conversed in low tones. Questions
about how this happened coursed through Lena's mind.
Wrath at the one who did this raged in every fiber of
her being, evoking the perpetrator's evil to slither within
her. So infuriated she was, she could have killed whoever
did this to Tobia herself. But who? How? In spite of all
her feelings, who was she to do anything? What more

could be done? Lena felt so powerless. All she could do was comply when her friend beckoned her near.

Lena stepped toward Tobia. With gray circles beneath the eyes, tubes connected from complex machines, alcohol doused everywhere, her chest bandaged up tight, she didn't look at all like herself. Needless to say, this feeble creature was a far cry from the woman who was so stalwart, wise, opinionated, and proud.

Except when Tobia attempted speech, her voice's clarity, even in a murmur, defied her appearance.

"You—you have to—to tell him, Le . . . na," she whispered.

Lena couldn't believe Tobia was thinking about her happiness at a time like this.

"Don't worry about me, Tobia. You concentrate on getting well."

Tobia closed her eyes hard, but opened them slowly.

"Don't . . . don't do . . . that. Let . . . me say what—what I have . . . to. Tell—tell him, Ro . . . bert, be—before it's too—too late."

"Darling, save your strength."

Tobia shut and opened her eyes again. "List . . . en. You're you . . . are harm . . . ing him more by . . . by keep . . . ing it—it from . . . him. Pe—people are prob . . . a . . . bly laugh—laughing be—behind his back. You're harm . . . ing Cor . . . dell and—and your—your . . . self, too, de . . . de . . . denying your . . . self the ad—advan . . . tages of com . . . plete . . . ly ex . . . per—experiencing your love. Don't—don't you—you want to have a . . . wed . . . ding and chil—chil . . . dren? Don't—don't . . . wait. Any . . . thing can happen. And now . . . look at me, I'm a . . . bout to do . . . this *thing* here."

"Stop! Don't talk like that."

"Girl—girl, I'm . . . I'm not fool . . . ing my—myself."

"Please, Tobia, stop!" Lena glanced over at Reuben and Cordell for support to her claim. Neither noticed. Cordell was patting Reuben on the back. Reuben's face was a mask of torment. She returned her concern to Tobia. Her friend was smiling and whispering over and over, "Is . . . isn't this—this fun . . . ny? I'm—I'm . . . a . . . bout to . . . do this *thing* here."

The instant Lena and Cordell stepped outside of Tobia's room, Lena embraced him like it was their last. Squeezing her equally as potently, Cordell's voice shivered hotly down upon her ear. "It's all right, baby. God won't take Tobia from us. Don't worry."

"It could happen. Anything could happen at any time."

"I know. That's why we have to live every day like it's our last. Get all the love and beauty out of every day."

"That's so true." She reared back, cruising across the features of his gorgeous face. Indisputably she had been wrong. Why did it take such a tragedy to make her see that? "Cordell, I want you to forgive me."

"I love—"

"Ssh." She pressed her fingers against his lips. "Let me say this. I want you to forgive me for being so dumb."

"You're not dumb, Lena. You just have a very soft heart. That's one of the reasons I love you."

"And I love you. And I won't do anything to disrupt our lives anymore. I'm going to tell Robert. He deserves to know so he can get on with his life. And I have to tell him, because we shouldn't deny ourselves anything else. I want to be with you completely. I won't be living with Robert anymore. And I'm going to tell him."

"Let me come with you."

"No, I have to do this alone. There are some things I have to say to him."

"What if he tries to hurt you?"

"Trust me, Cordell. He won't hurt me. I won't let him. Not physically or anything else. Your love has made me so much more stronger."

"I don't think I should have all that credit. The strength is all yours. It was there all along. It was just waiting to come out. But I really don't trust him. Although I do want to abide by your wishes. So we'll compromise. I'll wait downstairs in the car. If you're not down by a specified time, I'll come up. Is that fair?"

She dredged up a smile. "It sure is."

"And I want you to forgive me for something, too."

"What's that?"

"What I said earlier about you and him, about *something being there.* I didn't mean it. I know what you feel for me. I know what we have together. You've showed me that over and over again. That was just anger talking."

As soon as Lena stepped in the apartment door, she was confronted with Robert's vilest leer. Standing in front of her with his arms folded, it was as if the civilized gentleman he had become in recent months had never existed.

"Where were you, Lena?"

"Robert, we have to talk."

"You're damn right we have to talk! I've been trying to get in touch with you for days. I came home earlier than expected. All I wanted to do was tell you that I was back home and tell you how much progress I made. I didn't want to disrupt your two-bit career!"

"Robert, we have to talk."

"We sure enough do! I called Tobia's house—that number where you said to reach you only in an emergency. Well, I called it several times and it was no damned emergency, either. I called it because you are my woman and I wanted you to come home! But that old sleepy-sounding husband of hers kept answering the phone and telling me you weren't there."

"You shouldn't have bothered Reuben." Nonchalantly Lena walked down the hall and into the living room. For some reason, she felt it was easier to tell him there.

Trailing her footsteps, Robert's ire breathed fire against her back. "What do you mean I shouldn't have bothered that punk? I'll call any damn body I please! Matter of fact, I even called your idiot producers, Shell and Michael. Do you know those punks wouldn't even tell me your schedule, or if there was another number besides Tobia's where I could reach you? Then I even tried to call your so-called manager at his law firm, and his secretary wouldn't give me any information, either. That is crazy!"

"Because I wanted it that way."

His eyes blew up. "You wanted it that way? *What the hell do you mean!* Don't act all uppity with me. I knew you when you were a little skuz-bucket in an insurance company. You're no rocket scientist who's too good for everyday folk. You're nothing but a singer. You're no more special than me or anyone else. A dummy can sing! The biggest dummy in the world can open their mouth and sing a note!"

"Robert, you're acting just as ugly as you used to. I thought it was gone." She sighed. "I thought you were on your way to being the way you were before. I'm so glad I'm leaving you."

"Leaving!" Straightaway, panic struck him, staggering him backward a few steps. "Leaving, again?" He paced around aimlessly and when his countenance finally faced her, she saw helplessness. Despite it, she refused to let it sway her intentions.

"I'm going, Robert. No more of these Lena-bashing sessions."

"I'm sorry, Lena."

"Your sorry is played out."

"Lena, baby, I don't know what got into me. I guess it was just that I felt like a fool not being able to get in contact with my own woman. Put yourself in my shoes. Then there's—"

"Then there's what?"

"Oh, I went on a job interview before I left. An administrator's position in a hospital. I thought it went so well, too, despite my lack of experience. But today they called me and told me I didn't get it."

"I'm sorry."

"Me, too. But you see now why I was going off like that. It wasn't really at you; it was me. That's why I need you to stay here and help me. I'm going to try again. Not only that, but I'm going to take that bar and pass it this time. But I need my woman by my side to help me do that."

"I—"

"I need you around to help me cope with everything, but most of all love me. I still want to marry you more than anything. I pray for these things, Lena. You might think I'm a devil, but I'm not. I pray a lot."

"Robert, this prayer is not going to be answered the way you want. I'm truly sorry about us."

"Sorry about us?"

"Robert, I'm not just saying I'm going to leave—I am leaving *now.*"

"No! No!" He was shaking his head. "You're not going to leave me again."

But Lena knew there was no more left to do, to hide, to share, except the truth. As the conviction built in her soul, there was no more waiting—no more hesitation for the proper time to free herself of this oppressive burden. There was the overwhelming relief of no longer having to lie.

"Robert, I'm in love with someone else."

Robert cocked his head to one side as if he heard wrong. He moved soundlessly and carefully toward a chair and sat.

"Did you hear me? I will always care about you. But I'm not *in love* with you anymore."

He was still cocking his head.

"When you say such horrible things to a person like you've said to me, it does something. Those words have so much power. All the love you feel for a person just gets chipped away by those words. You have no idea how much they hurt me. Sometimes I would even think that maybe you were right. Maybe I was all the things you said. That maybe I was stupid or untalented or weak or deserved to be humiliated and hollered at and put down. I gave you so much power, and you gave me so much pain. As a result, my love for you just dwindled away. But I'll never forget you were good to me once."

He nodded and gazed up as if somehow just awakening to what was happening. "I was, wasn't I?"

"Yes. I will never forget that."

"Who is he?"

She debated whether to say at this time. Then suddenly, "My lawyer."

"Your lawyer?" His eyes widened with surprise. "Your lawyer? Isn't he married?"

"He's getting a divorce."

Robert shook his head. His eyes circled the room, but somehow Lena knew he couldn't see a thing in it.

"Are you all right, Robert?"

He didn't answer, but a concern was thought aloud.

"Everyone knew, didn't they?"

"What do you mean?" But Lena knew what he meant.

"Everyone knew?" He sounded amazingly calm. "Shell and Michael. Patty and Manuel, your band, the other producer. Now I remember the way they looked at me. Tobia, too, she knew. And that time, what Manuel said to me . . . now I know why."

"I'm sorry. I never wanted to hurt you. You gave me some beautiful, beautiful times, and that's what I will look back on when I think of you. The preciousness we shared. Not the bad."

"Not the bad . . . me, either . . ."

"When I met you and fell in love with you, I wanted it to last forever. But God knew otherwise."

"But God knew otherwise . . ."

"Yes, he did. And we did treasure each other, and learned things—wonderful things—about each other's hearts and souls. Our time together wasn't in vain. No one's time together is. There are reasons people are put together and come into each other's lives, regardless of

how large a reason or how small it may seem. There is
something you're supposed to experience, learn, feel. I
firmly believe it."

"You firmly believe that . . ."

"Ours was an experience that God wanted to happen
until we arrived at a new level of our lives. Now we can
let go, but we can let go with peace—and love, too."

"With peace—and love, too . . ."

"I'm so, so sorry, Robert."

"So sorry . . ." Abruptly he stopped repeating and really saw her. "You're sorry?" He looked dazed, sounded
soft as cotton.

"I am."

"Me, too. This here is really something." He laughed
dryly and balled up in a knot in the chair.

"Are you okay?" Lena called to him several times, but
he didn't respond. The smile also faded away. In an instant, he had entered a world that couldn't be disturbed.

After gathering her things in the bedroom, the dining
room, the living room, all through a storm of silence,
she looked once more at Robert knotted up in the chair.
He remained in that private world. In his mind-set, Lena
was no longer there. "Have a nice life," she uttered anyway. "I'll send the movers for the rest of my things."

When finally she closed the door and found herself in
the empty hall, she expected to hear cursing or throwing
of things. Neither. There was silence. A startling quiet
lingered on.

Baggage in hand, Lena walked to the elevator, pressed
the down button, and it came very quickly. She rode and
stopped and rode and stopped, somehow unaware of anything at all. There was solely the picture of a man balled
in a chair, who wouldn't leave her mind. She struggled

to make him unfamiliar. Someone she didn't know so well. Possibly he could be an easy fact to read past in two years of her life. It didn't work, so soon she strove to completely will herself away from all that had happened. Once outside, she looked at stores, frank carts, people, street lights, buildings, animals, but not long after, each was a distorted prism, each disfigured by the stubborn water standing in her eyes.

Finally "Lena," Cordell startled her, jerking her blurred sight to him standing behind her. Promptly he pecked her lips but afterward noticed the clouded eyes.

"Baby, is everything okay? What's wrong?"

"Nothing."

"You don't look like it's nothing. You look like you're about to cry. Did he do anything to you? Anything at all? I'll break his neck."

"I'm fine. He just looked pitiful, that's all."

"You're sure, that's all?"

"I'm sure. Let's go. It's over now."

"Good."

Picking up Lena's luggage, Cordell pointed to where his Jaguar was parked down the block. Escorting her there, he talked eagerly about their wedding, honeymoon plans, and an oceanfront home he saw not far from the Cliffs. Soundlessly she listened. Remarkably water remained upright in her eyes.

The baggage was soon loaded in the trunk. Cordell opened the passenger door and expected Lena to slide inside. But still reeling in the disbelief of the moment, she turned back toward the apartment building. A tear that was standing finally tumbled from her eye.

* * *

Days later, Cordell packed the last item in his suitcase and fastened it shut. Wordlessly Hope had been looking on, and only when he neared the front door did each feel the need to speak.

"I guess that's all of it." She spoke first.

"I think so. Thanks for letting me come back to get the rest of my things."

"You don't have to thank me."

"Well, I wanted to. I'm also very sorry—"

"Don't be sorry. And please don't feel sorry for me. You've done that enough."

"I don't feel sorry for you, Hope. Somehow I know you'll be fine."

"You think so?"

"I know so. Do you have any type of plans?"

She smiled and there was calmness about her entire face, her entire demeanor. It relaxed him. It made him truly feel that the best was working out for everyone.

"Well, sometimes I don't feel like I have anything to look forward to. Then there are those times that I do. In those certain times it's because of all that television I used to watch. I learned something from it. It's not such a waste of time as people think."

"Why is that?"

"There was an advertisement about an orphanage in Boston. They need people to help with the children. People who love children—love them like nothing else or anyone else, like I do. Sometimes I think about getting out of New York and going there. One of these days, I'll get the nerve to go."

"That's fantastic."

"I just hope when they check into my background, that my past problems don't hinder me."

"I'm sure once they meet you and see your love for the kids, they'll see that you're very capable."

"You're always so sure of things. And most of the time you're right, too. I'll take your word for it."

"And you have to be sure of yourself. You're going to be fine."

Her eyes were sparkling. "I really want to. It kind of makes me feel excited."

"And I'm excited for you. Be happy, Hope."

"You, too . . . Cordell."

He pecked her on the forehead. They shared their last look. The air whispered goodbye.

Eighteen

They were the sweetest days Lena had ever known. Everywhere she went, her voice exploded from somewhere. Radio, car tapes, clubs were all playing her distinct sound. Far more magical than any of this success, though, were the feelings Cordell was filling her with each day. She didn't have to wonder anymore about what it felt like to have a soul mate, the one born in this world perfectly for you, the one who touches you in a place in your heart and soul that you never knew existed.

With Robert, she was so far on the other side of that perfect kind of love. Never was it like what she was feeling with Cordell. The contrast of the past and present showed how much one's life could turn around. And it was like a divine plan that each of her songs topping the charts personified as much as mere words could, what Lena had experienced with one man and what she was now experiencing with another. It was her greatest wish that her music inspired someone. Either they would leave a negative relationship with the firm belief that there were brighter days ahead. Or they would savor the blessings of love so rapturous it was unlike any other. Yes, Lena's music made a powerful impact as it raced up the charts. More than that, Lena understood the meaning behind the words. For she had lived them and was living them then. The sultry ballads were everywhere . . .

Released July 1996, "Never Felt This Before"

No one can know,
What's behind my smile.
No one could possibly know,
How you make me alive.

Sharing our intimate world,
Is so incredible.
What you've brought to my life,
Never dreamed was possible.

Never felt this before,
A love so real like this.
You are the one for me,
Bring me such happiness.

How can I explain,
To anyone this love.
Rapture, joy, passion,
But mere words aren't enough.

Never felt this before,
A love so real like this.
You are the one for me,
Bring me such happiness.

Never felt this before,
A love so real like this.
You are the one for me,
You bring me such happiness.

Released September 1996,
"Just Because I'm Here Now"

Sometimes I feel we'll be together forever,
Then again I feel we won't last another day.

You've been in my life for two years,
And you hurt me again and again.
Like a child in your own world,
But you still want me to be your girl.

Just because I'm here now,
Don't think I'm going to be here forever.
Just because I'm here now,
Don't think I'm going to be here forever.

Your sweet loving keeps me going,
But your empty promises leave me lonely.

If you really loved me, why didn't you show it?
How long can a girl hold on?
Someone's been trying to lure me from you,
And I've been true, but no more.

Just because I'm here now,
Don't think I'm going to be here forever.
Just because I'm here now,
Don't think I'm going to be here forever.

Just because I'm here now,
Don't think I'm going to be here forever,
Just because I'm here now,
Don't think I'm going to be here forever.

Released December 1996, "You Touched Me"

I had heard about this feeling,
Just knew it wasn't true.
But oh what a feeling,
And it's all because of you.

You're magic and beauty,
You're food for my soul.
You're the one that leaves me breathless,
And I'll never let you go.

You've touched me in a place,
In my heart and soul.
Before you touched me,
It was a place I didn't know.

You've awakened life in me,
Life I never knew was there.
You're inside me so deep,
And our kind of love is so rare.

You've touched me in a place,
In my heart and soul.
Before you touched me,
It was a place I didn't know.

You've touched me in a place,
In my heart and soul.
Before you touched me,
It was a place I didn't know.

Released January 1997, "The Dreamer"

Couldn't find the right man,
I'm kind of hard to understand.
I didn't want to be with someone.
Just to keep from being alone.

Can't have my body without my soul,
Needed something real I could hold.
Then suddenly you appeared,
You loved me and really cared.

I am the dreamer,
Whose dream came true.
I am the dreamer,
Whose dream is you.

You're more than I thought you'd be,
Baby, you're so good to me.
Forever I will love you,
Always I'll be true.

I am the dreamer,
Whose dream came true.
I am the dreamer,
Whose dream is you.

I am the dreamer,
Whose dream came true.
I am the dreamer,
Whose dream is you.

Released March 1997, "You Don't Know"

I had so much to give you,
All of my love.
I just wanted to thrill you,
And be all you thought of.
But you hurt me.
We went our separate ways,
But now here you are wanting to love me again.

After breaking my heart,
Throwing it away,
Tearing it apart,
'Til I cried all day.

You don't know what you have,
'Til your well runs dry.
You don't know what you have,
'Til you're asking yourself why.
You don't know what you have,
'Til you've said goodbye.

I wanted to make you so happy,
Each and every day.
Always thought of ways to love you,
Make you pleasured in every way.
But you hurt me.
We went our separate ways,
And now you're here wanting to love me again.

You don't know what you have,
'Til your well runs dry.
You don't know what you have,

'Til you're asking yourself why.
You don't know what you have,
'Til you've said goodbye.

You don't know what you have,
'Til your well runs dry.
You don't know what you have,
'Til you're asking yourself why.
You don't know what you have,
'Til you've said goodbye.

Released May 1997, "Can't You See"

Sometimes I see something in your eyes,
And I think it's all in my mind,
That you're feeling what I'm feeling.
So much emotion,
I hardly know you.
But I want you so,
And I know it shows.

Can't you see,
Can't you see,
Can't you see,
I'm in love with you.

Ever since I saw your face,
My life has never been the same.

Like a precious fantasy,
That's what you are to me.
And if you were mine,

I'd do anything to make you happy.
Can't you see,
Can't you see,
Can't you see,
I'm in love with you.

Can't you see,
Can't you see,
Can't you see,
I'm in love with you.

Released June 1996,
"Taking the Higher Ground"

You say I've grown away from you.
I say you don't understand me.
And we argue,
Cry in our ways.
And it seems it's about over,
After our long time together.
But I'm stopping the fighting,
And I won't cry no more,
Explaining myself again is out.
And those troublemakers in our lives,
I pray their misery goes away.

Because I'm taking the higher road.
The road where God only knows
My pain, my heartache.
I give it all to him.
Are we meant to be, or not,

In a higher ground of love.
You're such a stranger to me now,
Like someone I don't even know.
Hardhearted as can be,
Wear such hopelessness.

But I'm stopping the fighting,
And I won't cry no more.
Explaining myself again is out.
And those troublemakers in our lives,
I pray their misery goes away.

Because I'm taking the higher road.
The road where God only knows
My pain, my heartache.
I give it all to him.
Are we meant to be or not,
In the higher road of love.

Because I'm taking the higher road.
The road where God only knows
My pain, my heartache.
I give it all to him.
Are we meant to be or not,
In the higher road of love.

Nineteen

"Where in the world is Cordell!" Lena yelled. *"Where is that man!"* Pump heels were clicking rapidly from one end of the dressing room tile to the other. From across the room, a head was bobbing from side to side with them.

"I don't know where he is." Tobia raised one brow. "But you yell at me like that again, and I'll give you a black eye to wear onstage."

Stunned, Lena ceased moving and gawked at her best friend.

Immediately Tobia exploded into laughter. She tapped Lena on the arm.

"Lighten up, girl. I was just joking."

"Oh, sorry I didn't get it. I'm a bunch of nerves, Tobia." She commenced stepping again. "I can't do this."

"Oh, yes, you will. Last time I looked out into the audience, Radio City Music Hall was looking pretty full, and they are all here to see one helluva singer, and that's you—Lena Durant! You can't bail out now. You shouldn't have had so many top-selling hits. You shouldn't have had an album that went double platinum. You're such a flop."

"Oh, you're making me more nervous. If only some-

one would kidnap me. Then I wouldn't have to do it. No
one would fault me either. You know anyone?"

Tobia mashed up her lips. "You scary poop."

"Call me what you want. And for God's sake, where
is Cordell?"

"He'll be here. Calm down. You're going to sweat your
makeup off."

"Oh, God, Tobia—I had no idea what I was getting
into." She clutched one side of her forehead. "It's one
thing to sing in a studio. And Centerfields made me nervous enough. And those TV shows with a good amount
of people in the audience weren't even this terrifying,
because the real audience—all those viewers—I couldn't
see. They were at home. But this"—she paused, now
clutching both sides of her face—"this getting up before
those thousands and thousands of people, and having all
these music critics waiting to rip me apart. It's too much."
Her hands dropped hard at her sides. "And to think I
have three more nights of this."

"Nobody told you to sing so doggone good and sell
out Radio City all those days."

Lena flashed her a sick smile. "You're too sweet. But
I tell you, you're not making me feel any better. When
I get out there, I'll be so scared nothing will come out."

"Believe me, you won't mess up."

"What if I forget the words, and I'm just standing
there with my mouth wide open. Oh, God!" She stopped
to form a mental picture, then began to speed walk.
"What am I going to do?"

"Girl, I'm telling you—you won't mess up! And even
if you do, just call on the Lord. He'll straighten it out
quick. I called him. That's why I'm here now. You know
that." She picked up a purple-beaded purse off the

dresser. "Now let me go look for your husband-to-be before you pass out. You sure need him. If I see him, I'll tell him to hurry back here before you give birth."

Weakly Lena smiled and hugged her. "Thanks, Tobia, you're one wonderful friend."

"I know." She chuckled. "And if I don't get back here before you go onstage, it's because of security. They are tight with you. Manuel and Patty tried to come back here, but they wouldn't let them back here. But I had clout. I wiggled my big man-calling hips." Exaggerating the swagger of her stride, she strolled to the door. A wink flashed at Lena before her buddy headed on.

As soon as Tobia was out of sight, Lena prayed, meditated, and did creative visualization exercises. All were efforts to sedate herself and bolster confidence. They were successful, too. That is, until the makeup artist paid her a second visit for the evening and initiated reapplying her makeup. Succeeding him, there was the hairstylist, who fussed with Lena's curls, all the while reminding her how large and boisterous the audience was becoming. Above all, there was no Cordell around.

When both vacated the dressing room, July's one hundred degrees outside seemed like it had somehow sneaked past the air-conditioning and erupted inside the room. The constant activity heard in the hallway didn't make matters easier. Backstage at Radio City, she could hear the set designers shuffling and shuffling. There were the musicians rehearsing their arrangements. To rankle her more, Shell and Michael passed by and checked on her, too. As well the other producer, who rehearsed the last verse of the new song with Lena, and when she saw him coming again to rehearse something else, she slammed the door.

Lena was mystified as to why she did it. Why was she
that rude? God knows, she didn't want to get on that
man's bad side. Yet she wasn't herself tonight. To make
matters worse, more and more people were peeking in,
notifying her that the audience was restless. Did they
think they were making her feel better?

Lena powdered her cheeks, putting a last touch to her
elaborate look. Nevertheless, viewing the woman in the
mirror she started to sob.

"I have to get out of this."

She shook her head and dabbed on a smidgen of wine-
colored lip gloss.

"I can't sing in front of all those people."

Turning her head from side to side, Lena examined
her hair. She didn't like the way the hairdresser had
parted it down the middle, leaving tendrils seeping down
to her brows. She grabbed the comb and parted it on the
side.

"And where in the world is Cordell?" She scrutinized
herself. "Is it my imagination, or do I look like a frog?"

Laying her head against the vanity table, the whimpers
came more forcefully. But where was all this coming
from? She didn't know, but then again she did. It was
nervousness—the kind you needed a loved one to soothe.
Undoubtedly Cordell's tardiness was irking her. More
than that, though, she mourned a heartache, too: her father wasn't there.

Fortunately there were many relatives attending. Be-
stowing all their congratulations, aunts, uncles, cousins
had called Lena for complimentary concert tickets. However, she had heard nothing from her father. Amid the
exposure of a double-platinum album, she expected to
hear something from him, even if he was out of the coun-

try. Furthermore, Lena knew her not hearing from him in six months wasn't because he was injured or anything. On several occasions, she investigated his whereabouts with his travel agent. Each time he was in some glamorous city, apparently having the time of his life—the last being Budapest. But why hadn't he written or called his daughter? Was her pursuing her dreams causing him so much difficulty that he chose to ignore her? Robert had always hammered that in.

"He doesn't believe in you. He dismisses your dreams as trash. As nothing!"

The worst thing about what Robert claimed was that it was proving true. From Lena's perspective, her father never considered music anything honorable. He deemed it a hobby. A whimsical thing to pass the time. Actually he even implied as much one day when she sang the lead role in a school musical. Lena could hear his voice ripping through her hopes and dreams precisely at that moment.

"Your cousin Louise won first place at the science fair, and one of the attorney's sons won a math scholarship to an upscale private school. You have to do better, too. You were good today, sweetheart, outstanding even. But don't get too involved with that music foolishness. You're wasting time there. Leave it for a hobby. You can do better than that. If you keep wasting your time with that, you could wind up being nothing."

Moreover, musical aspirations were a bunch of nonsense when Lena first shared her dreams of it as a career.

"Sweetheart, you have to get up and do something with some respect," her father stressed, *"something using your brain power. Black people have to stop singing and dancing to feel important and get ahead. We have to stop*

*singing for our supper. That's nothing you want to do
there, if you want to sing. That isn't anything except an
empty dream. Think of something else you want to do
with your life. Something that's going to mean something
to the world."*

Just then, knocking at the door interrupted her journey
into the painful past.

"Come in," Lena beckoned, praying it was the love of
her life. "I'm decent."

"Your wish is my command." Smiling, Cordell strolled
in the dressing room, causing her insides to flood with
warmth. Along with the impassioned sensation he summoned
forth, he brought the kind of excitement she worshipped—the
kind that pushed jangled nerves aside. Practically leaping on
him, Lena kissed him deep and lustfully.

"Ooh, you taste so good," he purred, biting his bottom
lip and holding her. Their mouths were unwinding so
they could get some breath.

"And you taste pretty delicious yourself."

He inched back some, his appreciation roving down
her voluptuous form. When their gazes intertwined again,
he was shaking his head with admiration. "You sure look
good. I am the luckiest man alive."

Again his kiss clung to her mouth. Probing softly at
first, he became hungrier for her, coaxing her lips open,
and painstakingly immersing every second of their en-
counter for all the rapture it was worth. Once savoring
her honeyed nectar, Cordell thought he would die from
pleasure. Equally so did she. A need for air made them
finally uncouple.

"Where were you?" she asked, peering at him dreamily. "Oh, God, you taste and feel so good." Her touch
kneaded the steel-like muscles of his arms.

"Remember I told you last night I was going to check that everything was perfect well ahead of time." He sounded breathless. "The speakers, the musicians, the seating, and everything else had to be checked on. I want everything to be perfect for your first concert."

"You're so good to me, Cordell."

"And you're like something I dreamed." He brushed a silken curl from her eye. "You don't have much longer, beautiful."

"I know." At that she felt a pang of the nervousness returning. Not surprising to her, being within his strong, dependable arms had made all worries slip away.

A hot, fierce, lingering kiss spellbound them again. Yet this time when they detached, Lena didn't relish the warmth of his embrace until she was ravenous for another trip to paradise. Wiping the lipstick off his mouth with a hanky, Cordell uttered, "Baby, I have a surprise." He looked suspicious. "There was this very dignified individual who was fighting with security to get backstage, who mentioned that he was a very close relative of yours. I was called to check him out, and I asked how close of a relative was he. I also explained that I had a right to ask because I'm your attorney and manager. So aren't you curious who this surprise person might be?"

"A male stripper?" she quipped.

"Not quite. But a male just the same." He stepped near the door, opened it, and motioned for someone to come in.

Anxious to see who it was, Lena unconsciously held her breath. Amazingly she held it even more when a shocking sight sauntered in and stood before her. Speechless, Lena stared, then looked at Cordell. She stared at the thinner, grayer person than she remembered and ogled Cordell again. Cordell was beaming.

"Hello, sweetheart," Angus Durant greeted his daughter.

"How are you, Daddy?"

He hugged her so tight, Lena didn't have any choice in exhaling. When they came apart, a thousand emotions seemed to shimmer from her father's eyes.

"Sweetheart, why didn't you tell me?" the judge asked. "Why didn't you tell me you were doing all this?

"I wanted to but—"

"But what?" He leaned forward for an answer.

Lena felt it safer to look at Cordell. "I—I wanted to, but—but—" She couldn't bear for her father to berate her dreams again, especially not on this dramatic night of her career.

Angus was about to express something else when Cordell interrupted by clearing his throat. "I'm going to leave you two to talk a minute. I'll check on things. Showtime soon, beautiful lady." Then he looked at Angus. "And again, it was very nice meeting you, sir."

Angus smiled and nodded. "You, too, son."

Lena's expression pleaded for Cordell to stay. She needed his support. Nonetheless, when Cordell departed, she was careful not to meet her father's gaze. Lena looked down and everywhere else to avoid him while he talked.

"He's a great fellow. He talked to me for a while about you."

"Did he?" She continued looking about.

"I really, really like him. He's the kind of man I always envisioned being worthy of my lovely daughter. He's far more suited for you than Robert. I never did feel right about him."

"I know."

"I knew you could have done better."

She was looking down. "I'm surprised you're here, Daddy."

"Well I had to be here for you. I had to tell you—"

Lena's head shot up. "That I'm making the biggest mistake of my life! I'm sorry I disappointed you. But this is my life. I enjoy singing. I'm proud of the album. I worked my butt off, and people love it!

"So don't go comparing me to this cousin or this one's son, because this is me! This is what I like! This is what I'm good at! God gave me a gift!"

Promptly her father came closer and gently held her arms. "You have me pegged wrong, sweetheart. I'm so proud of my little girl. Your mother would be, too, if she could see what you're about to do—if she could see what you've accomplished."

Lena was dumbfounded.

"Sweetie, I am very, very proud of you. Didn't you read my letters or get the phone messages I left with Robert?"

"What letters or calls? The last letter I received from you was Christmas, and you didn't mention anything about being proud. You acted like you didn't know I had a music career."

"I didn't back then. But shortly after, I passed a news-stand in Budapest, and there I saw your face on a magazine cover. It was among several others on the cover of a music magazine. They were talking about up-and-coming artists under this particular record label. Anyway, my heart nearly leaped out of my chest. My little girl was this beautiful woman on that magazine cover. I opened It up quick so I could read the article. After that, I showed it to everyone, telling them about my talented daughter. Then I wrote you a letter."

"Letter? There was no—"

"And to top that off, the next day when I picked up my morning paper, I opened to the entertainment page, and there you were again, posing with some people. As soon as I could, I called you. But you weren't home, and I left a message with Robert."

"There was no message . . . or letter, for that matter." But instantly Lena recalled all the occasions she was out of the apartment working on the album or spending tender moments with Cordell. Robert had plenty of access to intercept the mail. She couldn't believe he had been so vicious.

The judge's hazel eyes narrowed. "You mean he didn't give you the message, and you didn't receive the letter? That was right after Christmas, and I was telling you how excited I was about your success. When you didn't respond, it crossed my mind that something was fishy. But I just thought you were too busy for your old man. That thought hurt like hell, too."

"Oh, no, Daddy. I'm never too busy for you. Never, ever."

"That louse."

Dazed with shock, Lena gawked everywhere in disbelief. "He never showed me anything from you and never told me anything."

"He never told you about any of the times I called?"

"There were many?"

"Oh, sweetheart, so many. I've been calling and writing you letters for a while now to tell you how proud I am. I would have rushed home and told you in person if my traveling companion hadn't broke her hip so badly while we were roller skating in Budapest."

Lena blinked. "Daddy, you were roller skating?" Her conservative highbrow father sure had changed. "You were roller skating with Mrs. Atwater?"

"I had a ball, too. Until her nasty accident, of course. She's still in the hospital there. That's why I couldn't come home to you, sweetheart. Grace was so bad off, I couldn't just abandon her. But for this once-in-a-lifetime occasion, she had to understand that I had to come. I had to see my baby light up the stage."

This new attitude of his was so incredible to her. "I'm glad you're here. I can't tell you what it means to me. Since you didn't stay in contact, I didn't know what to think."

The judge looked puzzled. "But I did stay in contact. As I said before, I wrote and called, leaving message after message with Robert. I even found out which record company you worked for and tried to contact you through them. But as soon as I told them I was your father, they took it as a joke. I couldn't believe the brush-off I received. It was like they didn't believe me."

"That's because they didn't, Daddy. Fans do that all the time, saying they're a relative, to talk to me. I guess they assumed my father could reach me at home if he wanted to talk to me."

Her father sighed. "Robert is really rotten. I'm so glad you're free of him." Unexpectedly, though, a scowl shadowed his features. "Though one thing about you troubles me Lena. Weren't you worried about me after you didn't receive any more letters?"

"Daddy, I tracked your whereabouts through the travel

agent. I always knew where you were and that you were fine."

"So why didn't you call and let me know about your new life if you knew where I was? You were too busy then?"

"No, not at all. It was just that I didn't feel like lying to you about what I was doing. I couldn't tell you I had quit my job to pursue a music career. You made it clear how you felt. You used to refer to my dreams as nonsense or a hobby! Do you know how that cuts into a child—the only thing she might be able to do well and your parent reduces it to nothing. It kills you.

"Sometimes when I was trying to convince you that singing was important to me, and that I might be gifted, you acted like I didn't say anything at all. Either you would talk about Aunt Lettie, or you would keep on talking about something else. And then there was that time I was first offered the contract and you were so against it."

Her father lowered his head and searched all around the room. Finding his daughter again, he stared at Lena with intense sincerity. "All I can say now is that I am human. I made a mistake. I admit it. I hurt you. I hope I can make it up to you. I hope my coming here to see you perform tells you that I'm proud. And I'm also proud of the man you chose to share your life with, too. Cordell Richardson is a good man. And not just because he's successful, either. Oh, I've heard of him in my legal circles. I know he's a brilliant lawyer. But he's a good man, because I can feel his heart. He has a good one. And he told me that he's divorced, and you've rid yourself of Robert, so you should just love each other, just overflow with love.

"After he said he was your lawyer and manager, he really talked to me about my career, his career, your career and his great love for you. When we finished talking, I felt like I knew that young man all my life. I felt for the first time in my life that I had a son-in-law. Cordell truly has a good heart. Whenever I leave this earth, I can feel good that I'm leaving my precious child in good hands. And, sweetheart, that's all any parent wants. The best for his child. That's why I did everything I did or said everything I said, no matter how wrong I was." His eyes filled with water. "I wish I could walk you down the aisle on your wedding day, but I understand why you wouldn't want that."

The door opened. Slump-backed, silently weeping, the old man attempted to walk away. However, Lena flung her arms around her father and nothing could tear them apart. "Daddy, please walk me down the aisle. Please give me away on my wedding day. I forgive you. All you did was love me. How can I not forgive you?"

Cordell entering the room drew them apart, luring their attention to him. "There's someone else here to see you," he stated, not looking particularly happy.

"Someone else?"

Her father pecked her on the check and patted Cordell on the arm. "I'm going to go get my front-row seat before someone tries to steal it. Break a leg, sweetie."

"I will, Daddy." Glowing with joy, she watched his thin form fade out of the door.

"I see you two have patched things up," Cordell observed, directing her cheerful expression to him.

"Yes, we did. Thanks to you. You're such a wonderful man. Remind me after the show to thank you properly." She winked.

"Oh, you know I'll hold you to that. You're my weakness," he mouthed breathily.

"But who is it that wants to see me now? Manuel? Patty?"

"No, Patty and Manuel are in their front-row seats with ear to ear grins."

"Who is it then?"

"It's me," a familiar voice announced.

"Robert," Lena gasped as he appeared in the room.

It was a long time since she saw him last, she thought. Ingrained in memory was him in that chair. Yet now, considering what she had learned about him tonight, Lena should have been disgusted by the sight of him. Quite the contrary, she wouldn't let his wickedness darken her spirit. She was determined to relinquish the ugliness of the past and embrace the light of the future. Too many wonderful things were happening to let animosity attach to her soul.

Face to face, Cordell glared at Robert. Robert glared at Cordell.

"Do you have the time, baby?" Cordell asked. "Otherwise, I can just escort him out of here." He glanced at his watch. "It's almost showtime anyway. Really, it's no problem to escort him out. Actually it would be my pleasure."

"I'm here," Robert informed him. "Don't talk about me like I'm not."

Lena stepped between them. "Cordell, I can talk to him."

"Alone, please," Robert contended.

She puckered her lips in a kiss at Cordell. Robert grimaced.

"Honey, just give us a few."

Reluctantly Cordell nodded and sauntered out of the room.

Robert inhaled deeply when they were alone. "You look gorgeous, Lena. Are you ready for it?"

"I don't think so. I have really been going crazy back here, and all these people keep peeking their heads in telling me how crowded and noisy it's getting. It's making me crazy. I'm about to jump out my skin."

"Oh, you'll be fine." He smiled. "You can handle it. Once you get into it, they'll be putty in your hands."

"I don't know. I'm shaking. Feel my hands."

He did, and with their contact he looked at her with longing in his eyes. "I really miss you, Lena."

"I miss you, too. Do you still leave the cap off the toothpaste?"

He laughed. "I can't stop doing that. It makes me remember you telling me to put it back on."

She smiled and looked him over. "You look good, too. How have you been getting along?"

"I'm fine. Just trying to build a good, purposeful life."

She was surprised at his choice of words. "Good. That's good, Robert. So did you pass the bar?"

"As a matter of fact, I did."

"Great! Oh, wow, you did it!"

"Yes, I did it. The only thing is now that I passed, I'm not so sure about a law career anymore. Actually I've been teaching."

"Where? What grade?"

"Just substituting. But I'm about to go away, too."

"You are?"

"Yes, I've decided to take a trip to some quiet place. I don't know where, but I want a place that is real peaceful. I want to just think, you know. Be with nature."

"I never heard you talk like this before."

"That's because I'm changing. I'm seeing things different. I realize I have to stop moving so much. It seems like I've just been going and going, without ever stopping to see where it is I'm headed to. I have to stop and think about what I want to do with my life. I can't do that by jumping from one thing to the other."

Lena smiled.

"What's funny?"

"I was just remembering something. What you said reminds me of something Tobia told me. You see, she lost her brother, but before he passed a priest told him, 'Flowers, some may bloom in the same season, but if you really watched them, really did, they don't bloom precisely at the same time. They have to sit—sit and listen to God first. Then they'll bloom. Each after it has listened. Each in its own time and way.' And it reminds me of you now. Sounds like you're getting ready to bloom."

He hugged her with all the energy he could muster. When they released each other, she intended to walk out with him. Hence she proceeded, but abruptly stopped when the door opened. A woman was standing there. She was waiting for Robert.

She wasn't pretty, or shapely, or anything special to look at. Although she possessed a warmth. Lena saw that when she revealed what a fan she was. Lena was grateful and gracious, too, when observing the woman grab Robert by the arm. A second later they strode off.

She was still facing their direction when Cordell stepped up to her. "I saw you watching them." His voice was low. The sentence hung there in the quiet for a while. Through the hush, Lena searched his face. He didn't sound jealous, but the way he looked urged her to explain.

"It's just so weird seeing someone you were supposed to spend your entire life with walking off with someone else."

"Do you want him back? He seems more together."

He still didn't sound jealous, but there again was something in the eyes, a veiled desperateness about him.

She stared at him harder. "How could you ask me that?"

"Because I'm so in love you, I don't know what to do with myself. Lena, regardless of what I'm doing, you're always there, in my mind and deep in my heart and soul. I can't imagine life without you. I'm *alive* now, because of you."

She kissed him, and from it there was rapture so intense, it could have easily made her forget that a lifelong dream awaited. It was only someone shouting her name that tugged Lena away from Cordell. That someone shouted her name, again and louder. Another person was shouting her name, too. And another and yet another.

"Lena, it's showtime," they all yelled.

Cordell had made a start to step with her, but unexpectedly he felt compelled to shift in front of Lena, tenderly cupping her face.

"Before you go on, baby, I just want to say that I'm so proud of you. I understand how hard it was for you to get to this stage. You always had the talent, but you had so much other baggage to deal with before you could show that talent. Tonight is ground-breaking, because it shows that no matter how much you want something in this life, you can get it. And from now on, you know that whatever you dream of in life—no matter how impossible it may seem—you can have it. You can have it and you go for it, and I'll always be right by your side."

"I love you, Cordell." A kiss brushed his lips as soft as the look scintillating in her eyes.

Thereafter Lena stepped and stepped, eventually winding up at center stage. She positioned herself behind the curtain and before the musicians. Again the apprehension returned, and Lena knew she couldn't do this. It was impossible to sing before thousands and thousands of boisterous strangers. Her heart was beating and then it wasn't. Her ears were throbbing and they were at times just deaf. Her legs were weak, and sometimes she wondered did she have any.

Hearing the uproarious audience, Lena was tempted to run. Absolutely she would make a fool of herself. Her voice wouldn't work. What if nothing came out of her throat? That could happen.

The announcer began his introduction, screeching clearly and energetically to the hysterical audience:

"You've seen her in the videos! You've seen her on television shows, interviews, and in many, many magazines—"

The fans cheered louder, louder, louder.

"Well, New York City—are you ready?"

"YES AND YEAH!" screeched from everywhere.

"Well then if you are, will New York City give a thunderous round of applause for the young lady with the *NUMBER ONE ALBUM IN THE COUNTRY, ON BOTH THE R&B AND POP CHARTS, THE SEXY LADY HERSELF, LENA DURANT!"*

The screams, roars, and applause were deafening. The band commenced playing. The curtain hadn't risen yet. The producers had rehearsed a special effect with Lena and the musicians. To heighten the suspense of the show, there would be several bars prior to unveiling the entertainers to the audience.

Accordingly, Lena didn't know how she did it, but the beginning of the seductive ballad sifted from her. The crowd's excitement multiplied. Because of the thunderousness, the lyrics were scarcely heard. They were entrancing words. While singing them, Lena had to gaze at Cordell. Standing by the side of the stage, he looked serious, worried, and at the same time exceedingly proud. His countenance somehow assured her his affection would remain until neither had breath in their bodies. Forever within her, there was that feeling that never steered her wrong, that forceful intuitive sense, which relayed wonderful sensations about him. Lena wholeheartedly believed in his love. And this message in this song reminded her of the best of them, alone, intimate, sharing body and soul. Lena shut her eyes and released the passion of what she felt and saw.

Heaven didn't have anything on the place Cordell took her to. Lena could never be in that place long enough. She wanted to know why God had not let her arrive there sooner. If he had, she would have never, ever wanted for anything. She probably wouldn't have yearned to be anything or anywhere. Everything she ever needed, and would need, seemed to be within Cordell.

First he would hold and rock her into this place. She would cling there, believing she might die if he let her go. She didn't die. She was sustained by this island. An island where soft lips cushioned. It was succeeded by words and encouragement, sweeter than any embrace.

They lifted her soul to a plane she never believed attainable for her. He soothed her farther and farther into his oasis of the heart.

His love was new. It was something and somewhere that never existed before. In all her years, Lena had not seen or felt it in any shape or form. Outside of this Eden, she knew it was located nowhere else. His love was precious. He started it with that lotion. Tongue, teeth, and lips slow dragging around her ankles and up the curve of her calves. She tingled. All of everything on her tingled as he sailed up, calling her name, making it sound like velvet. She was filling up. She was bursting by the time he kissed each space above her heart. Then he bathed her—bathed her neck and face in what had to be the warmest, most invigorating bath there ever was.

His love was magic. Filling in hungry caves that she never knew were barren. Releasing those sensations from the nerves that raised her up and out of her mind. Freeing and freeing all that which had not ever been there, until they were discovered by him, only him. His brand of love created exotic scents, rainbows, angels, and unbelievable things.

It raked up seas and volcanoes at the base of her stomach. Tears and more tears cried, that laughed, laughed, laughed, laughed and laughed inside her. Tongues climbed cheekbones that were mountains never before explored. Eyes became rivers lost in hypnotic depths. For this, her weakness for him made her crumble into powder. For him, she made her hair a waterfall for all eternity. Cordell made her feel so unbelievably good, she would have killed for the time to stop when they were together. This way she could survive. To feel pleasure. To feel all life's joys. To feel love.

* * *

Lena opened her eyes, and the curtain was rising. To her, the audience's love was as frightening as it was flattering. More importantly, it was as lasting as her noteworthy position on the record charts would be. Even so, this season of life was indelible—precious and incredible. Her love for herself had transported Lena from a fantasy in her mind to this stage before thousands, just as her love would be there to nourish her spirit when nights like this one were memories almost too sensational to have been real. More than that, her love would be there when she needed strength in the dark hour and encouragement in the weak one. This night was her guarantee that all that she needed to not only survive, but thrive, was within her. The power was hers. Her soul was hers.

The music sashayed into the first verse. For the first time, Lena's eyes beheld the sea of faces. Lights were on them, switching from hues of red to midnight blue and lastly purple. It was a stark awakening. There she was, with nothing left to do but unleash the fire, which she was destined to do. People were waiting to feel sexy, and in love, and electrified and human and relaxed and away from troubles. And more than she could describe, Lena was excruciatingly grateful to be the bearer of these gifts to them. They wanted to feel, even if for a second, that emotion which was as good as good can be in life. So Lena threw back her head, closed her eyes, and met with gripping command the haunting, tantalizing, dangerous curves of the melody. Yes, she had a song to sing—this song of all love.

Epilogue

The sun reached down looking more potent than the feathery caress it pampered against their skins. To thank for that, there were turquoise waters crooning sweetly ahead in the distance. It dusted a coolness over the rows and rows of elaborate white chairs filled with friends and family, who sat erect and careened forward, whose smiles seemed everlasting, whose eyes smiled most.

At the inception and ending of each queue of seats, there were massive, oblong-shaped vases, their surface unusually decorated, sheathed with satin fabric the hue of buttercream. Leaping outwardly from each was a biblical bouquet. Colorful gladiolus, hyssops, lilacs, red roses, chrysanthemums, and stately orange tulips were topped by an embroidered page of the Old Testament. Its exquisite arrangement complemented the white Easter lilies strewn stunningly in a sequence along the pathway.

The picturesque setting was further embellished by a beige brick mansion that stood expansively, perching three stories against the ocean-kissed sky. Moreover, the lovely scene could have been mistaken for a wedding. There was all the grandeur of such a sentimental occasion. Except the love being shared at this sacred moment was the love for a beautiful baby boy.

The minister had just finished the blessing when he

took Cordell Jr. and handed him to his first godfather. Manuel snickered at the little fellow, whose curious eyes boldly looked up at him. The reverend removed the child, prayed, and placed him in the arms of his other godfather. Embracing the newborn, searching throughout his cocoa brown face, Patty beamed with gladness. Taken from his reluctant arms, the infant was again blessed, then cuddled in the arms of godfather number three. Nestling the chubby bundle to his chest, Michael Grierson's glasses fogged up.

Succeeding him, there was Shell. Squinting down at the baby, nuzzling its apple cheeks, he formed that unforgettable, hurtful smile. Lastly of the godfathers, there was Reuben. Closely observing him, Lena and Cordell prayed he wouldn't just doze off. They exhaled when he didn't. Reuben simply cooed at the youngster before presenting him to Tobia. A kiss sprinkled his forehead from her trembling lips. Hereafter, he was showered with the affections of his two other godmothers, who were Cordell's sisters.

A few heartwarming moments later, there was a vast buffet table with an assortment of edibles, soft beverages, and wines. Seafoods, broiled meats, spicy rice dishes, pastas, salads, and southern-cooked vegetables lured many with delicious smells. As well, oldies but goodies Motown music commenced to play. It roused the urge to dance in many, while others mingled, talked, laughed, or merely rocked their heads and shoulders to the funky or lagging beats.

The judge's willowy arms were encircling the baby when Lena, Cordell, Manuel, Patty, and Tobia besieged the pair.

"I think my grandson looks just like me," the old man asserted with a chuckle.

"I think he has Cordell's eyes and complexion," Lena voiced, captivated by her adorable bundle, then switching the fascination to her handsome husband. She winked at him.

Cordell rolled his tongue across his lips at her.

"No, I think he takes that weight problem after his godfather," Patty teased, drawing light laughter from all of them, even the baby.

"Look at that," the judge marveled. Baby Cordell was all gums. "He's laughing at Granddaddy."

"Yeah, just look at that." In awe, Manuel was shaking his head. "He looks like Lena to me. That smile is definitely hers. He just needs some teeth, and it will be Mommy's smile all the way."

There were sniggers.

"No! No!" Tobia exclaimed. "You have it all wrong. That baby looks like me. His figure is identical to mine. We both have that pleasing excess on the bottom!"

Everyone laughed and laughed. As they sobered, Manuel pulled Lena aside.

"Lena, I found something of yours the other day." Long, slim fingers fumbled through his pockets. "It was at the club in that corner by that little table. You know, the one where you and Cordell used to sit?" Finally he pulled out a charm. "You lost it once before, and I found it for you. Remember?"

Lena was looking amazed. "I remember. I lost this the last night I performed at Centerfields. Didn't realize it was gone until I came home." She nodded, accepting a part of her old key chain. It was that heart-shaped charm she'd purchased from a street vendor years ago.

"This old thing after all this time," Lena remarked, realizing she hadn't seen it in what seemed like ages. However, suddenly seeing it again, she recalled the old street merchant who peddled it to her. Mostly she remembered the tale the man had shared:

If the owner sees her eyes sparkling when she inspects its glimmering veneer, then one day they will sparkle before the man of her dreams while she's in his arms.

Studying the trinket, Lena was beaming. "Thanks, Manuel."

"You're welcome."

Promptly he rejoined the gathering, leaving Lena holding up the heart, thoroughly inspecting its veneer.

"Hey, good-looking." Cordell surprised her, luring her interest to him. A light peck on the lips threw her hands inadvertently to her sides.

"Yummy," she purred. He was rearing back to get a better view of her.

"You look beautiful, baby."

"You're not too bad yourself, Mr. Richardson."

"Are you happy?"

"More than ever. And I'm so glad that we've decided to take the baby on tour with us."

"I wouldn't have it any other way. But believe me, I will make time to be alone with you."

She eyed him devilishly and rolled a tress of spiraling hair. "And what will you do to me, handsome?"

"This and a whole lot more." Strong arms fiercely locked her within, allowing Cordell to entrance Lena with deep, soul-drenching kisses, which thrust her over and over in a river of paradise. The pit of her abdomen welled with desire as did the lust raging within him. When their lips drew apart, he was lost in the haze of

her sensuality. Much the same, she was mesmerized by
him. It all made her recall the significance of the heart.

"Are my eyes sparkling, Cordell?" She was near
breathless.

"Like they were the stars," he whispered.

Bliss exuded from her every pore. "Then it's true."

"What's true?"

"This man told me something that I thought was a
tale. But now I know it's so true. My eyes are sparkling
before the man of my dreams, and I am in his arms."

About the Author

Louré Bussey is a graduate of Borough of Manhattan Community College. She wrote over 50 romantic short stories for romance magazines such as *Bronze Thrills* and *Black Confessions*. She enjoys singing, songwriting and acting. She has also written a forthcoming novel, *Most Of All*. She lives in Brooklyn.

Look for these upcoming Arabesque titles:

January 1997
ALL THE LOVE by Bette Ford
SENSATION by Shelby Lewis
ONLY YOU by Angela Winters

February 1997
INCOGNITO by Francis Ray
WHITE LIGHTNING by Candice Poarch
LOVE LETTERS, Valentine Collection

March 1997
THE WAY HOME by Angela Benson
LOVE BUILDER by Layle Guisto
NIGHT AND DAY by Doris Johnson

TIMELESS LOVE

Look for these historical romances in the Arabesque line:

BLACK PEARL by Francine Craft (0236-0, $4.99)

CLARA'S PROMISE by Shirley Hailstock (0147-X, $4.99)

MIDNIGHT MOON by Mildred Riley (0200-X; $4.99)

SUNSHINE AND SHADOWS by Roberta Gayle (0136-4, $4.99)